Wicked Words 7

A Black Lace Short-Story Collection

Wicked Words 7

A Black Lace Short-Story Collection

Edited by Kerri Sharp

BLACK LACE

Black Lace books contain sexual fantasies.
In real life, always practise safe sex.

This edition published in 2004 by
Black Lace
Thames Wharf Studios
Rainville Road
London W6 9HA

Originally published in 2002

Design by Smith & Gilmour, London
Printed and bound by Mackays of Chatham PLC

ISBN 0 352 33743 5

Contents

Introduction

I am delighted these wonderful Black Lace erotic short story collections are getting a new lease of life, and in such fabulous eye-catching new pop-art covers, too! The series has been hugely successful, and sales of *Wicked Words* anthologies have proven how popular the short story format is in this genre.

As we all know, sexual tension is the best precursor to great sex. The greater the compression, the bigger the explosion. How much sweeter the feast after a period of abstinence! Good erotic writers know the power of delaying their characters' gratification. Imagine the scenario: man and woman meet at a party. They agree to have sex immediately. They do. The end. It may by a mini adventure, but it sure as hell isn't making the most of the dynamics that exist out there in the real world between potential lovers. This collection abounds with stories that feature a high level of sexual tension. In *Action Painting*, the central female character is kept waiting and wondering if the stunning young artist she's modelling for is even into women. The air is electric with longing. Cracking dialogue and modern observation as ever from Maria Eppie. There's tension too that comes from the differing power dynamics between characters like the bank manager and the very overdrawn account holder in Kate Stwerat's *Payback Time* and, in no fewer than two stories, between a cop and someone who is 'helping with enquiries'. Mythology is thrown into the equation in Anna Clare's witty and clever *Judging by Paris*, where a young man has to choose between three very different, very beguiling women. There's also the marvellously unusual *Clawing at the Temple Doors*, which taps into some deep-seated desires in the sexual psyche of an ex-cabinet minister. Very naughty indeed is Sara Jane Fox's *The Father of the Groom*, where one young bride-to-be gets an inkling that she's going to get on very well with her future father-in-law. Fabulously inappropriate behaviour!

There is just room to tell you about what is happening with the *Wicked Words* collections next year. As from February 2005, we will be publishing themed collections – which will be a fun way of diversifying the list. The first books will be *Sex in the Office* and *Sex on Holiday*, and after that we will be having *Sex on the Sportsfield* and *Sex in Uniform*. I can't wait! In the meantime, *Wicked Words 8* is also published as of this month – November – and the first six books in the series should be in the shops now. If you never got the chance to buy all the books when they were first published, you can now complete your collection and be the envy of your friends! Look out for the colourful covers – guaranteed to stand out from everything else on the erotica shelves.

Do you want to submit a short story to Wicked Words?

By the time these reprints hit the shelves, it will be too late to contribute stories to the first two themed collections, but the guidelines for future anthologies will be available on our website at www.blacklace-books.co.uk. Keep checking for news. Please note we can only accept stories that are of publishable standard in terms of grammar, punctuation, narrative structure and presentation. We do not want to receive stories that are about 'some people having sex' and little else. The buzzwords are surprises, great characterisation and an awareness of the erotic literary canon. We cannot reply to all short story submissions as we receive too many to make this possible. Competition-style rules apply: you will hear back from us only if your story has been successful. And please remember to read the guidelines. If you cannot find them online, send a large SAE to:

Black Lace Guidelines
Virgin Books
Thames Wharf Studios
Rainville Road
London W6 9HA

One first-class stamp is sufficient. If you are sending a request from the US, please note that only UK postage stamps 'work' when mailing from the UK.

Action Painting Maria Eppie

You know, I never much liked Art, so it was ironic that I bumped into him (literally) in the bar at the ICA. The Institute of Contemporary Art was hardly normal territory for me, but I'd been dragged there to see an evening of utterly incomprehensible short films by a pair of friends. Three hours of culture and I was dying of thirst and boredom. The thirst bit speaks for itself, natch. The boredom bit is tied up with my friends innate ability for non-stop intellectual analysis fatally combined with their recently confirmed status of being born again couple-positive.

This latter disease is a terminal affliction which, sadly, is beginning to infect most of my close acquaintances. They pair off, they move in together, they spend two years decorating their new home, they stop going dancing and start attending lectures with titles like 'Rejuvenation Through Tofu'. Next, they're nagging you about your lifestyle, about clubs, about drugs, about promiscuity. Repressive! Then, before you know it, they're trying to pair you off with Julian's friend Charlie or some such dork. 'Oh, you'll love him! He's something in the City, really, and he's *dying* to settle down.' And these are the ones that haven't even started breeding yet. Depresses the shit out of me, I can tell you.

Anyway, the friends (now consigned to that fast growing pile marked 'gone strange') had each got off home to their significant others and left me to look after myself, which I do very well. I was fighting my way through to the bar in dire need of another margarita when we crashed into each other. I was all set to turn him to stone with my watch-where-you're-going-fool glower, when I heard this voice, a husky voice with a little catch in it, say, 'Oh, I'm sorry.' Even though, actually, it was my fault. I looked up and I was gazing into two deep dark pools. And I thought, I wouldn't mind some of that. The thought went right through me like an electric shock. He might not have been quite my normal type but, then again, my normal type does not invariably qualify for the category 'absolutely bloody gorgeous'. High cheekbones, neat, short locks and a very muscular back. Kinda raggedy-scruffy looking in an artful way (but then he was an artist, so he claimed). Sexy-dirty, definitely. And those eyes. I'd never seen eyes as dark as that and that's what did it for me.

We got talking. Well, I wasn't going to let this opportunity pass me by. Raphael ('Call me Rafe') came on all laconic and intellectual at first, the way twentysomething boys seem to do when they're intimidated by a sexually experienced woman. For God's sake, I thought, if I wanted intellectual conversation I'd still be sitting with my weird friends. However, I stuck with it because, I admit, he was the best-looking thing in the entire bar. So I gave him the full-on, wide-eyed you-artists-are-so-romantic-and-thrilling treatment, which of course he lapped up. And, after a while, he got less arrogant and I thought, he's actually quite sweet. He seemed interested too.

It was coming up to closing time and we were being herded towards the door but he still hadn't made a move. A guy of about the same age came over and joined us. Dan, his name was. Another artist, maybe not quite as fit as Raphael but young and elegantly handsome too. I was just starting to get some rather saucy ideas when, all of a sudden, it was, 'Nice meeting you. See you around sometime.' No phone numbers, no nothing. I don't think so. I'd invested a whole evening on this Raphael by now and I was not going to let him get away that easily. So I said the first thing that came into my head. 'I could model for you, if you wanted.' OK, corny, but could you do better? He just said, 'Yeah, right,' as we squeezed out of the glass door and on to The Mall. 'See you then,' he added and headed off with his friend up the steps towards Piccadilly. I stood there, guppy-mouthed and mortified! He paused at the foot of the steps, looked back at me with a blasé stare and said, 'Guess you'll want my address then.' Cheeky sod! But we exchanged numbers and, as I watched his tight little arse clamber away on up, I resolved to give this Rafe a lesson in manners.

So when I went round to Rafe's studio that first afternoon, I'd already decided that I wasn't going to let him touch me. I was going to pay him back for acting cool with me in public. I was going to make him beg for it. His studio was in an old warehouse in Curtain Street. I stripped in a crudely partitioned-off area that served as a bathroom and came out in a silky dressing gown. I let the gown slip to the floor and said, 'How do you want me?' He swallowed and just pointed to this cruddy old arm chair. I sat down on the edge of the chair, all stiff backed and tits out, while he started arranging paper on the floor. As he moved around, I got to check out his body which, yep, was still gorgeous. He was wearing these old paint-stained combats with a rip where the arse should be. Each time he squatted, he flashed a sizeable hunk of very firm, very neat, very rounded caramel-coloured bum at me. Then, preparations completed, he stood up and stared at me.

He stared at me for ages, looking very intense, then

walked over and positioned me in the chair without saying a word. The tips of his fingers only barely brushed my skin but I was covered in goose pimples. It was so cold that my nipples were pointing to the ceiling. Maybe it wasn't just the temperature. Maybe, I considered, I wouldn't make him beg me for it for *that* long. He arranged me in a sort of ball and I was tense with excitement because I thought (I hoped) his fingers might need to move my thighs. If they'd gone within six inches of my pussy, I'd surely have come there and then.

Two hours later, I was still waiting and hoping. One side of me was blue with cold and the other was fried from the crappy electric heater he'd stood next to the chair. Then he said, 'OK, Julia, thanks, you can go get dressed now,' and started talking about the next session. Next session? He expected me to spend my time freezing my tits off just for Art? I threw on my gown and flounced to the bathroom, but he put his arm out and my stomach walked on into the palm of his hand. His handsome face bent very slightly towards me and my insides just went whoosh, like that very first rush down the big dipper. About time, I thought. At last, this is it. He's gonna kiss me! He did, but ever so lightly on the side of my mouth, and I felt his tongue flick softly against mine. So softly, I wasn't even completely sure it had happened. Then he looked at me with those black eyes and said, 'Thanks, Julia. Next Tuesday?' That was all.

Of course I agreed. OK, so he *was* interested; he was just scared off by the direct approach. I'd have to act more demure. It wasn't my natural style but I thought I'd give it a go. By the time Tuesday came around, I'd worked out a game plan. I thought that I'd let him coax me a bit and so acted a bit sniffy about taking my knickers off. The bastard didn't seem to care – said that

I could keep my pullover on as well and that he'd just draw my hands and face and feet. I didn't know what game he was playing, but he was very good at it because he had me completely out-manoeuvred. I practically ripped my clothes off, jabbering, 'No, no, it's OK, I enjoy posing,' and flopped breathlessly into the armchair with a 'How do you want me then?' The bastard just pursed his lips and said, 'That'll do.'

I decided to relax and play by my own rules with this Raphael. He sat opposite me with his sketch pad, so I could look directly at him over my body, which was still nice and brown from last summer. He seemed to be staring straight into my pussy and I wondered if he was scared off by my hairy bush. For a while I'd had a Brazilian – you know, the plucked-chicken-totally-nude look – but I got bored with it and I decided to let it grow out. And, boy, did it grow! It's now a mass of dark curls. I like it like that, just a deep, sweet, luxuriant valley where those who dare can delve. My legs were wide open and I was beginning to feel more than a little slippy, and I was certain it was noticeable. It made me think about my particular weakness for oils and lotions and all things wet and creamy and I imagined a juicy trickle slowly slipping between my cheeks till it reached and moistened my other hole. Every so often Rafe's gaze would lift and his black eyes would lock on mine for just a second longer than necessary. I was certain no male could resist my luscious invitation and I imagined the pillar lurking in his combats, huge and aching, perhaps already leaking a little moisture itself.

It would soon be time for some serious deep-down delving, so I considered the interesting positions that the actually surprisingly comfy armchair offered. Like kneeling, arse flexed, or the splits, toes pointed at the ceiling, or even (and I rated the possibilities that this one offered best of all) pussy up and on my shoulders, supported by the chair back. Then he could draw me any way he wanted – he could paint his hands on my tits and his tongue up my crack and my mouth round his dick. Oh, fuck the Art, I thought, come and fuck me! The boy was either a mind-reader or I'd said it out loud because he suddenly put down his pastel crayon and stood up. I could see a telltale bulge straining the buttons of his fly, even the suggestion of a moist patch of pre-come on the worn material of his combats. He squatted down before me and I groaned in anticipation of that first flick of the tongue. My clit felt like it was hugely swollen and I spread my thighs even wider, mentally urging him to lick it, to bite it right off if he wanted, as long as he stopped the ache. I'd had enough of game playing by now; I just wanted him to bury his face deep in my pussy and lap up my juices.

But the lick didn't come. Instead Rafe took hold of my ankles and, in one motion, yanked them up and apart. My body slumped back into the chair with my weight pushed on to my shoulders. My legs were stretched high above me, salaciously doing the splits, my pussy laid bare to his gaze. Almost exactly how I'd pictured it. The boy was indeed a mind-reader. 'Can't see your cunt for all that hair,' he muttered by way of explanation. The phrase sounded filthy and shocking in Rafe's husky, gentle voice. I realised how little I knew about him. I was exposed and vulnerable before him and he could do whatever he wanted to me and I was such a slut, that's all I actually wanted. He stood over me, looking down into my spread-eagled slit then transferred both my ankles to his left hand to free the other. Then, he slowly unbuttoned his fly and took hold of his engorged cock. It was more solid, fuller, thicker than I'd even dared imagine. The tip seemed to be as big as the fist that was lazily wanking it over my exposed arsehole. 'I'm gonna have to force this in the only hole I can see, if that's alright with you?'

My ribcage was so constricted that I could barely speak, but I managed to croak, 'Yeah, sure, that's OK.'

'Did you say something?' Raphael asked in that maddeningly sexy voice of his.

The bastard was going to make me beg. I was beyond caring. 'Yeah, it's OK. Please,' I murmured again.

'Julia?'

I smiled and tried to open my legs further, tried to display myself even more wantonly for him.

'Julia? Would you keep the pose?' What? I opened my eyes and found myself staring into his wicked black eyes. 'You've lost the pose. Your, erm, hand . . .'

I'd slumped in the chair and my fingers had wandered south to twirl very gently and not a little provocatively in my bush. Ohmygod, was he laughing at me? I couldn't tell if he was or wasn't. But, either way, one thing I couldn't believe. There I was, lounging longingly in front of him and his only thought was of Art? Keep the pose? What was it with this man? By the end of the session, I'd realised he was gay. I thought I'd maybe just check out the sketches he'd been working on and, if they were any good, I'd take one in lieu of payment, then, fuck it, I'd be off and I wouldn't be coming back.

Good? They were amazing! He'd done a whole series of dusty, pink and brown pastels and they were so incredibly beautiful. They made me look astonishingly svelte and sexy. (Which, of course, I am. But it's something else to have your sexiness immortalised, isn't it?) When he said, 'Next Tuesday?' I decided that maybe I didn't mind suffering for Art if it made me look this fine, so I said, 'OK.' I asked him if I could take one of the pictures and he nodded.

Then, after I had picked out the nicest one, as I straightened up, I brushed against his hand which, almost by accident, seemed to stroke me all the way down my back to my arse then sort of guided me towards him and I thought, *Yes!* I just melted into him and thrust my mound into his groin and he was hard. Very hard. Very, very hard. But he only kissed me and, apart from a definite play with his tongue, that was it. I tell you, I was completely ready, able and willing. My pussy was practically gulping. No shame, I was even going to ask him for it, straight out, 'Please, Rafe, fuck me, will you?' But, before I'd had a chance, he'd broken away and was talking about the next session and everything was very businesslike again. Well, as businesslike as it can be when you're naked and moist, and in the presence of an extremely husky, rock-hard male.

That moment was with me all the way home. By the time I arrived, I had decided I was dusty and sweaty and thought I'd better take a shower. Actually, I just wanted to take my clothes off again. I stripped as fast as I could and walked round the flat naked for about a quarter of an hour, thinking about the situation. I wanted to feel like I was back there in Raphael's studio and to analyse the confusion of those events again. Part of me was angry and perplexed. I mean, this man had some nerve! I was not used to this kind of treatment. *Au contraire*, as is well known, it's usually me that's dishing it out. And, though I say it myself, it is not my experience that, as and when I make myself naked and available, men take no notice. Being a well-shaped, uninhibited sex-bitch, red-hot carnal passion is the regular response, varying between total loss of self-control to terrified submission by the male in question. Occasionally I've known fumbling incompetence, I admit. But casual indifference? Hah, never!

On the other hand, the bastard did have a beautiful body, firm and compact, and it was that I was thinking of as I soaped myself. There was no doubt about the hardness of his erection when I pressed up against him, or the dimensions of his cock (which I was beginning to suspect might be in the category of 'worryingly large'). Either that or he was storing a giant tube of oil paint in his underwear. He moved like a cat and he'd got a look of his own – stylish and dirty at the same time. He just looked like he was a great fuck and I'm not just talking about the feel of his cock or his muscular shoulders or the tautness of his buttocks or the texture of his skin. I mean, some men seem to radiate sex, don't they? Well, this one radiated it like a furnace.

I rubbed shower gel over me, all the while thinking of him. My skin was silky and shiny and sluiced and lubricated by the gel and I just went off into a little dreamworld where I was trying to picture the size of his dick, what sort of head it had, how it curved into his groin, how much curly hair grew round the base. You know the sort of thing. I must have spent a couple of minutes there before I realised I had actually been spending most of my time soaping my pussy and I was by now decidedly warm, wet and ready. I worked a finger in a bit. There was a distinct juiciness around my hole. After a bit of creative fingering, I had a better idea. I switched the shower head to jet massage and aimed the spray between my legs.

This was fun, except that the drawing feelings in my sex and belly were so strong that my legs kept wobbling and buckling. So I sat on the side of the bath, propped against the tiled wall, and squirted the jet directly at my clit, using my left hand to hold my lips wide apart. The squirmy sensations built up again pretty quickly and I was soon breathing really fast and lightly. I looked across at myself in the big bathroom mirror; my mouth agape and panting, my high little tits all taut and pointy, my fingers spreading my pinky red pussy and the silvery water cascading all over it and my tummy and my slim brown thighs, while all the time my bottom was rocking in an irresistible rhythm, back and forwards on my little ledge. I love watching myself. It makes me feel like a whore giving a sex show performance. God, I looked such an irresistibly dirty little slut, I fancied me myself. I really wanted Rafe to see me too. That'd put a stop to all this 'keeping the pose' nonsense. I took the jet in real close and let the shower head just brush against the hood of my clit. I imagined it was the swollen end of his dick, rubbing me faster and faster. That did it. I came with such strong pulsing contractions that I dropped the shower and slid down into the bath. I didn't get dressed for the rest of the evening and, later on, I gave myself a good moisturisation with body lotion. That set me off again so that I had to lie down on the bed and finish myself off properly. I slept well that night. Maybe I'd got him out of my system.

For a week, I was pondering whether to go again or not. Why was I wasting my time chasing after this youth who didn't seem at all interested? Was I making a fool of myself? It was no use turning to my friends for advice because the answer from them would be a resounding yes. In fact, it was the thought of my grown-up sensible friends and all their well-intentioned match-making with endless Charlies and Simons and Julians that spurred me on. I like being single, I like sex and there is absolutely no reason whatsoever that I can see why the two should not be highly compatible. My friends act as if, when you hit thirty, you're supposed to renounce carnality and take up yoga instead.

Well, I don't think so. If I'm gonna twist my body

round into some weird and complex shape, I'm gonna do it with some other body that's warm and brown and close fitting. For as long as I am able. Rafe was a consenting adult and he was very cute. The only marginally negative thing about him was that he's way too serious about this Art thing. He needed to lighten up a bit. Perhaps it was his way of seducing me. Well, perhaps the guy just didn't realise he'd won that battle on day one. I could not make him out at all. I was tired of all of the game playing. He either wanted to fuck or he didn't; simple as that, I decided. Why hesitate? It was time to sort this business out once and for all, and let's all stop being coy about the fact that, Raphael, I badly want to fuck you.

When Tuesday came round again, it was a beautiful day. It was as good a day as any to go round and ask him straight what game he was playing. I thought it only fair to show Raphael exactly what he'd be missing if he didn't get his shit together and I dressed accordingly.

I was gorgeous. I wore this Op Art minidress I'd got from the Vintage Clothing Store, some knee-length white boots and a dab of Kenzo and nothing else. I never wore any undies when I modelled for him anyway. He didn't like the marks they left on my skin as he needed the flesh smooth and perfect, which was fine by me. It felt like I was in one of those sixties films, some groovy chick on her way to her modelling session. My nipples were rubbing against the fabric of the dress and the breeze was blowing up my dress and ruffling my pubes and I noticed quite a few men were looking at me. I mean, *looking* at me. I was hot! I had this sort of weightless feeling in my belly and by the time I got to Rafe's, I was squirming.

I was determined to cut straight to the chase but

Raphael beat me to it. He seemed excited, more animated than usual, and he was keen to get me out of my clothes. For a second, I contemplated making him wait but then remembered that I'd had enough of games and obligingly stepped out of my dress. I left my boots on. I wasn't going to give up the extra three inches they gave to my legs. I positioned myself in my chair, legs spread over the arms and said to Raphael impatiently, 'Come on then! I'm ready.'

He seemed distracted, glancing at the door and saying, 'Not yet, we have to wait.' There was something going on here and I didn't have long to wait to find out what it was. The door opened and in strolled Dan. Now, I'd only met the guy once and there he was, getting a gynaecologist's view of my pussy. I wriggled myself into a less compromising position, but Dan studiously avoided looking in my direction anyway, like he was afraid of what he'd see or something. He walked straight over to Raphael and hugged him. Now the penny dropped. Yep, Raphael *was* gay. I felt appalled. I'd been such an idiot.

'Hallo, Dan,' I said cooly, 'what brings you here?'

I thought I caught a nervous glance in Rafe's direction and he said, 'The project. You know. The painting?'

I hadn't a clue what he was talking about. I was totally confused but I figured that the only possible way to escape the situation with any pride intact was to pretend that everything was cool and this thing with Rafe (whatever it was) was only ever about Art all along. So I said, 'Yeah. Of course.'

Rafe helped me off with my boots, while Dan spread a big canvas on the floor. Then he positioned me in the middle of it. I was beginning to smell a rat and I said, 'Rafe, what exactly are you doing?'

He looked at me really seriously. 'Action painting,

Julia. It's a Retro thing, very hip in the forties. Jackson Pollock?' Then he threw a gallon of paint over me.

They poured paint on me, they squirted paint on me, they flicked paint on me, while I stood there gasping and dripping. When finally they stopped, I recovered just enough to ask, 'Now what, you bastards?'

It was Dan who said, 'Now you lie on the canvas and squirm.'

As I'd come this far, I decided that the only thing to do was to stick with it, so I lay down on the canvas, as instructed, and squirmed. At first, I was so intent on keeping the gunk out of my hair that I didn't notice my arse being lifted into the air. When I looked to one side, Rafe was kneeling beside me. We were on an equal footing now because he was also naked. Then I felt a dollop of something wet slop on to my bum. As it trickled down, it was gently smoothed into my crevice, which was not unpleasant. In fact, it was so not unpleasant that it reactivated my weightless belly thing. I've already told you I've got a weakness. I turned to look at Rafe's face. He had this expression of total concentration. I began to giggle. Next thing, paint was being smeared into my tits and I raised my head. Dan's dick was about three inches from my face and it was very pleased to see me. Enough!

I knelt up and faced the pair of them. 'If you two want to get it on together, just do it. You don't need painting as an excuse. Or me,' and I tried to get on my feet. I immediately slipped over and ended up on my arse, splashing paint everywhere. Rafe started laughing.

'Julia! Keep the pose,' he spluttered, nearly in hysterics.

'You bastard,' I shouted, but now I was having trouble keeping a straight face too. Rafe grabbed my ankles and yanked me towards him. I wriggled but slid helplessly over the rainbow coloured mess till I reached him and he was kneeling between my legs.

I pushed myself up, laughing out loud now, till I was face to face with his groin, which was an attractive mixture of Indian red and ultramarine. Something heavy and multicoloured swung between his thighs. It grew firmer and straighter until it became a handsomely stiff cock, pointing directly at me. My suspicions in the dimension department were confirmed and I stopped giggling now; it was my turn to swallow. Then I looked up at him and asked, 'You're not really gay, are you, Rafe?'

Raphael just laughed gently and bent forward and kissed me, then he stretched me out in the paint and buried his face deep in my pussy and, while Dan returned to working paint into my tits, my tummy floated off into space as my knees spread ever wider and wider. Raphael's jaw was firmly clamped on to my sex and a wet, muscular tongue was rhythmically working over my aching clit. My hands reached down and gently rubbed paint into his locks as I hauled his handsome head into me, till I must have been practically suffocating him. Manfully, he didn't complain but his tongue continued darting in and out of me, picking up my moisture and dragging it up to the taut, shiny skin at the top of my groove. Meanwhile, Dan's fingers were teasing and squeezing my swollen nips till I could no longer differentiate between the pleasures being wrung from my various little erections. Two or three minutes of this and my hole was pulsing and pleading; even though I'd come, there was still an agonising void that needed to be filled, urgently, this second and right now. Raphael, if you don't mind . . .

Next thing, my hips were slowly being rotated and Rafe flipped me on to my knees. A very thick pillar of paint-smothered flesh was being slowly eased up into my cleft till, unexpectedly, it slid in. 'You bastard, Rafe,' I managed to moan. He slowly began to move against me and I arched and flexed my back against the pushing. One hole was now just about as stretched as it could feasibly get but, annoyingly, I was still achingly hungry inside.

I looked around for Dan, to be faced with a vivid cadmium yellow cock. I looked up into his face. 'Non-toxic,' he croaked hopefully. I didn't care. I pulled him down so that he slithered beneath me on his back and I felt his cock work snugly upwards into my empty cunt. Then, with a last firm shove, Rafe went in deeper than I thought possible. The hungry void was finally filled. I had no idea how much I'd been missing with this Art thing, I thought, as the rest of the afternoon melted into a rainbow world of cocks, a wet and slippy world with a superabundance of everything swollen, where I didn't have to wait any longer for anything I wanted, till I no longer knew or cared who's what or where.

OK, so that was *Action No. 1*. It sold for eight hundred quid. I negotiated a temporary lease on the empty shop down below the studio and we opened a gallery there. It's crammed full of work. I've discovered that, besides a certain penchant for making Art, I have a definite knack for selling it. Perhaps it's the way I describe our technique. There's several dozen more paintings upstairs and we're churning new canvases out almost by the day. Oh yeah, we're being very, very creative. I say we because, well, Rafe and Dan have insisted that I work with them now.

Ironic really. There was me, bitching about all my girlfriends getting cosy with a nice young man and I seem to have gone one better. But at least it ain't coupledom, and, let me add, I take Art very seriously now. I am actively considering several offers from other artists who are equally interested in working with me. Of course, as an artist, it is essential that you are free to collaborate with whom you wish. Why not try a little creative collaboration yourself? You might enjoy it. Maybe you'd like to assist on the next canvas? There's always room for extra input. But I should warn you, it is a bitch getting the paint out of your hair afterwards.

Oh, yeah, did I tell you how we autograph the canvases?

Playtime Rachael Baron

Alison could feel David's eyes on her body all evening.

The free-flowing wine already had her feeling warm, but it seemed like every time she glanced around the room of partygoers for someone new to speak to, David was looking back, and that was making her feel overheated. The colour in her cheeks flushed still deeper as she caught his eye. He smiled as he steadily held her gaze and winked. A couple of times, he made himself useful, making the rounds with a wine bottle and topping up glasses. Both times he overfilled Alison's glass. She asked him jokingly if he was trying to get her drunk. He just smiled, brushed the back of her hand and moved on to the next guest.

It was growing late, and the party was starting to break up. The hostess was busy retrieving coats, ringing for cabs and seeing guests to the door. Joanne shooed away any offers from Alison to be helpful, preferring to deal with all the important people on her own. In fact, no one there seemed to take much notice of Alison. No one except David. She thought it was time to get going. She drained her wine glass and headed up to the loo before the long tube ride back to her flat.

As she washed her hands, she regarded herself in the mirror over the sink and tried to see in herself what David saw. Her dress was cut low enough to accentuate her full breasts without being too revealing, her hair piled on top of her head with a few loose tendrils gracing the curve of her neck, and her full lips were painted a lush red. She had to admit the overall effect was alluring. The added flush of colour to her cheeks from the alcohol and the openly lustful stares of David made her glow. She needed to get out of there fast! The flirting was getting a little too much for her to bear.

Alison knew the house well, and took the back stairs down to the kitchen. She thought perhaps she could sneak out the back way and avoid any awkward 'good nights'.

David was waiting at the bottom of the stairs. He held on to both railings and blocked her way, smiling up at her as she descended, watching her chest bob up and down with each step. Alison stopped a few steps above him, just beyond his grasp.

'Where's Joanne?' she whispered. Stupid question: she could hear her voice in the front hall entrance.

'She's seeing off some of her cronies. Don't worry ... she's forgotten we exist.'

'I doubt that. How could she forget about you?'

'You give her too much credit, Alison. All she cares about any more is her business. I've simply become an accessory at parties. London's newest star literary agent and her tall, dark and presentable husband.'

The smile faded as his voice took on a bitter edge.

'You're more than just presentable,' she mumbled, shifting her feet on the stairs.

David noted her discomfort.

'Forgive me. I know this must be awkward for you.' He turned to a side table and retrieved a couple of glasses he had waiting. 'Here ... have one last Christmas toast with me before you go.'

With one hand on the railing, Alison leaned down and accepted the proffered glass of brandy. She was a bit too tipsy for comfort as it was, but did not see how she could politely refuse. Feeling a bit dizzy, she sat on the stairs with her drink. David stood at the bottom of the staircase, one foot resting on the step. She felt her eyes drawn to the obvious bulge in his trousers and fought not to be caught staring. Alison snuck a peek with each sip as he talked.

'Yes, it's sad but true,' he continued, swirling the brandy around in his glass. 'Joanne is consumed by her work with her precious agency, and there is nothing left for me at the end of her day.'

'I can't believe that. You two have always been so happy.'

'Not for some time, Alison my pet. Joanne spends all of her energy on wheeling and dealing for foreign rights, film options ... I know that my profession doesn't hold the least bit of interest for her, but if it weren't for the stodgy old insurance business, she wouldn't have this house, and she sure as hell would never have been able to start up the agency without my backing her financially. Sorry ... this must sound awfully dull. You must already know all of this.'

'That's OK.'

Alison took another burning sip and felt herself slip into a deeper state of inebriation. Joanne's voice was still ringing out in the front hall and, from what Alison could make out, it didn't sound like her conversation was going to end very soon. She could afford to linger a few more minutes and hear David's troubles.

'Oh, and I have made the effort. I began to woo her like before we married with sweet gestures: flowers, silly notes. She didn't seem to notice. Then I tried to spice things up by ... no. I can't say.'

'Go on ... you "spiced things up" how?'

He grinned and winked, taking a deliberately slow sip of brandy.

'David! That's not fair. Don't keep me in suspense. Please.'

'I can never resist a pretty woman who begs! Right then ... I went out and bought her a few ... toys.'

'Toys? What kind of toys?'

David choked back a laugh at Alison's sincere confusion.

'Don't laugh at me! What are you talking about?'

'Toys, my dear girl. A whole little arsenal of things –'

His voice dropped lower, and she was forced to lean down to hear him. He recited his list to her with a gleam in his eye.

'A vibrating egg. Nipple clamps. A butt plug. And a long, fat vibrating cock.'

He looked mighty pleased with himself. Alison felt her breath deepen. Her hands shook and she had to cup the glass hard between them to prevent it from falling.

'Are ... are you joking?'

Her voice was shaking as badly as her hands. He pretended not to notice and went on.

'I brought them all out and laid them on the bed for her to find when she was finished her bath. I sat in the armchair and waited. When Joanne came into the bedroom, she stopped dead. "Which one would you like to try first?" I asked. I was so excited, I didn't know how I was going to contain myself.'

David's bulge gave a twitch and lengthened before her eyes.

'What did she do?'

'She just stared at them and didn't move. "Here," I said, "I'll help. Take off your robe and lie back." I thought I could apply them to her one at a time, starting with the nipple clips, then run the egg over her clit until she was dripping. Ease her hips on to a pillow and slide the butt plug into her arsehole. Then give her a choice: my cock or the dildo. Doesn't that sound good?'

Alison couldn't believe she was having this conversation. It was well past the understood boundaries of their long-running innocent flirtation, and she knew she should have told him to stop, but she didn't want to. Her nipples were tingling and straining against her lace bra as she imagined David giving his wife the lascivious instructions. No boyfriend had ever talked to Alison that way, and such blatant sex-talk from a sophisticated man fifteen years her senior was unbearably arousing.

'Which would you have wanted, Alison? Would you have chosen the vibrator, or the real thing?'

Her eyes widened as he openly cupped his erection and watched her face intently for her reply. Alison's lips parted to speak, but no sound seemed possible.

'I'll tell you what I think: I think you would have taken the real cock and kept the vibrator to play with in private. Am I right?'

Alison found a voice. It came out unrecognisably low and husky. 'But what did Joanne do?'

'Wouldn't even touch any of it. She told me to "put the disgusting things away".'

'Oh –'

'But never mind what she did or didn't do. You haven't answered my question yet.'

Alison couldn't answer.

'So, you'd rather I guessed? How unfair. You could at least give me a hint. How would you have reacted, Alison? Would it have turned you on? Tell me. No, show me.'

It didn't seem real what was happening. Alison didn't even know herself as she set down her glass on the stair beside her and held his gaze steadily with her own. His hand still gripped his cock through his trousers. She grasped the hem of her dress.

'Go on,' he prompted.

She eased the skirt of her dress up, gratified to see David turn a shade redder in the face. Slowly, she hitched the dress further upwards, revealing the tops of her stockings and suspenders. She kept her knees locked tightly together until the dress was gathered around her waist. Alison ran her tongue over her lips before she spoke.

'Would you like to see how wet I'd be if a man – if you – offered me such toys to play with?'

It was David's turn to be speechless as he nodded. He glanced over his shoulder towards the front hall. Someone was laughing with Joanne at the front door. Emboldened, he stepped up and gently took a knee in each hand, his face level with Alison's crotch. He prised her willing legs apart and they both heaved a great sigh.

'Hmm, hard to tell through the black knickers in this dim light, Alison. How will I ever know the answer? Maybe if I lean in a bit closer . . .'

Alison was pulsing. Her pussy lips were pouting and she could feel the juices seeping into the crack of her ass. David's breath was hot on the crotch of her knickers and it was almost as though he was stroking her with a feather-light touch.

'How do we solve this, Alison? Tell me.'

Alison's head dropped back, her mind spinning with lust and shame. Her lips formed soundless words.

'I can't hear you –'

'I said, "Touch me" –'

David's hands slid up the inside of her thigh. There was a pause that seemed to go on for hours before he stroked the length of her sex with the merest touch of one finger. Alison groaned and bit her lip to keep herself quiet.

'Oh dear. I still can't tell – the material is so slick and smooth. Are these satin?'

He stroked again, lightly scraping over her clit so that her hips jerked.

'David . . . please –'

'Wait. I know what to do for a clear view.'

He slid his hands up and grasped the waistband.

'Knees together, dear girl,' he ordered. She obliged, and lifted her hips as he removed the final barrier to his quest.

'Now, let's have a look.'

Alison's knees dropped open and she peered down at him through slitted eyes. He was smiling.

'Yes, I see. The idea does make you wet, doesn't it? I guess different women react differently to the same things. And so beautifully open.'

His hand started to reach out for her again. Alison could feel the heat of him as his forefinger grazed down over her clit and nestled into the opening of her quim, barely touching her at all. It was maddening. She braced herself, dying to feel his finger plunge all the way in.

The front door slammed. Joanne's voice called out.

'David? Where are you hiding?'

Alison scrambled to pull her dress back into place. David watched coolly, winking at her shocked expression as he slipped her wet knickers into his jacket pocket. They had just enough time to recover. Joanne found them amiably chatting and sipping brandy, Alison perched on the stairs and David leaning against the railing.

'Alison! I'm sorry, pet. I didn't realise that you were still here. I could have hooked you up with the Stephensons for a lift home.'

Alison stood up and hoped that she didn't look half as shaky and guilt-ridden as she felt.

'That's OK. I'll just get the tube. It's still running.'

'Are you sure? I could call you a cab.'

'No, no. I could use a bit of night air. This brandy has had quite an effect.'

David just watched her and smiled. As Joanne turned to fetch her coat from the cupboard, he lifted his hand and sucked his finger into his mouth. Alison barely managed a 'goodnight' before she ran down the street towards the tube station.

'Oh, my God,' she thought, 'what did I just do?'

Alison stood on the platform. The next train was approaching, stirring up a breeze between her damp, naked thighs. She clambered into the carriage and sat as far away from the few other passengers as possible. She had never felt so horny before in all her life, and her knees jiggled up and down with frustration. She wouldn't get to her flat – or her own vibrator (she wasn't as ignorant of 'toys' as she had let on) – for at least half an hour, and she knew that she wouldn't make it home without going mad.

Alison took a quick look up and down the carriage. A few girls were chattering at the far end, oblivious to anyone but themselves. A woman sat with her back towards Alison, reading a magazine. A young businessman was slumped just a little way down and across from her, but he was sleeping with his head tucked into his chest.

Oh, why not? she thought. I've already gone further than I ever dreamed was possible.

Alison shifted forward slightly and opened her legs as far as she could and still appear normal. She slipped a hand into her coat pocket and groped about for the hole in the lining she kept meaning to mend, but somehow never got round to, and nestled a couple of fingers over her wet cunt. She wished she could hitch up her dress and not have to rub herself through the barrier of material, but beggars can't be choosers.

She feigned a neutral expression, ready to stop if anyone got on and sat near her, praying that no one would. Please, God, just give me a minute or two. She didn't need a lot of time. She was primed.

Alison frigged with quick short strokes, imagining David's fingers. Her clit felt ready to burst.

The climax hit almost immediately. It was intense, shooting bolt after bolt of pleasure up her spine. She clamped her eyes shut and bit the inside of her cheeks to keep from crying out, but couldn't help jerking her head back and giving a low moan. Her body sagged and she opened her eyes to see where they were as they pulled into the next station. She was glad to see that she had a couple of stops to go and set about pulling herself together. Alison straightened up and noticed that the sleeping man was wide awake and looking in her direction. He stood up and stepped to the door nearest to her seat as the train slowed to a stop. Alison was mortified at the thought that he was on to what she'd been doing to herself, but at the same time she found unable to break away from his gaze. He gave her a little smile as the doors opened.

'That sure looked like fun, love,' he said, and stepped out, walking off along the platform without a backwards glance.

Alison got through the holidays in a haze, distracting herself with a visit home to see her family in Bristol.

But once New Year was over, she knew that she'd have to go back to work and face the music. There would be no avoiding Joanne.

It was complicated enough that her husband had done his outrageous best to seduce her under his wife's nose, but Joanne also just happened to be Alison's boss.

Alison got back from Bristol to find the message light flashing on the answerphone. Joanne had left a long rambling message telling her that they would be going to America for a week on business just after the holidays, so she would be left to 'hold the fort' until their return. Alison couldn't have been more relieved. The longer the stretch of time between that crazy scene on the staircase and her having to face Joanne, the better. Exciting though it had been, it was treading on very thin ice, and it was not a game that she could afford to continue playing if she wanted to be able to survive and pay her rent. David would tag along with Joanne as usual, and have a bit of time and space for himself to forget about what had passed. He wouldn't have been stupid enough to tell his wife, and Alison felt sure that Joanne had not seen anything at the party.

The next morning, Alison took the tube to Highgate and let herself into the empty house with the spare key. Joanne had most of the ground floor converted to office and entertainment areas, and the top two floors were the private living quarters. She found a long list of tasks waiting on her desk in the small front room, and sighed to see that it was Joanne's usual leftovers consisting of unpleasant phone calls to be returned and a backlog of bookkeeping: all the things she couldn't be bothered to handle on her own. Her boss had an annoying habit of leaving things to pile up until they got to be a strain to put right.

But at least she'd have the place all to herself for a

week. Much easier to concentrate without Joanne – or David – around.

'PS,' said her note. 'Sorry, pet, but the downstairs loo is broken, so you'll have to use the one upstairs. (Could you arrange for a plumber?)'

Typical, thought Alison.

And now that she'd been reminded, she did need the loo.

Alison stopped at the bottom of the stairs and rested her hand on the railing just as David had on that strange night in December. She looked at the stair where she'd been sitting, trying to picture the display she must have put on for him. In proper daylight, alone and sober as she was, none of it seemed like more than a wet dream.

Did she really sit there with her legs spread like a whore, begging him to touch her, her juices running down her crack? Yes, yes she had.

Alison's mind slipped into a fantasy: What would have happened if we'd had a few more moments to ourselves? He would have sunk his finger into my depths, and then what? Would he have dared to lick me? He'd looked hungry enough to have risked it, and I had been too far gone to have stopped him. Even if Joanne had walked in and found me writhing on the stairs with her husband's mouth suckling at my cunt, I wouldn't have cared if she fired me at that point, just so long as I had time to come before she threw me out of the house!

Alison's head was spinning. She tore herself from the spot and hurried up to the toilet. She noticed a wet patch of excitement in her pants.

As she went back out into the hallway, she cast a curious glance towards the closed door of the master bedroom at the other end. Alison had never been in the room, having only ever glimpsed at it once when the door had been left ajar on one of the rare occasions she'd gone upstairs on an errand for Joanne. Half expecting to find the door locked, Alison walked down the hall and tried the doorknob. It turned. She stepped into the bedroom.

Her breath caught in her throat as she approached the bed. It was king-sized with elaborate wrought-iron posts and piled high with extra cushions. Very luxurious. Hard to believe that such a decadent bed was only being used for sleeping these days. One side table was stacked with hardcovers. Alison recognised the names on the spines as some of the authors from the agency. She moved around to the other side of the bed.

David's side.

Alison touched his pillow and tried to imagine his head lying there, his greying chestnut hair tousled from sleep – or sex. She shivered, despite the growing temperature in the room, as her hand drifted to the closed drawer of his side table.

I wonder, she thought, did he keep those toys Joanne had rejected?

Alison felt that it would be a shame if no one ever got to use them.

She slid open his drawer and gasped out loud. It was stuffed to the brim with magazines, their covers turned discreetly over, but she could guess what they were. A musky scent emanated from the pages and made her nostrils flare with longing. She took out the top magazine and flipped it over to see a lurid photo of a naked woman offering her oiled breasts to the viewer under the heading *Fantasy Letters*.

So, this must be what passes for David's sex life.

This was too much for Alison. She looked up at her own reflection in the wardrobe mirror, gave herself a coy little smile, and stripped herself as naked as the girl in the magazine before she pulled down the covers to prop herself up on David's side of the bed. She dug around in the drawer under the stack to see if she could find any sign of the toys, but it was not to be. Resigned to using only her fingers, Alison settled back on David's pillow, balanced open the magazine on her splayed lap, and began to read the outrageous 'true life' accounts of wild sex. The idea that David had already used these stories to wank himself off turned her on even more.

Her pussy was deliciously aroused. Alison was aware of her juices seeping down on to the bedclothes and felt a twinge of guilty panic. But no, it would be fine. If need be, she could wash the sheets. Or else leave the traces of her scent for David to accompany his sessions with his private stash. She ran her wet fingers along the side of his pillow so that he would dream of her.

Alison wanted to take her time and really enjoy this. Her heart was pounding as that familiar tingle began to spread upwards from her toes, warning her to slow down. She forced herself to leave her throbbing clit alone for a couple of minutes to stave off the crisis. Dropping one leg over the side of the bed, she half-turned to look at herself in the mirror again. There she was, naked in David's bed. The sight made her feel giddy.

Alison set the magazine aside and watched as she ran her hands over her breasts, pretending that it was David touching her, pinching her nipples and making them hard. She stroked lower over the little round swell of her belly and raked her fingers through her damp pubic hair, pulling her lips open so that she – and David, in her mind's eye – could better see the juicy pink interior.

'Touch me, David,' she whispered.

Slowly, lightly, just as David had on the back stairs,

she glided her fingertips over and around her clit, and then (as he had not the chance to do that night) pushed one finger deep up inside her. She retracted it with a moan and raised the finger to her mouth to lick and suck it dry of her juices before returning her hand to resume the gentle swirling around her clit. Alison closed her eyes and dropped her head back on to David's pillow, releasing a whiff of his scent with her movement. It wouldn't be much longer.

'Oh, yes,' she sighed. 'Lick me, David.'

There was a faint sound at the doorway of the bedroom. Alison turned her head languidly in the direction of the noise, and her eyes widened to see David standing there. With a little shriek, her hands flew to grasp at the bedclothes. In two steps, David was across the room, his hand holding her wrist, preventing her sudden modesty.

'No, don't you dare cover yourself up.'

His face looked stern. His left hand captured her other wrist and pinned her flailing hands still. His elbows kept her thighs open. Mortified, Alison looked past him towards the door in terror of seeing Joanne, but thankfully he seemed to be alone.

'Silly girl! We trusted you with the care of the house, and just look what you get up to behind our backs when you think the coast is clear. In our own bed ... and going through my private drawer.'

'David, I'm so sorry –'

'You mustn't be sorry, Alison,' he said. His expression changed.

'Were you searching for those toys I told you about? You won't find them. They're long gone. You'll have to settle for this –'

Alison's fear and embarrassment melted into pure joy as she saw him lowering his face into her cunt. Once he could tell she would not resist, David released her hands and she sank her fingers into his hair to urge him on. His tongue lapped her from bottom to top, sucking up the taste of her before he danced circles over her clit. Her back arched up as she felt his fingers tease the entrance, only plunging in after he had made her beg.

David's mouth hovered over her as he worked his fingers in and out.

'Tell me, Alison. What do you want now?' His tongue darted out to tease her clit with lightning-fast jabs.

'David ... fuck me.'

'What with? I haven't got that vibrator any more. Such a pity. You would have loved it – it was so long and thick.'

'Don't ... I'm so close ... please –'

'Don't? Well, if that's what you mean then I'll stop.'

Alison felt his hands and tongue move away. Don't tease, she had meant! She squeezed her eyes shut and cried out for release. David stopped teasing. He tore off his clothes as fast as he could and threw himself down on top of Alison. She was so hot and wet that his cock needed no guiding hand and he plunged up to the hilt into her cunt. Alison was a wild thing, digging her fingers into his back and buttocks, pressing him further inside as he pounded hard in his own urgent need to climax.

Alison gave in to the sensations and bucked her hips up against him as the ecstatic waves finally broke the surface. Her head dropped to the side and watched in the mirror as David rode out her orgasm with her until he reached his own. She smiled at her reflection to hear him call out her name, just as she had cried out his as she came.

They curled into a spooning embrace, David's head

tucked on to her shoulder. He watched in the mirror as his hands roved her body in long, lazy strokes. Alison sighed her contentment.

'So,' she murmured. 'What are you doing home from New York so soon?'

David shrugged. 'I felt unnecessary. I felt I should be in London doing my own work. And I felt like surprising you. To be honest, you've been the one full of surprises! You lewd girl – imagine playing with your cunt when you're meant to be working, and it isn't even noon!'

'Sorry to ruin your surprise.'

'Don't be. I loved it.'

Alison writhed her back against him, feeling his cock twitch back to life. He licked her neck and whispered hotly into her ear.

'In fact, I'll prove to you how much I loved it, and then –'

Alison reached around to grab a firm hold on his hard cock.

'And then what?' she asked, giving him a squeeze.

'And then we'll go shopping. I think I've finally found someone who could appreciate a few of those sex toys.'

The Jewel Carrera Devonshire

'Darling!' Anthea sweeps towards me across the elegant marbled hallway of her Belgravia town house. She plants two kisses in the air beside my cheeks. 'That dress is divine,' she purrs.

She should know. She designed it.

My boss has no difficulty recognising her creations. She could pick one out in a coal-mine without a torch. But pretending a dress is not hers is one of Anthea's favourite games. It allows her to sing a sly chorus of her own praises, giving her a veneer of modesty that fools no one.

'And you look lovely in it,' continues Anthea with a beneficent smile. She turns me towards a towering gilt-framed mirror and we both survey my reflection. I have to agree. The dress is fabulous, and it does suit me very well. It's cut from fine crêpe de Chine in the darkest possible blue and falls to just above my ankles. Boned and lined to perfection, the fabric flows over the curves of my hips, slithering deliciously over my thighs and bottom. It scoops too low to wear a bra, but is so well tailored that it easily supports my breasts. They rise up – plump and luscious – above the plunging neckline.

'But it needs something else,' says Anthea, frowning as her gifted mind grapples to identify the missing ingredient. 'Some decent jewellery perhaps.'

Jewellery is Anthea's passion. Fortunately, after thirty years at the top of the international fashion business,

Anthea has made a substantial fortune and is well able to indulge her taste for expensive trinkets.

She reaches behind her head and unclips her necklace – a single tear-shaped diamond suspended on an aged gold chain. Standing behind me, she fastens the necklace around my neck. I feel an almost erotic thrill as the flawless stone slides down my throat and nestles at the top of my cleavage.

'Oh, Anthea.' I reach up to touch the magnificent gem. 'May I borrow it? Just for tonight?'

Anthea laughs. 'Of course, darling. But do take great care of it. And now, let's take your wonderful dress and your wonderful necklace out for an equally wonderful night on the town.'

The evening is everything Anthea promises. A treat for her staff at the end of an exhausting but highly successful London Fashion Week, Anthea entertains me, and the rest of her team, in grand style. Dinner in one of London's most illustrious restaurants is followed by a whirlwind tour of the city's fashionable clubs.

When I return to my flat in the early hours of the morning, I fling myself on to my bed. But I'm too excited to sleep. I lie quite still, the memories of the evening spinning in my head. I remember the diamond against my skin. The powerful charge I got from wearing it. I remember how its sparkling beauty had drawn attention to my breasts. And how I had enjoyed the admiring glances.

Slipping my hands inside the top of my dress, I ease my tits from the bodice. Bound by the fabric, they cleave and bulge attractively. As I look down I can feel my breath against the creamy white curves. I watch my nipples harden as arousal grows.

I draw up my knees and the dress tumbles up my

legs, sliding slowly up my stocking-clad thighs. I run my hands over the sheer nylon, enjoying the contrasting tones of the steel-smooth fabric and the firm flesh beneath. Above the stockings I am naked and my bare skin tempts me. My fingers float up my legs to drift over the down of my pubes.

For a while I'm content with this gentle tease, but as my desire builds I need more. My sex grows heavy with want and I ache for relief. I can't resist any longer. I press one finger down between the plump lips to meet the throbbing bud that is my clit. My finger swirls, tormenting the tiny erection into a hard point. I dip my thumb deeper into the oily wetness, sighing at the moment of penetration.

I turn on to my stomach, and I feel the slightest roughness in the sheets against my nipples as my breasts fall forwards on to the bed. Parting my thighs, I moan out loud. At first I move slowly, my body undulating to a languid tempo. But soon I become more savage. As I near my end, I can't help thrusting my hips, and I hump my own hand, my need to climax becoming urgent. The position is undignified and my masturbation is not pretty. But I don't care. Nothing but my orgasm can stop me now.

I plunge my dress between my thighs, and the fabric saws at my sex, splitting the swollen flesh. This is the trigger to my orgasm and I reach my peak, my sex spasming gloriously against my knotted fingers.

As the last ripples of my climax fade, I reach up to touch the chain around my neck. It is only then I realise the jewel has gone.

There is nothing else to do. I must buy another diamond. Anthea ranks carelessness as a cardinal sin and I can't face explaining the loss of the jewel. I spend Saturday morning scouring the West End for a replacement. At last I see it – a stunning tear-shaped gem – resplendent in the window of one of Bond Street's smartest jewellers. A liveried doorman stands aside as I step into the shop.

There is just one other customer, a man, looking at a display of gold-encrusted glassware. He catches my eye and smiles. The smile is fleeting but full of promise and something about it sends a ripple of pleasure through me.

I ask to see the stone. An assistant brings it to me, laying it on the satin-topped counter with a flourish. I reach out to caress its cool, smooth surface.

'How much?' I ask. The jeweller regards me with barely disguised contempt.

'Ten thousand pounds, madam,' comes the snooty reply. My heart sinks. There's no way I can afford that amount of money.

'Oh,' I stammer. 'That's more than I'd hoped. I'll have to leave it.' Hot tears prick my eyes as the shop assistant moves to put the jewel back in the window.

'No, wait.' I hear a voice and turn to see the customer standing next to me. 'I want to buy it.' The impulsive shopper tosses a platinum credit card on to the counter.

He is tall and broad. His expensively casual clothes hang stylishly on his well-proportioned body. As he leans forward to sign the credit card slip, his dark hair flops forward over his handsome face. I stare after him as he tucks the jewel into his jacket pocket and leaves the shop.

But outside on the pavement he's waiting for me. He's leaning against the shop window in an attitude of studied indifference.

'I really wanted that diamond,' I say. A flicker of amusement crosses his lips.

'I know. And you shall have it. In return for spending

tonight with me.' His bizarre proposition takes me by surprise and I stare blankly at him, unable to think of a reply.

'What's the matter?' He lifts a graceful hand and runs the tip of his finger over my mouth. Involuntarily my lips part and I taste his skin against my tongue. 'I have something you want,' he says. 'You have something I want. It would be a fair exchange.' He fixes me with dazzlingly blue eyes. 'What's wrong with that?'

'Nothing,' I reply. 'I'm just a little shocked.'

'And if you can shock me tonight, you can have your diamond.' His name, he tells me, is Sebastian.

Shocking he wants and shocking he shall get. I've prepared for my date with great care and, as I check my reflection, I am more than satisfied with my appearance. My make-up is perfect. My eyes are rimmed with black, my lashes mascara'd to an impossible length. My lips are painted deep crimson. I fluff up my blonde hair to create a look that's part Barbie doll, part porn star.

My outfit, purchased hastily this afternoon in one of Soho's less respectable shops, is a million miles from my usual understated style. My feet are squeezed into ridiculously high-heeled black patent boots. Rising to halfway up my thighs, they force me into a slightly unsteady gait, giving me an air of rakish abandon. I'm wearing black fishnet stockings, which rustle seductively as my thighs brush together. When I move, I catch an occasional glimpse of white flesh between their deep lace tops and the hem of my black latex skirt.

I have never worn rubber before but now, as I see what it's done for my figure, I understand its charms. Polished to a glasslike shine, the latex emphasises every curve of my body. As I ease my hips forward, the swell of my mound is clearly visible beneath the glossy fabric.

My cropped top is also made of latex, lashed tightly together at the front by a leather lace to create a wonderfully deep cleavage. My breasts are barely contained by the tiny scrap of rubber and they almost spill out of the indecently restrictive garment. The outfit is finished by a black leather collar around my throat. I look like a tart. And I love it.

Waiting for Sebastian, my stomach flutters with excitement at the challenge that faces me. I want the diamond. I want to win. But most of all I want to play the game.

When Sebastian arrives, he makes no comment about my appearance. We speed off through the London streets in his long, low sports car.

Sebastian takes me to a smart restaurant in Mayfair and my outfit causes a stir as I stride across the crowded room in my spiky boots. There's a lull in the conversation as I pass tables of corpulent, suited diners. Men gawp, forks laden with food poised in front of their open mouths. I imagine them dashing away from the restaurant to masturbate frantically. Or fantasising about my latex-encased body as they fuck their fat wives.

We dine well. Good food is washed down with quantities of champagne.

'Where to?' Sebastian asks after the meal.

'Perhaps a film?'

'Anything you fancy?'

'Oh, yes,' I say.

The private cinema club in a seedy back street is almost deserted – its only customers a few drab-looking men dotted around the darkened auditorium. As we enter, no one looks away from the movie. I too am transfixed by the action as we find our seats.

On the screen is a close-up of a large cock pumping mechanically into the anus of a woman. As the shot widens, we see her squatting above her lover, her head thrown back, her mouth open in pain or pleasure. Her fingers are thrusting into her sex, her thumb rakes feverishly against her clit. She may be faking it, but her masturbation looks very convincing. I long to be touching myself in the same way. Her partner pushes her away as he nears his orgasm and we see him come, his spunk arching up to splash against the lips of her wide open cunt. Two rows in front of us, a balding businessman groans as he too climaxes into his coat.

I slip to cramped space on the floor between Sebastian's legs, my back pressing against the row of seats in front. In the darkness he can't see my face, but he understands my invitation. With one hand he reaches down and unzips his flies. He slips his hand inside his boxer shorts and takes out his cock. Turned on by the porn film, he is already semi-erect. As he fingers himself, I watch in fascination as he fills and thickens further still. I lean forward and feel the head of his prick bounce lightly against my lips as he masturbates. I breathe in the manly, warm scent of him.

The film and the touch of his own hand fuel his need and he shifts his hips, eager for more. I bend over him and lower my lips over his now solid shaft. He lets out a little moan of pleasure as I take him into my mouth, my lips sliding down to the shadowy base of him and then back up the glistening surface to the very tip. I devour him, feasting greedily on his succulent flesh while he watches the film. Curling my fingers around him, I use one hand to double the sensation. I reach down into the darkness and stroke myself, my free hand picking up the rhythm as I wank us both.

Quite suddenly, he reaches down and grabs my hair, holding me still against his cock. I wait, knowing what the stillness means. Then a tremor runs through him and I feel his cock jerk as his come foams across my tongue. His orgasm is long and strong and he pumps spurt after spurt of delicious liquid into me. I gulp it down, enjoying the flavour of him. As I swallow the last drop, I too begin to climax into my hand.

When finally we are finished, I stand up and kiss him, pushing my tongue past his lips while the taste of him still fills my mouth.

'Shocked?' I ask. But Sebastian only smiles.

Walking back to his car, we talk about the film. I hear his breath quicken and his voice deepens with renewed desire as we discuss what had turned us on.

'What was your favourite bit?' I ask. He laughs, almost shyly, and does not reply.

'Go on,' I coax, 'I'm not easily shocked.'

'I liked the bit where she peed herself.' He speaks quietly, his voice hardly above a whisper. 'The expression on her face as he watched her do it was really lovely. She looked so vulnerable. So exposed. It's such a private act; I'd love to see a woman soak her knickers like that.' I stop walking and he turns to meet my steady gaze.

'Really?' He holds his breath as I back into an unlit doorway and slowly lift my skirt. 'Like this?'

I plant my legs apart and lower my body into a squat, my thighs spread wide. He recognises the position.

'Jesus,' he mutters. 'You're going to piss.' I let myself go. He watches as I urinate, golden liquid flooding through the black lace of my panties. The release is almost orgasmic and I groan again as relief seeps through my veins. The final drips splash from me in little spurts.

I have barely finished before he grabs me by the waist and shoves me deeper into the shadows. Then, ripping my wet underwear to one side, he pulls me on to his rampant cock. His climax begins even before he is fully inside me.

Later, at his riverside loft, we lounge on sumptuous sofas and sip cognac. I sit opposite him, deliberately placing myself where I can offer him the best view. I spread my legs wide. Now I am wearing nothing under my skirt but he doesn't react as he eyes my naked mound. His phone rings and, with a polite 'Excuse me', he takes the call.

I yawn ostentatiously, letting him know that if he won't amuse me, I will do something to amuse myself. As he talks, I reach up to unfasten the lacing on the front of my top. It's so tight that, when I untie the knot, the latex slides open almost on its own. He carries on watching as my bosom comes into view. I shrug off the top and my breasts sway as I shake my shoulders. Still talking into his phone, he surveys my bare tits, and I can tell by the slight smile on his face that he approves. I reach down and caress the ample curves, lifting one breast and then the other, letting him see them shift and ripple beneath my touch.

'I've received the paperwork,' says Sebastian, 'I'll sign it in the morning.' My hands move further down the plane of my stomach and over the diminutive skirt. Bracing my legs apart, I slide my fingers through the curls of my pubes towards my clit, which is again yearning for attention. I let my finger flutter in the lightest possible caress. The pleasure is intense. As I sweep my finger over the tiny bud and the hot opening of my sex I can't contain a sigh.

'Yes,' I hear Sebastian say, 'the deal should be concluded by the end of the week.'

My lids flutter and then close as sensation leaps

through my body. But I can feel his eyes on me as I lie back and roll my hips. I hear a slight unsteadiness in his voice as I raise one hand to my mouth and lick my fingers. I run my tongue the length of each, savouring the taste of my own wetness. Then I slide my damp palm back down my body and use one finger to fuck myself. Sebastian's call ends, but I am too turned on to stop touching myself. I arch my back and grind against my hand, giving him the show I know he wants to see and which I am now compelled to perform.

Sebastian speaks first.

'What are you doing?' There is a hint of outrage in his voice.

'I'm sorry,' I say, feigning contrition. 'Is it rude to masturbate in front of a man on a first date?'

'Yes,' he mutters. 'Oh, God, yes.'

I open my eyes to see Sebastian standing over me. His cock is in his hand. Once again, it is hard and huge. He rubs it furiously, holding it close to my face – so close that I can hear the moist slapping of skin against skin. He is staring fixedly at my hand as my fingers move lazily in and out of my sex. His face begins to distort and, hunched over his swollen cock, he masturbates hard. I wonder what it will look like to see him come at such close range.

Neither of us hears the door open. But, aware that we are being watched, I look up into a pair of eyes that are the same blue as Sebastian's. They belong to a girl, who stands as if frozen. By embarrassment or fascination I cannot tell.

'Sorry, Sebs,' she says, 'I didn't realise you were ... entertaining.'

Hurriedly, Sebastian shoves his cock back inside his trousers. I make only a token effort to cover my own bared breasts and pussy.

'This is Diana,' he stammers. 'My sister. She's staying with me for a few days.' Sebastian's introduction is almost dismissive, as if he has never noticed Diana's obvious good looks.

Diana has clearly been out partying. She's wearing a short pink dress, which flashes at least a yard of tanned leg. Her feet are bare and a pair of high, strappy shoes dangles from one finger. Her sleek magenta hair is trimmed into a neat bob – the kind of cut that falls back into place, no matter how wild the night.

She sits, perching on the edge of a chair, and we chat. But underlying our polite conversation is the knowledge that I am naked beneath my slut's outfit. Diana, I can tell, is curious. When she gets up to go, I know she does not want to leave.

'I'll just get myself a drink then I'm off to bed,' she says, throwing a knowing smile at Sebastian as she crosses the room. She moves with easy grace, long limbs rippling like a fit thoroughbred. After sloshing an inch of Sebastian's cognac into a glass, she turns to go.

'No, wait.' I lean forward and place my hand on Diana's knee. She jumps slightly at my touch, and for a moment I hesitate. But, as I inch my fingers to the inside of her thigh, she makes no attempt to move away.

'Stay,' I whisper. 'Just for a little while.' I slide my hand further up her leg. Her flesh is warm and slightly damp. I meet her gaze and see alarm in her eyes. But behind it there is something else. The first spark of desire. As I move higher I'm not sure if I feel her step slightly further apart. Emboldened, my hand rises again. Diana holds her breath. So do I. Finally I reach her mound and, almost casually, as if by some wicked accident, I run my finger gently over the satin-covered swelling. The sensation of female underwear against my fingertips sends a new and thrilling buzz through me. I linger, stroking, coaxing, until Diana's eyes close and she begins to sway against me, her hips taking up a beat as old as time.

I reach up to take the glass from Diana and place it on the floor. Taking hold of her wrists, I ease Diana's body over mine. Poised above me, she looks into my face, awaiting my next move. I reach up to the fine straps of her dress and inch them over her shoulders. As the fabric slides down her arms, her breasts are slowly revealed. One deep pink nipple then the other is bared. The sight is breathtakingly lovely and for a moment I can only stare. I reach down and dip my finger into the brandy. Then, with a wet fingertip, I trace a tiny circle around each dark nipple. I marvel as the liquid-chilled tips pucker and point.

Sebastian groans as I pull Diana towards my face and begin to lick, lapping at the pert, brandy-flavoured breasts with long, slow strokes. I draw one erect nipple into my mouth and flick my tongue against her in a teasing caress that I know I would so enjoy myself.

Diana arches against me, and I feel the subtle but insistent pressure of her mound against my stomach as she seeks the contact she so clearly now needs. I move my hands down her body, and lift her dress to reach her minute, and now very damp, panties.

As I ease the fabric away from her sex, I am gratified to hear a soft whimper from Diana. The whimper becomes a low sigh of pleasure as I slip one finger into the wetness. Instinctively, I know what to do. I touch her as I would touch myself, the pace and pressure increasing as Diana's pleasure builds.

It is almost too strong. She leans heavily against me, sliding down my body and on to the floor in a daze of ecstasy. Sprawled face down over the edge of the sofa,

Diana looks magnificent. With her dress flipped up over her bottom and her panties in a little bunch around the tops of her thighs, she is ruthlessly exposed. I am transfixed by the full lips of her pussy. She is as tempting as sun-warmed fruit and I long to sink my teeth into her delicious flesh. I wonder if Sebastian feels the same. I glance up to see his erection pushing up hard against the front of his trousers, distorting the fabric into a strong bulge. Oh yes. His feelings are clear. He stares at Diana's inert body, his eyes glazed and fixed on the dark shadow of her sex.

I run one hand casually over the curve of Diana's buttocks, letting my fingers stray towards the pink crease between the tops of her thighs. Her flesh parts like a ripe peach as my fingers move lower. The inner folds glisten with her juices. I move my hand underneath Diana's trembling body and she writhes against my fingers as I find her clit and begin to fondle it once more.

'Look,' I say, easing her thighs further apart so Sebastian can see clearly how splendid she is. 'Don't you want her?' Sebastian is staring at her, eyes dark with lust.

'But she's my sister.' I raise an eyebrow. Surely he's not shocked?

Diana has no such qualms. She moans with increasing passion as I continue to stroke her swollen clit. She's so high, I know it won't take much to sweep her away. Soon she is trembling with need. She is desperate to be fucked – even by her own brother.

'Please, Sebs,' she whimpers. 'Please put it in me. Please fuck me.'

Still sitting on the sofa in front of us, Sebastian observes her mounting arousal with an interest he can't disguise. I watch him struggle with his conscience. But desire is spurring him on and he's not in control. Unsure, he shoots me a nervous glance. I nod, giving him all the encouragement he needs.

He looks back at Diana's proffered body. He can't resist her. He kneels behind Diana and, scrabbling to untangle himself from his clothing, guides the tip of his prick to her waiting cunt. I watch as he slides into her. Diana sighs with bliss as he slowly fucks her, burying his cock deep, his hard stomach pressing against her upturned arse. Their faultless bodies flow together, rising and falling as one. The silence is broken only by the occasional low moan and the faint, almost imperceptible slurp of cock dipping through willing wet cunt.

But soon I too am overcome by the need to be filled. The divine cock slipping in and out of Diana becomes necessary to me. As necessary as my next breath. I climb astride Diana, my booted legs straddling her bare thighs. On my hands and knees over her, I ease my skirt up over my bottom and part my legs to offer Sebastian my sex above Diana's. Faced with two cunts from which to choose, Sebastian can't conceal his delight.

'Oh, girls,' he sighs. 'You are so beautiful.'

He takes his prick out of Diana and stands up behind me. I feel him ease into my surrendered sex, a craving emptiness slowly and perfectly filled. As he begins to thrust against me, my body is rocked, pressing my clit against Diana's lovely bottom. My breasts slide over the smooth skin of her back. I reach down and slide my hands under her, wanking her with my new-found expertise. She moans and her trembling pleasure thrills me. My power over her is a strong aphrodisiac – it is as much as I can do to hold back the orgasm that threatens to engulf me.

Greedy as a schoolboy in a sweet shop, Sebastian is finding it hard to make up his mind. Bending his knees, he lunges into Diana again. Then it's me. He plunges into one and then the other, enjoying us both to the full.

It is Diana who climaxes first. At first it is the merest shiver, then her orgasm builds and powerful spasms ripple up my fingers. As I feel her coming against my hand, I can restrain myself no longer. Grinding myself against the pert globes of her arse, I reach my own orgasm, moaning with pleasure as each delicious wave washes over me.

And now Sebastian is free to give way. It is Diana he chooses as he reaches his end. I feel him shake as he pours himself into her forbidden body.

The next morning I awake in Sebastian's bed after a dreamless sleep. Yawning, I stretch my legs against crisp linen sheets. Sebastian and Diana are gone, but on the pillow beside my head is a small leather box. I open it and see the diamond, cushioned in blue velvet. Next to the box is a card. I pick it up and read: 'You shocked me!'

Nearly a week passes before I see the diamond again. Anthea wears it to work. It sparkles enticingly against her black cashmere sweater, as beautiful as ever. I can't tear my eyes away and I find myself staring at it as Anthea moves about the office.

Catching me looking at her, she walks towards my desk. For a ghastly moment I wonder if I've been rumbled. But Anthea is smiling at me. She covers the gem with a manicured hand.

'You like it very much, don't you?'

'Yes,' I stammer. 'Very much.' I know I won't be able to relax until I'm certain she hasn't noticed the switch and I risk a question.

'Is it part of the collection you bought at that Cartier auction last year?' Anthea tosses her head and laughs.

'Good Lord, no!' she says. 'I got it from a stall at Camden Lock market. Only paid five pounds for it. But it's so pretty you'd almost believe it was real, wouldn't you?'

'Yes,' I say, the word catching in my suddenly parched throat.

'But if you love it so much, you must have it.' Anthea lifts the chain from her neck and presses the diamond into my hand. My fingers close around the cold stone. 'Please. Keep it,' she whispers.

And I will.

After all, I earned it.

Helping With Enquiries

Ruth Fox

My heart thumped with excitement as I walked under the blue light, then through the double doors that lead into our local small-town police station. I know its not every girl's cup of tea but for me the authoritative figure of a hunk in uniform is the ultimate turn-on and the anticipation was exquisite.

I had longed all my life for an excuse to get closer to a copper but it had never happened. Even on New Year's Eve, when all my drunken friends grabbed the officers on duty in the town square, I was far too intimidated. My interest, which had almost climbed to fetish proportions, wouldn't allow me to ask for the customary kiss because I was convinced I would make a fool of myself. I even had a pair of handcuffs to fantasise with and a keyring that stated to the world that I was willing to 'come quietly'. But I hadn't been quite prepared for this.

The civilian at the desk was a disappointment to me but I decided that, as I was here for such an embarrassing reason, I should be grateful. I waited my turn and then told the girl that I was there to make a statement about a burglary at my flat. I felt sure that the culprit was my landlord but, when I called the police, it was suggested that I came and gave a statement.

The girl behind the counter gave me a very reassuring smile then asked me to take a seat; someone would be with me in a minute. I had been waiting for about ten minutes when the door to the inner sanctum opened and a very horny-looking copper in full uniform came out and walked over to the desk. His shoes were so shiny you could have made up your face in them, his shirt was crisp and white with the dark contrast of the epaulettes immediately setting him apart from your everyday ordinary bloke. He had a flat peaked hat with a chequered band tucked under his arm and a very broad grin on his face. As he turned and looked me up and down my heart fluttered. He chatted for a moment to the girl behind the counter, called goodnight to her as she collected her bag from her chair and left the station, passing me with a smile.

'Miss Johnson?' he queried. 'Would you come with me?'

I chuckled inside, thinking how surprised he would be if he knew how I would have liked to answer that question. God, how I would like to come with him, straddling his truncheon if possible. I followed him down a hospital-like corridor, watching his bum in the dark serge trousers while he explained that I was lucky to catch him in. Apparently the station closed in forty minutes. Then I followed him into a very bare room that only housed a Formica-covered table, two chairs, one each side, and a security camera attached to the wall. There was a grubby ashtray on the table and a bin in the corner. That was it.

I had a chance then to examine him closely as he laid out paper and pens from a drawer in the table and adjusted the amazingly sexy belt around his waist. The wide black belt was covered in paraphernalia that sent the blood pounding in my temples. There was the black side-angled baton that hung from his body like a weapon of torture, pouches with things in them that I could only begin to imagine and a rigid leather case to hold his handcuffs. My eyes were riveted on those handcuffs. All my resolve to behave in an adult and grown-up way went completely by the board when he unbuckled the belt and laid the whole thing on the table in front of me.

'Hope you don't mind, love, but it is such a treat to get the weight off.'

I stuttered pathetically, which caused him to look at me properly for the first time. He looked directly at me, taking in my tight short denim skirt, skimpy summer top and high strappy sandals on bare brown long legs. He quickly looked back to his paper; I am sure to regain his composure.

'Are you OK?' he asked me, looking up again and searching my face for signs of a problem, but I managed a smile and brushed it off.

'Would you like a glass of water?'

'That would be lovely, thanks, I am a bit nervous.'

'You don't need to be nervous. I promise I will be gentle with you.'

I looked into his eyes to see if he was playing with his words but he appeared to be totally innocent of all knowledge of the effect he was having on me. I fidgeted in my seat to relieve the intense discomfort between my thighs and licked my lips that had gone dry with I don't know what. Either nerves or arousal, but I wasn't sure which reaction was most in the forefront of my mind. I did know, however, that I found PC North, with his knowing eyes and his tall lean body encased in the complete turn-on of his uniform, absolutely irresistible.

He left the room to go and get my water, leaving me with his belt and my thoughts. I longed to touch things, to see what the other pouches contained, but I was too scared he might come back. I did have to touch the handcuffs though. I leant forward and tentatively stroked the shiny silver metal as the fantasy of being trapped in them crashed through my conscious thought. The idea of PC North locking me in them was even more thrilling and I allowed my thoughts to run away with me as I slid them out of the case. They weren't like the cuffs I had seen before but both cuffs were in a rigid line with a square of black hard plastic in between. I could only begin to imagine how helpless a prisoner would feel in them. Just as I tucked them back into their case I heard a soft whirring noise. I jumped back in my seat as I frantically looked around to see what had made the sound. The camera on the wall was moving almost imperceptibly, but when I looked up it stopped and I almost believed I had imagined it.

PC North came back with my glass of water and sat, passing me the glass. As I leant forward to take a sip my heart stopped. PC North was taking the handcuffs out of the pouch and turning them round. He grinned at me very knowingly and replaced them. I was mortified. I knew then that he had seen me playing with them and I instinctively looked up at the camera, but it sat innocently still.

The moment was broken and almost forgotten when PC North asked me to tell him what had happened in my flat the night before. I began to explain that I had arrived home from work to find that things didn't feel right. Too many things had been moved for it to be my imagination and when I had looked into my bedroom I knew someone had been there. He asked how I knew that someone had touched my things and I explained that clothes in my wardrobe were facing the wrong way, a way that I would never put them.

'Hmm,' he agreed. 'I know what you mean. Its very obvious when something you know well has been tampered with, isn't it?' While he asked this very leading question he put his hand firmly on the handcuff case on his utility belt and waited for my answer. It was obvious that he knew I had fiddled with his things but luckily, for some reason, he was happy just to embarrass me. After a second or two of revelling in my discomfort he changed the subject.

'Has this happened before?'

'A few times, but until yesterday I always thought I imagined it. This time he actually took things.'

'Have you brought a list of the stolen items, Miss Johnson?'

'Er ... no, I didn't think.'

'No problem. I can make out a list now to save time.'

'Oh, God, do I really have to? Its so embarrassing,' I cried.

'Look, Miss Johnson.' He then looked down at his paper and changed it to, 'Look, Beth, I am a police officer. There is nothing you could tell me that I haven't heard before. The sooner we get started, the sooner we can finish and we can both get off home.'

'Well ...' I stammered, 'there was at least ten pairs of knickers and one or two bras.'

'Would you give me a description of them please,' he asked with an almost smug look on his face. I brazened it out then, hoping to put him on the spot but, as I reeled off the list of lacy G-strings, shiny thongs and wispy items of lingerie that I thought would only ever be discussed with a partner, he looked me right in the eye. He asked the colours, the sizes and a more intimate description before asking if there was anything else. The item he lingered on longest was a PVC black bustier, one of my favourites.

'Was anything else taken?'

I had never realised just how transparent I was until I mumbled 'No' and he admonished me for lying and asked again if there was anything else that was missing.

'If you aren't honest with me, Beth, I won't have a true picture and the chances of ever catching the person who violated you will be next to nil. Now, come on, you have come this far, you might as well tell me it all. How about I go and make us a cup of tea while you think of what else you have to tell me?' With that he left the room, but within a few seconds I clearly heard the camera move into position. I knew without a doubt that I was being watched. To test my suspicion I got up and moved about the room, standing on tiptoe to look out of the barred window and leaning against the wall by the door. Each time I moved, the camera moved with me, following my progress then silently awaiting my next move.

Thoughts fought for supremacy in my brain. Was it PC North? If so, was he just checking me or was there a more intimate reason for his observance of me? Perhaps the camera automatically scanned the room at regular intervals? I was quite apprehensive about what appeared to be happening but also extremely aroused. The idea of PC North watching me unseen was such a turn-on that I felt myself flood with need. The sticky juices oozed from me to dampen the crotch of my knickers. I decided to test him. I stood in the centre of the room and bent over to supposedly adjust the buckle on my sandal. I knew that my breasts were bulging over the top of my T-shirt and that, if the camera was angled right, the watcher would be able to see up my short skirt to my disgustingly wet knickers. The reaction of the voyeur camera was immediate, focusing on me instantly and confirming my suspicions. I knew that if it had been PC North then he would return in seconds, so I hurried back to my chair and sat with my legs crossed and the chair pushed well away from the table.

'Here we are then,' PC North said as he placed the tray on the table between us less then a minute later. 'Are you ready to tell me everything now?'

He looked down at my legs where they crossed and cleared his throat. He ran his finger inside the collar of his shirt and looked decidedly uncomfortable, so I decided to call his bluff.

With the least inflection in my voice I could manage, I looked pointedly at the camera and asked if we were being filmed.

Poor PC North looked very sheepish then. He couldn't meet my gaze as he answered that of course we weren't being filmed – actually we were the only ones left in the station. He tried to persuade me that I could tell him anything and I longed to tell him things that would blow his socks off. I wanted to explain in detail how my pussy was wet and my nipples were hard under my T-shirt, how I longed to have the nerve to lean over and undress this very horny officer of the law. The play with the camera had awoken a devil in me that would not be quietened.

I scooted my chair up to the table, rested my arms on the top and leant forward to give him a taste of what I was feeling, but I think it was unnecessary. PC North looked very uncomfortable as he tried to keep his eyes on my face, but every few seconds his hungry gaze would stray to my breasts as they spilled forward.

'I had a few intimate items in my bedroom that have gone missing. I kept them under my bed in a small case but when I came home from work yesterday they had gone and the case was on top of my bed empty. It's so stupid; they are not the kind of things a burglar would steal, so it must be my landlord. He is always leering at me through my windows when I am getting undressed or I catch him lurking in the hallway or just generally watching me.'

'Do you encourage him, Beth?'

'Of course I don't,' I replied, red faced at his suggestion.

'So how does he see you getting undressed? Do you leave the curtains open? Surely if you undress in front of an open window ...' he enquired, leaving the sentence unfinished but with such weighted suggestion in his voice that I blushed.

'I can't help it if I forget sometimes, can I? Sometimes I just do things I shouldn't, without thinking of the consequences. Anyway, that doesn't give him the right to let himself into my flat and help himself, does it?' I questioned, angry that he appeared to be on the wrong side.

'No,' he agreed, drawing out the word until it sounded just like a disagreement. 'But it does seem to me that you do things without thinking, which might cause events you don't necessarily want.' With that he looked from the camera to his handcuffs.

Before I had a chance to respond, and while I was still blushing profusely, he insisted that I tell him exactly what was in the case that I kept under my bed. By that stage I really wished I hadn't reported the theft at all. I was very uncomfortable. It was obvious he had been watching me touch his things and also that he knew I bent down to taunt him. I was torn. Should I tell him? My toys in the box were for my private use and no one knew about them. How could I tell this gorgeous man about my vibrator and the pretend handcuffs that I fantasised with when I masturbated? I couldn't. It was as simple as that.

'Look, they were very personal items that I really

don't feel able to discuss. I can tell you that they didn't have any value. Not monetary value anyway.' I turned away and muttered under my breath that I would really miss them though.

'You might as well come clean, Beth. It's obvious they were sexual items so you might as well just tell me. If you don't, I will have to guess, won't I? And that would be even more embarrassing. Embarrassing for you and for me. Come on, we all have toys we play with.'

'Yeah, right. Of course you do,' I snapped. Even though I was very embarrassed by the conversation I was also very excited at the image of him having sex and using toys. I almost groaned at a vivid picture in my mind of him, still in uniform, standing over me, with me handcuffed to my bed.

We batted questions and innuendoes backward and forward for another ten minutes. I longed to just tell him about the toys, and that I fancied him like mad and, if I am honest, that I wanted him to fuck me but I wasn't quite sure how he felt. I couldn't bear the thought of getting it wrong. I was almost convinced that he felt the same way as me but he had to be so careful that I knew he would probably never make the first move.

PC North stood up and excused himself and left the room; I was again left on my own with his 'toys'.

Within a few seconds I heard the camera whirr into position and I knew it was now or never. I faced the camera and looked right at the lens. I took his long black side-angled baton out of the belt that still lay on the table in front of me. I stroked the cool length of it from top to bottom suggestively. I gripped hold of the mushroom-shaped handle and ran my hand down the short side that is designed for holding and the other end that must have been at least fifteen inches long. Then, without another thought, I opened my legs and slid it between them. Clutching the rock-hard weapon between my thighs and knowing he was watching had to be the most exciting feeling I had ever experienced. I gyrated it backward and forward, sliding the length of it over my wet knickers while clutching hold of the side angle, lost in my fantasy now.

I had totally forgotten PC North as a hunger for more engulfed me. I closed my eyes to enjoy the feelings more intensely, imagining his handcuffs controlling me. The click of the door shocked me back to the present and I blushed profusely as he strode across the room. I was convinced he was going to do something awful but he just grinned at me and slipped his cuffs from their pouch. He retrieved another pair from his back pocket and, without a pause, took the baton from my hand and held it up to his nose.

That wicked PC breathed deeply of my smell then groaned with pleasure. He took one of my wrists, gave me a second or two as he looked questioningly into my eyes, then rested the edge of the cuff firmly against my flesh.

'Oh, God, yes,' I moaned shamelessly.

The pressure he put on the cuff released the clasp and it trapped my wrist effortlessly. I expected him to attach it to the other wrist but he took the second pair and did the same. I stood there weak-kneed as he steered me towards the table. When the edge was pressing against my hips he pushed me forward until I was stretched over the tabletop. He then walked so calmly around the front, knowing I wasn't going anywhere. How arrogantly he assumed that I would just wait for him to make his next move. When he fixed the spare ends of the cuffs to the front legs of the table I was stretched out like an insect specimen.

The feeling of being so completely helpless was all I had ever dreamt of. I was stretched out so tightly that I could only just breathe comfortably. The sinews in my arms were taught and my head lay sideways on the cold Formica as I felt my insides flood out in a tide of perfect need, soaking my knickers and dribbling down my legs. I couldn't believe how turned on I was and he hadn't even touched me. Neither of us had said a word when he picked up his baton and weighed it in his hands. He automatically twisted it into place under his arm and almost stood to attention before he walked around the table to stand behind me. I felt every inch of its length as he laid it along my back but I knew he had freed his hands for a reason. I gasped out loud as his hands firmly took hold of the hem of my skirt and wriggled it up to my waist. He grasped the top of my knickers and, without any ceremony, removed them.

By this time I was grunting loudly into the table, the sweat was pouring from me and my legs were flailing helplessly, trying in vain to protect my modesty. I am not quite sure why I wanted to protect myself because I craved this exposure with every fibre of my being.

He picked up the baton again and I felt the cold end press against my pussy from behind. Instinct made me close my legs even though I was desperate for something inside me, violating me.

'Open your legs, Miss Johnson.' His amazing voice took complete control of me.

I fluttered a bit, moaning my pleasure at his barked instruction, so authoritative, so different to earlier.

'Now, Beth,' he ordered.

I obeyed without hesitation. I opened my naked legs as far as they would go, knowing I was exposing everything. I felt the end of the long baton push through my sticky lips and into my pussy and I wriggled with acute arousal. The girth of it was huge as it stretched me wide, forcing its welcome entry. I thought I was going to come on the spot but delicious PC North managed to keep me on the boil with his impressive rod of hard plastic, so like my lost vibrator at home but three times the length. I thought I would pass out with the excitement as he pushed it further into me.

I had never felt so full, so stretched, so incredibly aroused. I tried to imagine how that symbol of all that excited me, the total symbol of police power, must look as it disappeared into my restrained captive body. I cried out as the pole was twisted and turned in my juices, sliding inside me yet further. It wriggled and wormed its way so deep inside me that I felt his fist against my bottom. He was clutching the stumpy side angle as he rammed the straight end into my desperately hungry hole.

I think I was wailing by this time, totally unashamed at my debauchery. I was finally living out my fantasy and I intended to enjoy every second. Without any warning my beloved PC North slipped the baton from between my legs and came around the table until he was standing in front of my face, brandishing the sticky length. My head slightly hung over the edge of the table. I could see his shiny black boots, his sharply creased trousers and the bulging zip on his fly. I tried hard to look up at him but could only just catch a glimpse of his white shirt and tie and the glistening black plastic 'toy' that he held between my face and his groin. Behind his shoulder was the camera that had started it all, sitting innocently on the wall.

I was shocked to the core when he placed the wet shiny end against my lips but I had no hesitation as I opened my mouth as wide as I could to accommodate the instrument of my greed. I sucked shamelessly as if it were human, which obviously gave him the same idea as me.

He unzipped his trousers agonisingly slowly then, true to my fantasy, just flipped out his cock from the opening. What a perfect cock in a perfect setting. It was all blue-veined, hard and purple-ended, surrounded by navy serge. Heaven. He moved forward and it surprised me how easy it suddenly was for me to raise my head. He grabbed hold of my hair and forced my head to a good position for him, as if I were just a receptacle. His hot cock slipped into my throat as neatly as his baton had seconds before. I nearly choked as almost immediately, after no more than ten thrusts, he pumped what felt like gallons of come down my throat and I gulped furiously.

Without a pause, his softening cock was removed unceremoniously from my bruised mouth and he zipped himself back up as he returned to the rear of the table and my desperate situation.

I felt my legs pushed apart again as he stood between them to get closer to me. He pushed the baton back into place until it filled me and slid his free hand underneath me to search for the button that would explode me. His knowing fingers ran around the edge of my stretched hole until they found the bit he was looking for. He ran what felt like two wet fingertips across and around my throbbing clit as if he had known me for years. Somehow the thought that he had probably done this many times before excited me more than I liked to admit, and kicked me into my orgasm. I felt my spasms start.

To allow myself to come in this situation was very intimidating and for a second I looked again at the camera and remembered how it felt to know he was watching me. The memory of the whole experience, together with the standard issue policemen's weapon, which was still buried at least ten inches inside me, was finally more than I could withstand and I think I screamed as I came. I flooded his hand and his weapon as I bucked and twisted against the bonds that still held me, groaning continuously.

As the last twitches tickled down my spine and my breathing began to return to normal, I looked again at the camera. As I stared at it the whole fixture rotated on the wall and the lens zoomed in and then back out again, mocking me.

PC North chuckled out loud as the camera continued its antics. He patted me on the bottom and removed the weapon that was still running with my juice. He walked around the front of the table as I heard the door open and booted footsteps enter the room. PC North bent down until he was at eye level with me and I saw another pair of navy trousers join his.

'I am sorry we can't release you yet, Miss Johnson, but we need you to help us further with our enquiries.'

Judging By Paris Anna Clare

There was a triptych at one end of the bar that night – blonde, brunette, redhead. Goddess, whore, queen. And they were bored out of their brains.

'You think you'd get over it.'

'You never get over it.'

'It's a bitch, babe. No mistake.'

'It used to be so easy,' sighed the brunette. It should have been easy for her, her companions thought, bitterly. Dewy of eye, rounded of limb, pouty of lip. Her slender little waist was enclosed in a broad silver belt worn over a gauzy low-cut dress – all shimmery chiffons and silver, like the foam on the sea on a sunny day.

She pursed her red lips and sipped from a bottle of some frothy pink concoction, the arch of her neck suggesting that she was about to put the whole bottle neck in her mouth in an obscene demonstration of just how damn good she was at giving head.

The blonde at her elbow tossed down another Martini and snorted. 'It's no use, dear. They don't make 'em like they used to.'

'That could be a good thing,' the redhead said. She was the broadest of build of the three, the oldest, although it was hard to put an age to that face of hers, a smooth, imperious mask, the faintest lines around her mouth indicating years of obsession, of pain caused by loving the wrong man too much.

'It's not.' The blonde pulled herself up to her full and considerable height, eyes dark in the smoky, noisy club, grey irises like the ring around the eclipse of her wide, black pupils. 'There's no guts in 'em any more, no balls, no *brains* ...'

'Oh, I think you'll find their *brains* are in perfect order,' the brunette sniggered, casting a significant glance at a passing waiter's crotch.

'Vee! Really!' The blonde – cool, snowy, patrician – swallowed a shocked laugh.

'Min, when are you ever going to accept that it's never been about their intellects?'

'Yes, but they don't seem to be so exciting as they used to be,' the redhead said, somewhat wistfully, raising a flute of champagne to her haughty, hurt mouth. Her dress was dark blue and green, patterned with peacock feathers, matching her huge dark blue eyes. She checked out a young man in chinos and a preppy shirt, mentally cataloguing his bank balance, his influence, his arse.

Nope. Dressed down, insipid, none of that spit and fire that her ex-husband had had. He'd been a lying, cheating bastard – screaming fights, hysterical declarations of hatred, bedroom power games that culminated in confessions of wild love and snarling sex. She supposed you couldn't have one without the other – if he hadn't been such a monumental shit there would never have been that electricity between them, the erotic tension rolling like distant thunder between them.

'June ... darling ...' The other two gravitated towards her. 'Sweetheart ...'

Her regret at losing him was like a dull moan that didn't quite escape her lips. The other two women picked up on the scent of loss like hunting dogs and patted and stroked and consoled. She shook them off gently.

'Thank you ... I know ... I know...' She sighed deeply. 'I'll be all right.'

'They're all bastards.'

'Gorgeous bastards, though.' It didn't take much to dent Vee's appetite. She glanced over at a young man leaning over the bar, whispering his drink order right in the barmaid's ear, or maybe it wasn't an order of a drink. Maybe it was a come-on, an invitation to get tangled up in the various permutations of love and lust. Vee shivered appreciatively at the crackling sparks between the two of them, feeling the heavy silver of her belt chafe against her through the thin fabric of her dress.

'Nice.'

'Flirtatious. Could be fun.'

Min, the blonde, took in his posture as he leaned back from the bar, propped one foot on the rail. 'That's not good.'

'What?' June flicked open a gold cigarette case, a work of art in itself, a birthday gift from her youngest son who was a goldsmith.

Min nodded. 'That pose. One foot on the bar-rail. It's a known fact that as soon as a male raises one foot two inches from the floor like that his bullshit motor is engaged. I've observed the phenomenon for years.'

The other two laughed, appreciating her wit. Sometimes she stung like a bee, but on nights of feminine solidarity like this, they loved her, smart as a whip, lean as a greyhound, her muscular, efficient body clothed in a tight white top, pale suede fur-collared jacket and white jeans, which gave her a luminous quality, like a ghost, like a barn owl gliding down from a beam, darting on its prey, never missing a thing with those bright, grey eyes of hers.

'They're all full of shit,' Vee said, with cheerful defiance, thumping the bottle down on the bar. 'But he's exceptionally beautiful. Look at him. Like smooth caramel . . .'

They looked. Vee saw the solidity of muscle, the shimmer of light blue eyes, the perfect smooth tan like a veneer on his skin, and saw how those eyes would light up in the dark, how those biceps would ripple and shiver as they rolled over and under and around one another in the sack, and how the streetlight from the window would catch the high, sweet arc of his cheekbone as his jaw went slack and his eyes closed and he moaned out at the point of orgasm.

Min saw his hands, long and slender, fingers curling around the stem of a wine glass, looked carefully at his mouth, examined the fine indentation of a frown line between his thick, arched eyebrows, watched for signs that he might be more than just a pretty face. His mouth was full and sensitive, but that could just be an illusion. She'd seen enough dumb beauties to last a thousand lifetimes. But he was speaking, flirting with the barmaid, his mouth shaping clever words, his free hand gesturing, long fingers describing and punctuating in the air. He had eloquence, grace, all indications of an agile mind. She liked that.

June saw something different – a beautiful man young enough to be her son, a man who would appreciate the experience of age, of marriage, of bitterness, someone who would stand back and admire the betrayal she wore like a diadem and offer to kiss it better. Someone who acknowledged her power, deferred to it. He looked pliant, a man who would not struggle and scratch and stray and come rolling into her bed like a tomcat in the middle of the night. A perfect pet, a prince who knew his place and knew his queen.

'Lovely.' They all three spoke at once, out of force of habit, out of knowing one another too well, and still laughed at their own timing.

Vee tilted her head. 'Shall we?'

'Well ... you know what happened the last time ...' Min said cautiously.

'Oh, really, dear.' June exhaled a bluish plume of smoke. 'You said yourself, they don't make 'em like they used to. They don't fight for the love of a woman any longer. All the fire's gone out of them.'

Oh, why not? They were out on the tiles, three women, Min, June and Vee. All dressed up and no place to go any more, discarded and unappreciated.

Min swallowed her Martini, peered at the pimento stuffed olive looking back at her like a fish eye from the bottom of the glass and popped it between her smooth, thin lips. 'OK, lets do it.'

Vee bounced on the lucite heels of her shoes, her breasts jiggling. 'Yay! Who wants to go first?'

Her doubts had stiffened her resolve. 'I'll go second,' Min said, stroking her sleek mane of blonde hair down. She knew the strategic importance of the middle ground, acting as a balance between Vee's flirtatious abandon and June's haughty, *noli me tangere* approach.

'You want to go first, June?' Vee twinkled, her hair seeming to crackle like black static and swirl up and around, framing her beautiful heart-shaped face, rendering her eyelids and mouth all the more kittenish and tempting.

June ground out her cigarette. 'Flip a coin,' she said, her voice lusciously throaty and Lauren Bacall with the tobacco.

Vee picked up a damp penny from the bar, wiped it distastefully on her hip and held it in one palm, the other hand palm down. 'Heads or tails?'

'Tails.'

She propelled the coin into the air, where it spun, fell, landed back in her palm and was flipped and pressed swiftly on to the back of her other hand. Vee removed her hand, looked, raised her eyebrows and presented the verdict with a small wiggle of one hip, so that she looked like she was cheekily thrusting out her hand for a lover to kiss.

'Heads.' She licked her lips. 'You're on, June. Go get him.'

'Marvellous. I get to be your warm-up woman,' June groused, sticking her roman nose in the air.

'You're gorgeous. Knock him dead.'

June peered past the optics behind the bar, checked her reflection in the mirror. 'More lipstick?'

'No, you're perfect as you are. Go ... go ...'

She laughed while Min and Vee spun her round and pushed her in the young man's direction, then snapped into seduction mode, producing another cigarette and smoothing down her peacock blue dress. 'It's an old tack ...' she said ruefully, holding up the cigarette.

'It *works*,' Vee sing-songed, her laugh like rippling water.

'I'm going in.'

'Best o' luck.' Min tipped her a military salute, making her laugh and threatening to wreck her well-practised ice queen act.

She walked up to the young man. 'Excuse me, do you have a light?'

He looked surprised, apologetic. 'Oh, sorry ... no. I don't smoke.'

'Never mind.' She took out her own gold lighter and lit up, letting the joke show in her eyes, but not in her mouth.

He laughed. 'You had one anyway.'

'Yes,' she said, coolly, sweetly. 'What do you make of that?'

His smile was shy, wrinkling his nose a little. 'Jonathan . . .' he said, holding out his hand.

She took it, slowly, peering down her nose, Bette Davis style. 'June.'

'June.' He tried the name on his lips. 'That's nice . . . rather . . .'

'Old fashioned?'

'Nothing wrong with that. All these babies popping out these days and getting called things like India and Chance and Brooklyn . . . June is nice. Pretty.'

'Well, Jonathan is rather older than June as a name.' She demonstrated aptly that she was in control. Cool, queenly, an old-fashioned screen goddess with just a slight air of loucheness, enough to make him think he could get close enough to touch her bronze skin and copper hair if he was good enough to ask permission.

'Yes. It's Hebrew.'

Min and Vee watched from a few paces away, watching June request champagne and getting it effortlessly.

'She's doing well.' Vee had the look of a hunting cat. 'Your turn.'

Min smiled to herself. So he liked the queen. How would he like the Amazon? She dropped her suede coat, slinked forward in her tight white top and white Versace jeans, high on her heels. She hooked one thumb into the back of her jeans, amusing her restless fingers with the texture of the little silver Medusa's head that sat just above her butt.

She swaggered over, rested her hand on the gold finial of the bar-rail, which came away in her hand – well, after a couple of good hard twists anyway.

'Whoops . . .' She held it up, with a surprised expression on her face. Perfect icebreaker.

'Jonathan . . .' June raised her eyebrows at the gold bauble in her hand, and she supressed a giggle. 'This is Min. Min, Jonathan.'

She took his hand in a strong grasp. 'Hello, Jonathan. Sorry about the destruction in my wake. Don't know my own strength.'

He laughed. 'Powerful grip you got there, Min.'

'I work out.' She snapped the words out, flipping her hair so that it fell like the feathered head-dress of a warrior on her muscled shoulders. No breathiness in her voice, no girlish wiles, just the promise of the strength and intellect that a woman was capable of, a challenge. Take me on. Dare ya. She had never been good at firing lust like Vee, or exuding imperiousness like June, but she commanded fidelity. Through love, through fear, she didn't care. Her will was iron, her wit mercury.

'So I see.' Jonathan was appraising the muscles in her bare arms, bound by silver bangles around each bicep. She could appeal to the hunter in him, give him something worthy of a chase. 'You've been here before?'

'It's possible.' She may have been. She couldn't remember. June was looking at the finial of the bar rail near her elbow, trying not to laugh. Poor June. At least one thing she hadn't lost through years of marriage to Min's father was her sense of humour.

'I think I've seen you before . . .' Min cocked her head and swept a quick, predator's glance over the man. He reminded her of someone she'd loved and lost many years ago – a smoother, unscarred, less beaten version, but with the same bright spark of intelligence.

'Jonathan lectures at the university,' June supplied helpfully, hiding her smile against the rim of her champagne flute.

'Oh. A scholar.' She smiled, darting a quick glance at Vee over her shoulder. Vee was frothing and foaming with irritation at how well they were doing, waiting to take her cue. 'I'm a military historian myself.'

'Really?' Jonathan looked fascinated. 'Which period?'

'Hellenic, Roman ... ancient history mostly.' She quirked a broader smile at that and got an 'oh really' look from June.

'Wow! My area is classical contexts of English literature.'

Delicious. Min savoured the rattle of intellectual sabres being drawn. June slouched back against the bar like a queen among her courtiers, nonchalant, waiting to be amused and entertained, but only if she could be bothered to enjoy herself.

Vee watched, thumped one heel impatiently against the bar-rail, her dress feeling more and more insubstantial and flimsy, the belt around her waist the only thing she could feel against her skin. Her fingers slipped between chiffon and silver, feeling the heat of her own flesh beneath the thin fabric. Min challenged, June commanded, Vee simply entranced, and she set out to do so.

She leaned back against the bar, stretching like a cat waiting to be stroked, holding her legs apart, hooking one heel behind the rail – a posture that pushed out her sweetly rounded belly and poked her barely covered tits towards the ceiling. Spotting a man looking, she reached for her bottled drink – something sweet and frothy, no substitute for nectar, but good enough for her purposes. She tipped her head back, turning her posture from merely slutty to pornographic, and the man came to heel. She deliberately let a dribble of cranberry juice slide between her breasts as she took the bottle neck out of her mouth and looked at him through heavy lidded eyes. No Adonis, but he'd serve a purpose.

'Hello.' He looked hungry, and slightly stupid.

'Hello.' She pushed the word out through a sigh, as

though she were recovering from a shuddering climax in the arms of a lover, and shifted the heel of her shoe this way and that on the rail, swinging the knee of her curved leg this way and that so that the thin sea-green chiffon rolled over her inner thigh like waves.

He looked a lot hungry now. And a lot stupid. She wriggled appreciatively at the salt scent of lust coming off him – that's what desire smelled like, like sea foam, like salt, like semen.

'And who might you be?' the man asked. A lousy line. She countered with one equally crappy, feeling better about using him as an ornament to her pose.

'I *might* be Venus.'

'Might you now?'

'Yes. Now. Ask me again later and I might give you a different answer.' She led him, practically by the dick, towards Min, June and the young man, kissed him firmly on the mouth and said, 'So ask me again in half an hour. I have some business to tie up here.'

'Whatever you say, Venus.' He backed away, blowing kisses, which she blew back, drifting like soap bubbles from her fingertips.

'Venus?' The young man smiled.

Vee turned towards him like a flower towards the sun, so absorbed in her routine that she missed the dirty looks coming from Min and June. 'Call me Vee.'

'Jonathan.' He laughed and picked up the gold finial that Min had snapped off. 'I feel like Paris right about now.'

June tried hard not to choke on her drink. Vee settled for looking pretty and clueless.

'I hear it's delightful this time of year,' Min said, drier than her Martini.

'No, no . . . I mean another Paris. See? We even have a golden apple of a sort.'

Jonathan cradled the gold orb in his hand, stroking his thumb over the jagged nub of metal where it had snapped away at the root under the dauntingly powerful hands of the blonde. He wasn't sure what the women were up to. His superstitious mother had always told him that bad luck came in threes and he didn't need any more bad luck right now. Not with love and lust weighing on his shoulders like the weight of the world on Atlas's shoulders – the signs, the confessions, the illicit meetings, the convoluted plaintive lies from Serena.

I love him, but I'm not in love with him. Do you see?

No he didn't see. He didn't bloody see at all. He didn't want her to have a drop of love left for him, wanted her to scrub the last seven years she'd spent as a married woman, greedy for her soul as he was for her body. All those nights running to shabby hotels near Victoria Station, looking for somewhere with four walls and a bed where they could pretend to be other people and they'd lose sleep for yet another night – fucking and sucking and chewing and devouring one another with licks, kisses and hands fisting sweaty sheets.

He hadn't known love could be so acutely painful and delirious since he'd fallen so hard for a married woman, and had sat for hour after hour trying to write love letters at his desk, his cock aching in his pants at the thought of how she rode him roughly, her long dark hair trailing, her heels digging into his lower thighs as she approached orgasm, spurring him on like a horse to follow her and come with her. It felt pathetic and hopeless, and to compound his feelings he'd been working on a seminar on Yeats, poor old WB, yearning for the love of a woman he'd never have, who would eventually deign to bed him but always deny him her heart and soul. He'd sent Serena a copy of one poem – 'Was there a second Troy for her to burn?'

She was Helen, her husband Menelaus, himself Paris, but now it was as though he had come to be judged by the three goddesses, three women whose witchy tang disturbed him and excited him.

The smallest woman, the brunette with the shimmery silver-green dress and the shimmery sea-green eyes, looked up at him with interest. 'Really? I've never heard that story.'

She was flirting – oh, hell, they all were – the redhead with the Roman chestnut skin, the cool blonde with the silver bangles and designer jeans, the little brunette with the boobs and the bottom and bouncy, wiggly Marilyn Monroe gait. Why not play along? It would be satisfying to cheat on Serena; he had no idea what scenario the women envisioned, but it was bound to be something exotic between the four of them.

He'd only fantasised about such things and imagined how it might be to have all three of them, to watch them enact some pornographic threeway on his bed and then be serviced one by one – as depraved as one of the emperors or potentates of Min's beloved antiquity.

'Well ... it's an old story, a Greek myth –'

'Greco-Roman,' Min, the blonde, chimed in.

'Um ... yeah. Greco-Roman. A golden apple was sort of tossed into the arena at the wedding of the demigods Cadmus and Harmonia, inscribed 'To The Fairest', and the three goddesses, Athena, Hera and Aphrodite, fought so hard over it that Zeus, the King of Heaven, insisted they find a neutral judge. So they found Paris, a young Trojan prince who was tending to his father's sheep on Mount Ida –'

'Aphrodite cheated,' the redhead said, peering down her nose again. She had the most extraordinary eyes, soft and wide, very round and dark deep blue. The blonde sniggered and the brunette pouted and scowled.

'Well, no ... they all did, to a certain extent.' Three pairs of eyes fixed on him, blue, green, grey – cool and affronted.

'Oh, did they indeed?' asked the blonde, and he found himself shivering, smelling something strange in the air, like blood and burning feathers – coppery and acrid.

He laughed it off. 'OK ... not exactly cheated. They all offered him things as bargaining chips.'

'Power, intellect ...'

'And did he take any of these things?'

'No. He took the third option.'

'Which was?'

'Sex.'

'That's so predictable.' Vee laughed. 'Really ... so typical.'

He smiled. 'According to the legend, Venus slipped her dress off and showed him her body.'

'Speak of the devil ...' Min cocked her head towards one of the speakers, which had started pumping out a bouncy dance version of 'Venus'.

'Oh, yeah!' Vee jumped and jiggled. 'Come on, let's dance.'

'Um ... really ... I don't ... oh ...' She had him by the hand and was leading him on to the crowded dance floor before he could even put his objections into a coherent sentence.

Vee savoured his frustration, his exasperation, and dragged him on to one of the podiums for good measure. No, he was quite right, he wasn't much of a dancer. She shimmied her hips, letting the skirt of her dress billow and shake, raised her arms in the air and gyrated, up and down, back up, arching her back and pushing her breasts up.

'You just have to *feel* it ...' She wasn't sure if she'd said the words or pumped them directly into his mind, but he got the message. He picked up the rhythm, swaying his hips, raising his arms, mirroring her movements. She swung and swayed with him, spreading her legs and wriggling her arse downwards in that 'shake yo booty' move she liked, coming back up to wrap her arms around his neck, her lips less than an inch away from his sweat-slicked panting ones.

Adrenaline surged through her veins, sparked up her nerve endings, sent an old, familiar shiver, whippingly sweet, through the lowest tip of her spine and between her legs, a strong reminder of her own power over men and women alike. She'd hooked him. He was taking off his shirt, giving into the dance, his torso surprisingly well muscled for a guy who said he spent most of his time in lecture rooms and libraries. Smooth, perfectly hairless except for that enticing little trail that led from the dimple of his navel and vanished into his jeans. Lovely. A bare-chested acolyte of Love herself. She'd smelled it coming off him in waves, his lust, his frustration with his mistress – like salt, like the sea foam, like the rich velvet, scented folds of a woman's sex.

She wrapped herself up in him, nose to nose, eye to eye, almost lip to lip, but no, no kissy – not for you, boytoy. You're just here to settle the contest once more.

'What do you *want*? Really? More than anything?' She ground her hips, and his hands gripped them, pulling them into his groin so that she felt the length of him through his jeans press and tickle against her pubic hair.

'Really? *Anything?*' he asked.

She tossed back her head and laughed, baring her throat, knowing he'd have to kiss it. 'Didn't you know, darling? I can grant wishes. Make your wish.'

He stepped back, looked regretful, and she smelled that frustration again. 'I want her to leave him,' he said. 'My lover . . . her husband . . .'

'Consider it done.' She leaned on the railing, arching one leg again, letting him see that her dress had slipped open and that she wasn't wearing underwear. 'And I get to take first prize?'

'I don't see . . .'

'The golden apple, silly.' She winked and twinkled, bright sparks glinting through her dark hair like moonlight on the waves, her eyelashes wet like seaweed.

'The piece of the *bar-rail*?' He laughed incredulously.

'You don't get it, do you?' she asked, musically, way into her stride now, loving the game and recalling old, old triumphs. 'Down on your knees.'

He had to obey. He was a man, and she was standing there with her legs parted and the core of her exposed. He'd have to get down on his knees to take a better look and he did.

'Closer.'

He shuffled closer so that he was kneeling between her spread legs. The music thundered through her flesh, increasing the tingles in her sex, and she helped them along, carding her fingers through the sweat-damp curls of black hair, opening the lips and showing him the slick redness inside.

His eyes were black, his lips parted. He was breathing in the scent of her, the salt scent of the foam from which she had stepped, a pearl inside a shell.

'Taste it.'

She shivered, anticipating, and let out a long moan of pleasure as his tongue darted tentatively out over her clit, wet and raspy and good. He sank back on his heels in dismay, tasting the salt and sea foam on his mouth.

'You *are* Venus!'

Her hair crackled and sparked wildly with the recognition, her mouth pouting and softening as she lifted one finger to her lips and closed one eye in a slow, wicked wink. 'Shh!'

It felt good to get the old magic back, if only for a moment. She splashed up a tide of foam in the poor man's face, and reappeared with aplomb at the bar, where the other two goddesses were looking distinctly disgruntled.

'Really . . . have you *no* shame?'

She did a quick twirl on her heels. 'Hel-lo, goddess of *Love* here!'

'Floozy!' Min said with grudging admiration. 'And you've done it again, haven't you?' She quirked her head towards a young, dark-haired woman sitting on a bar stool looking so antsy and nervous that she looked as though the heel hooked into the stool was the only thing holding her to Earth.

'Whoops!' Venus smiled. 'Yes. Very probably.'

Jonathan emerged from the dance floor, shirtless, covered in foam and looking bemused. He didn't even look at the three of them. He sort of shook off his confusion like a dog shaking itself dry and homed in on the girl.

'Serena! What are you doing here?'

'Jonny . . . oh God . . .' She flew off the stool like a black moth, all dark velvet eyes and adoration. 'I've done it . . . I've left him. I told him it was over.'

'Oh, my darling!'

'My love!'

The three of them watched with a kind of happy cynicism as the happy couple rushed off to find the nearest bed without a backward glance.

'Well, that was rude,' Minerva said disdainfully.

'Yes. Didn't even say thank you.' Juno sipped her champagne. 'They're all the same, you know. Bastards.'

Venus triumphantly picked up the bar-rail finial. 'I won again.'

'*And* you've probably started another war, you minx.'

'You love me really.' She tucked the gold orb into her silver belt and poked her tongue out defiantly. 'Let's blow this joint, girls. I hear Dionysus has opened a new place.'

'Oh, you have *got* to love Dionysus' parties,' Juno groaned wistfully.

The triptych dissolved, vanished, leaving nothing but an owl feather and a peacock feather floating in a small puddle of salt water on the bar. Nobody ever saw them come and go any longer, discarded and tossed aside as they were, replaced by the strictures of sin and monotheism, but they were always willing to help out the faithful.

And they'd always have Paris.

The Love Machine Barbie Scott

I had paid my fee and I knew they would come eventually. What I didn't know was the time and the manner of their coming. But that's all part of the attraction, isn't it? – the spontaneity, the surprise of it all.

Dr J's service wasn't cheap. It was no singing telegram-type affair of maximum embarrassment and minimal turn-on. Nor was it a dial-a-shag gigolo-for-hire sort of thing. No. This was the business – a class act. It had all the elements that gave it top marks in my book: unexpectedness, yet constant anticipation; discretion, yet with a hint of public humiliation; and a hefty slug of S&M. No, it wasn't cheap, but I knew it would be worth it.

Every morning when I woke I would glance out of the window, twitching the curtain aside furtively, searching for any sign that they were coming. What I would have done had I actually received warning of their arrival, I don't know. But the possibility of detecting some portent sent shivers running through me. Goose bumps prickled across my cold skin. Hairs rose at the nape of my neck. My legs would tremble and my pussy clenched with delicious fear.

Oh, Dr J was the most revered practitioner of his art. He knew exactly the level of pleasurable terror to inflict. The data I had tapped into his website questionnaire had been extensive. He knew everything about me, everything relevant to my carnal satisfaction anyway. He knew all the tricks that lovers took months to learn, all my secret fetishes, all those little eccentricities I kept locked tightly in my loins.

Every morning, after checking the street and the hallway outside my flat, I would shower, obtaining great enjoyment from the sensation of the soft water caressing my tense body. My enlarged nipples were hard with erotic expectation; my pussy lips swollen by the blood my body sent pounding to the area, in readiness, like a defending army, to tackle intruders. I kept the front door unlocked, the bathroom door ajar, in case they should choose this time to arrive. I wanted to be ready for them, even though I knew I never could be. Dr J was far too clever to allow that. He would not send them when I expected them. They would come at the very moment my guard was relaxed.

After my shower I dressed, always with one eye on the door, always giving some thought to which clothes would be most suitable to be taken in. A tight skirt that would have to be rolled up to my waist, exposing my smooth buttocks? Trousers that could be pulled down to my knees? A brassiere? Sensible knickers? I had heard stories of a woman who had been taken while wearing a peek-a-boo bra and split crotch see-through panties, and who had been made to walk through the streets in them, her nipples bursting through the revealing holes, her juices dribbling down her legs. Exciting as this sounded, I didn't require such exquisite shame as that.

I moved tremulously through the days, ever alert for the sudden intrusion, the tap on my door, the noise in the hallway, jumping at every sound, holding my breath at every footstep. I dared not allow myself to dwell on what would happen when they came – what they would do, how I would react. I had requested the de luxe service, and serviced I knew I would be.

At home in the quiet evenings I would turn off the

television to listen for half-heard noises. I would turn down the CD player, using the remote control, and sit stiffly upright in my chair, imagining scufflings in the doorway. My body was constantly alert, constantly in a state of arousal, tense, fearful, *ready*.

Nights were long. Sleep was impossible. Hollow-eyed, I would welcome the dawn. What game was he playing, the infernal Dr J? Why didn't he send them? Send them and get it over with.

A month after I'd booked, I decided to cancel. I couldn't stand the suspense any longer, the waiting was proving too nerve-wracking; I was limp with exhaustion.

'Dr J's office. Miss K speaking. How may I help you?'

'I want to cancel a booking,' I said.

There was a short silence.

'I'm very sorry, madam, but that's impossible. Once a booking has been made with Dr J, it cannot be cancelled.'

'You can keep the fee,' I said. 'I don't care about that. Just cancel the appointment.'

There was another silence, muffled sounds, whispers, a hand placed over the mouthpiece perhaps? 'I'm afraid there can be no cancellation.' The woman's voice was sharper. 'But the request will be noted on your file.'

I knew then that I had made matters worse for myself. No cancellations. A scribbled note on the bottom of a document. A telling reminder of my weakness and cowardice. And still they would come. Nothing I did now could prevent it.

And so they came.

They were gentler than I expected. They did not break down the door at midnight, nor barge into my office and take me there and then before my astonished colleagues. No. A quiet tap one evening when I was not long in. A neighbour delivering a misdirected letter? Someone collecting for charity? I had almost begun to believe they would never come; that my cancellation had been accepted after all; that the icy refusal was merely another of Dr J's devilish little touches. How easy it would be for him to make a recidivist regret such back-peddling and live in fear forever after, never knowing if one day the order would be fulfilled, the goods finally delivered. Even the strongest mind could crack under such pressure. Better to get it over and done with.

In the event, I opened the door without thinking, distracted as I was by the myriad petty chores requiring attention on my return home: feeding the insistent cat; removing outer garments; checking the machine for messages; opening the door to Evangelists.

When I opened my front door, there were indeed two of them, but they were not Evangelists, unless the good news they had come to spread was that the hour had finally arrived. They took me as I was, coatless and in stocking feet. I was wearing a knee-length black dress, very simple, very stylish. One of them slid his hand up my thigh under the fine woollen material, while the other looked on, impassive.

'Delivery to go to Dr J, I believe,' the first one said, his finger stroking the damp gusset of my briefs. I was transfixed with terror – delicious, tremulous terror. I gawped up at the man but, of course, I could not see his eyes. I knew they always wore dark glasses. Dark glasses, dark suits and neat, professional hair, so slick with gel that the colour was indiscernible. They were interchangeable – six feet tall, broad-shouldered, passive of feature, their faces carrying only a hint of what they could – would? – do to me. For a moment I thought they would fuck me right there in my own hallway, with the front door open and people passing by on their way home from work. But no, that wasn't what I had ordered. De luxe means just that. I was going for the big one. The luxury deal. It was expensive but I knew I deserved it.

Removing his finger from my crotch, Number One smiled briefly. Then they took an arm each and escorted me forcibly to their vehicle. I was glad I had already fed the cat. The de luxe could take quite some time, I had heard. They pushed me into the back of the gleaming black limousine and closed the door. There were no handles on the inside and the windows were blacked out, so I could not see where I was being taken. I sank back into the leather seat, shaking violently. A glass partition separated me from my captors; I could just make out their chiselled profiles as they exchanged glances.

Then we were off.

The journey was short, which surprised me – a smooth-running, purring ride of no more than ten minutes. I had probably walked by the place many times without ever realising I was passing the headquarters of the mysterious Dr J. What innocuous facade did his power centre present to the world? A Victorian town house? A thirties semi? A modern office block? I was not destined to discover the answer to this question. As the car slid down a ramp, I heard the sound of gates closing behind it. When they opened the door to pull me out, I saw that the vehicle was parked in an enclosed space, dimly lit and smelling of oil. The walls were a smooth featureless concrete, the ceiling low. It could have been a suburban garage, a seedy lock-up or part of some larger complex. I could not tell.

A small lift took us up unnumbered floors – two perhaps? Three? Four? I felt cramped, crushed between the two large men, who stared silently over my head. Sweat began to gather in my armpits. When the lift stopped and the door slid open, the first man gripped my elbow and escorted me out. The reception area was quietly carpeted, hushed; elegant. A young woman sat at a curving desk which carved the room in two. Miss K, I presumed. She wore a blonde wig piled high on her head and winged diamante glasses. Her lips were scarlet, her nails blood-red. She did not smile.

'Delivery for Doctor J,' said Number One.

The woman picked up a white telephone and murmured something into it. The oppressive silence of the room seemed to thicken as she listened to the response, the receiver pressed against her ear. My entire body was now damp with perspiration. Surreptitiously, I rubbed my stocking soles against my legs. The soft carpet would show the imprints of my feet, I felt sure. The woman turned her back on us – my captors and me – and looked at a flickering computer. She tapped something into it and said over her shoulder, as though in afterthought, 'The Doctor will see you now.' Without granting us the courtesy of a further glance, she raised a red talon and pointed to a door which, until then, I had not noticed. Set flush into the wall, it was almost invisible. I held my breath as it slid silently back to reveal an elderly man waiting on the other side.

At last, I stood face to face with the diabolic Dr J.

There could be no mistaking him: the white coat, the gold-rimmed spectacles, the fob watch. He was a walking cliché – wild professorial hair, eyes gleaming with an enthusiasm just this side of madness, fingernails well scrubbed. I had heard all the rumours, all the stories. The man who stood before me could be no one else.

'A pleasant package this time, Doctor, if I may say so,'

said Number One. Number Two had still not spoken but now he reached behind me and slid down the zipper of my dress as the door hissed closed.

'Ah, good, good,' said Dr J. 'That's right. Yes. Get it unwrapped.' He made fussy little movements with his hands and hopped from foot to foot. Looking down, I noticed that his feet were small and neat. He wore highly polished brown shoes which I was certain he had not shined himself.

'And the rest. And the rest. Yes. Yes,' he said, fluttering his hands to indicate the removal of my clothes.

Number Two now stepped in front of me, his eyes still mysterious behind the dark glasses. Taking hold of my undone dress by the shoulders, he pulled it forwards with a sudden snapping movement, which almost knocked me off my feet. The dress came off my arms, slithered down my body and fell to the floor. Nerves jangling, I stepped out of it. My pussy twitched, clenched, jerked. Though bathed in sweat, my skin was icy.

Number One, who had turned to a table to retrieve something, now turned back and smiled impertinently, right into my face. In his hand he held a large pair of scissors. I drew in a sharp breath as he advanced them towards me. Slowly, almost delicately, he eased the cold blade under the shoulder strap of my bra. Snip! He eased it under the other strap. Snip! I held my breath as he slid the blade up between my breasts, nestling it in my cleavage for a moment. I was hypnotised by the glittering blade. Snip! He cut my bra in half between the frothy lace cups and it fell to the floor like a dead bird. My breasts swung softly forwards, my nipples hardened by the cool air and the chill of fear. I licked my parched lips and studied Number One's face. Still smiling, he lowered the scissors until they were level with the tufts of pubic hair curling over the top of my flimsy white knickers. He slipped the long blade inside my briefs, from left to right; I felt the cold steel slide along my pubic bone. Snip, snip, snip. I quivered internally as the soft cotton crotch dangled limply, like the gusset of a leotard with the press-studs undone. The blade slid up and under again, from the cut edge of my knickers to the lacy elastic top. Snip, snip, snip. And they were off.

'Ah, good, good.' Dr J was fussing again. 'Over here. Over here.' He led the way to a padded screen off to the right. One and Two took my arms again and dragged me forward. I confess that at that moment, had I had the use of my legs, and had it been remotely possible, I would have turned and run.

'No! No!' I jammed one foot against the edge of the screen and tried to wriggle from their grip.

'Now, now,' said One, good humouredly, 'you asked for this and you're going to get it.'

Two cupped my chin in his free hand and squeezed my cheeks. 'No sense in struggling, darling,' he said, his voice oily with menace. 'You're past the point of no return. You passed that point the moment you first contacted the eminent Dr J.'

Together they lifted me off my feet and bundled me, naked and trembling, into the nerve centre of Dr J's empire. The screen, which was metal beneath the cream leather padding, hid from casual view the apparatus of Dr J's profession.

I gasped when I saw it. Usually, advance information renders actuality disappointing. Hype can take all the surprise out of things. But not this. All the stories, all the rumours, had not done it justice. It was worse – no, better – than I could ever have imagined. No dream, no nightmare could ever do it justice. My mouth dropped open in fascinated horror.

'That's right, sweetheart,' said Two. 'We like to see all the orifices open wide.'

I snapped my jaw shut. What had I done? Why had I subjected myself to this? I tried to remember the stories, the tales of satisfaction, of orgasmic release. The blissed-out expressions of people who had undergone the de luxe. I recalled a woman interviewed on late night television. How distant and dreamy her eyes had been – almost as if she were in love. She spoke of Dr J in reverential tones, her voice barely above a whisper. 'He's a genius,' she said. 'He's the Einstein of carnal gratification. The Oppenheimer of sexual explosion.' She sighed deeply. 'My orgasm was like an atomic bomb – and I'm still experiencing the fallout.' She had hugged herself then, smiling, ecstatic. Yes. Almost as if she were in love.

Dr J fussed around the machine. He blinked as the two men dragged me closer, as if he had forgotten my presence. 'Yes, yes,' he said. 'One moment, please.' He twiddled a knob on the control panel while I stared up at the celebrated instrument of delight: The Love Machine.

Gleaming chrome? Yes. Fine leather straps? Yes. Brushed steel? Velvet padding? Electric sensors? Yes, yes, yes. Everything your fantasies show you. Everything you shy away from. Everything your veneer of civilisation denies. It was all there, made real, glinting in the bright lights of the studio. I gazed in awe, my eyes sliding over the smooth surfaces, the polished implements, the curved elegance of its construction. It was like an expensive car, hiding its power behind grace and form, yet never truly disguising the brute force, the potency, housed within.

Dr J peered at the display, adjusting his spectacles. He checked some readings, fiddled with some knobs, glanced at his watch. 'Yes, yes. Very well. Place her in position.'

It was then that my knees finally gave way. My bladder loosened, my bowels threatened to evacuate.

'I think she needs to take a moment,' said One, pushing me towards another, smaller screen, behind which there was a stainless steel toilet and a handbasin, like those in an aeroplane, or a prison cell. 'Do what you have to do,' he said. 'I'll be right here.' He folded his arms and, mercifully, turned his back.

Fear made it easy. I gave no thought to the three men standing only feet away as I sat on the loo. My mind was numb with terror. Were there to be no preliminaries? Was I to be forced without further ceremony straight on to the machine? Now? I splashed my burning cheeks with cold water, patted myself dry on a towel as soft as angels' wings, and stepped from behind the screen. Number One smiled again, almost gently this time, and stood aside to allow me to pass.

I raised my head and examined again the instrument of sensual gratification, the merry-go-round of pain and pleasure for which I had purchased a first-class ticket. My sex was wet with anticipation, my nipples erect. But as I gazed in awe and wonder, my fear dissipated. My eyes misted with tears. At last I was to experience the delight I had always dreamed of. The day had dawned: I too was about to fall in love with Dr J.

The two men, now as gentle as lovers, helped me up on to the first platform. Before me, at hip level, was a crimson velvet cushion, deeply studded, like the arm of a Chesterfield, or the cylindrical bolster of a chaise longue. Number One stood on the platform to my left, Number Two to my right. Easing me into position, they bent me over the cushion. The silky velvet was firmly padded, like an erect cock, softened by smooth skin and spongy glans. Number One ran his hand over my left buttock and allowed a murmur of appreciation to escape his lips.

'Now the wrists,' said Dr J. 'Into the straps with them. Yes. That's right. Yes.' I could no longer see him as he was now behind me at his console, but I was aware of his presence. He emanated a nervous energy which rubbed up against the edges of my own fizzing aura. On his instructions, each man took one of my arms and placed them on velvet armrests. Soft leather straps were fastened around my wrists. I felt my sex tremble, my clit flicker, as the straps tightened and the tongue of the buckle penetrated the metal eyelet. My chin was lowered into a cupped chin rest and a broad leather strap was fastened around my head, tightly enough to prevent movement, but not so tight as to cause me pain. That would come from another source.

As I knelt on the lower padded support, I felt, but could not see, my ankles being clamped into suede-lined metal shackles. I was now completely at the mercy of Dr J, his assistants and his magnificent machine. Number One slid his finger into my drenched cunt while Number Two tweaked my right nipple briefly, before slipping a blindfold over my eyes.

'Stand clear,' said Dr J, and when the two men stepped down from the platform, the machine began to move. With a smooth, almost soothing movement, I was tilted forwards until my nipples came into contact with a cold surface. The surface opened like a flower and my breasts were sucked into a steel brassiere which adjusted to fit me perfectly. 'Testing,' said the Doctor. A tingling sensation surged through my nipples and I clenched my buttocks in surprise. 'Testing,' he said again, and a further shock jolted through me, making me squeal. 'And now – the other end.' Dr J was surprisingly coy for a man who provided orgasms for money.

The machine moved again and my ankles were gently spread apart. I was now bent over the machine, face down, with my thighs open and my throbbing pussy revealed for all to see. I heard another movement and braced myself. I knew what was coming. I knew. I knew. And oh, it came, sliding, slipping inside me, like a speculum, a steel shaft, cold and hard entering me as I quivered and half fainted in delicious agony. Not that it was painful going in – I was so slick with juices that a submarine could have entered me. No, the agony was akin to ecstasy, mental, fevered, erotic. When the shaft was snug inside me, I felt a smooth clamp rise up and fit itself over my clit. I tensed, expecting Dr J to test this new instrument of enjoyment too, but no shock came. Instead, I felt the slender steel cousin of the cigar tube inside me nudge towards my bumhole. Loosened with fear as I was, it too had no trouble gaining entry.

'Good, good,' said Dr J. 'All set. Stand well back.'

How can I describe what followed? Give me a second to gather my thoughts for, from that moment on, I was subject, for I don't know how long, to the most delectable, most excruciating joy and anguish that a human being can endure without becoming unhinged with pleasure.

A whip cracked across my exposed buttocks at the same moment as electric shocks screamed through my tits and clit. Again and again the whip cracked. Again and again the jolts shuddered through my most sensitive parts. My clit was swollen and throbbing. I was desperate to rub myself but I could not move. The clit clamp fizzed and sparked and spread a warmth throughout me. The steel pikes vibrated inside me, touching multiple G-spots I never imagined I possessed. Then the clamp began to vibrate too, agitating my stiffened clit until I believed I could take no more.

Oh, but I was wrong. I took much much more.

The whip was joined by a thin swishing cane and together they played a delightful tattoo on my stinging behind. The machine was a feverish drummer, maddened by a marching tune, and I was the taut drum. My buttocks were hot and smarting; my nipples wincing; my cunt quivering. I writhed and contorted within the constraints of my bindings. Suddenly, I heard myself sing and cry out as my first orgasm tore through me. My nipples tingled inside the metal cups, my clit was aflame. The pistons pumped their rhythm and the drummer hit rim shots that sent me into spasms of ecstasy. My flesh shivered and sobbed; every tiny hair on my body was rigid; my lips, upper and lower, inner and outer, coursed with hot blood. Rolling waves of energy pulsated through my tormented flesh. My clit was the epicentre of a volcanic eruption; the tremors spread outwards to my scalp and my toes and my fingertips. When I thought it was over, aftershocks spasmed through my cunt and sent me swinging again into the clutch of a climax so frantic that I was almost hysterical. Hot thick juices coated my inner thighs; the walls of my sex clenched and squeezed. I was filled to capacity, fore and aft. I was racked with a searing, exquisite frenzy. My eyes rolled upwards behind my closed lids, behind the blindfold. Every inch of my body was on fire.

And just when I thought nothing could add to my delirium, the machine began to move. I felt myself tilt and tip as I whirled through space on a roundabout of pleasure, a fairground wheel of rapture. Music pounded in my ears – 'The Ride of the Valkyries'. Oh, Dr J was a prodigy, a superman, a genius. Nothing could ever top this. I was sizzling from head to foot as wave after wave of delicious orgasm swept through me. It was unsurpassable, glorious, dazzling. My brain was bursting with rapture. I was euphoric. I called hosannas to the angelic host; I cried hallelujahs of joy. Tears of exultation streamed down my burning face. Never in my life, before or after, have I experienced such bliss. At any moment my spirit might leave my body; I would become detached, etheric, lost forever in the realms of delight. Truly, I was in Heaven, Valhalla, Elysium; truly, I saw visions of Paradise, witnessed scenes of jubilation on high. The machine waltzed me through the upper air of Dr J's laboratory, turning and swooping. Oh, Dr J, Dr J!

I came more times than I can count. Indeed, it was not possible to count the times because my climax was a series of inseparable seismic shocks, coming so fast and furious that they overlayed each other and became one long orgasm. Uncountable. Unnumbered. My nerves twanged like a zither, like a harp. My orgasm was a trumpet blast of delight. I flopped, limp and soaked, over the velvet supports, well beyond mere satisfaction. The electric shocks stopped; the whip and the cane ceased their rat-a-tat-tat. I relaxed in expectation of a bewitching post-coital slumber as the machine slowed its gyrations to a gentle dance.

Then the black silk blindfold, which had been but loosely tied, slipped from my eyes. Slowly, I dragged them open in time to see a screen sliding back across a picture window set into the wall of Dr J's pleasure dome. Behind the glass sat a mixed audience, their faces rapt and lascivious, their mouths open, drooling.

'Every one of these people,' said Dr J, as my public were slowly hidden from view by the sliding screen, 'will receive a complimentary video of your performance. You will be a star.' As the machine swung me into his line of vision, he removed his spectacles and wiped them on the hem of his lab coat. 'That's a little something extra I devised especially for you. Call it a cancellation fee.'

Payback Time Kate Stewart

'He can't have spent all this.' Amanda stared at the computer printout, praying that it was either a mistake or a nightmare, but the evidence was too clear for her words to be anything except a plea. 'There's no way I can pay this back. It wasn't my fault. You've got to understand that I didn't know what he was up to.'

She knew she was babbling, but this had been a nightmare from the moment she'd taken the phone call from the bank and found out why she hadn't seen a bank statement for months. It had been bad enough to have lost a boyfriend, without finding that their joint account had been plundered. And, now she'd discovered that the bank could even sell her home, it was all she could do not to abandon pride and sit there and howl.

She didn't know why she was expecting sympathy from this hatchet-faced manager. He kept staring at her, and his expression made her skin crawl. She wished she hadn't worn this short skirt that she'd put on back when she'd been sure of her ability to charm her way out of this mess, and determined to make the right impression. She'd have felt less vulnerable if her legs had been covered, although she wasn't sure that even a yashmak and those voluminous black robes that Arab women wore would have helped much. When he looked at her it felt as if he could see right through her clothes to the body that was as toned and trim as three trips a week to the gym could make it.

'You signed the documents.' His voice would have frozen boiling water.

'Yes, but I never expected to have to pay anything like this.' Inspiration struck. 'Wasn't there insurance?'

'If he was dead, or redundant, yes. Not if he just . . .' The man let the words trail off, but the implication was all too clear. Her ex had bolted, leaving her in the shit right up to her ears.

'I don't know what to do,' she whispered.

'If you don't pay, it will go to our Collections Department, and they won't be as understanding as I am.'

She was about to snap that he hadn't been understanding when the combination of what he'd said and how he was looking at her sunk in. If that had been anyone else she'd have said that was an invitation, but it couldn't be. Not a manager of an old, respectable bank like this.

'I don't understand.' She licked her lips nervously, taking a good look at her tormentor; and liking what she saw.

He wasn't as old as she'd first thought, and that close-cut grey hair just accentuated his austere good looks. If it had been any other time and place, she might even have thought how sexy his strong, cruel face with the eyes that were as steely as his hair was. His hands clenched and unclenched on the desk in front of him, but he wasn't nervous. He was intent on something; and that something was her. She'd been chatted up by men before, much better-looking men too, but no one had made her feel this way – scared and nervous and excited. As if, somehow, she had no control over what would happen to her next – and she didn't want any either.

'There might be another way to pay me,' he said slowly.

'You what!' She stood up and headed for the door, aghast as her suspicions turned into reality, but not as horrified as she knew she should be. She knew she ought to storm out and denounce him, but she didn't want to. She didn't like him, but there was something about him that she couldn't resist. When he watched her she felt something she had never felt before. Something tight in her stomach, something that left her wondering what it would be like to submit herself utterly to him. No, of course, she couldn't do that, even if he'd wanted her to, which he couldn't do; but what else could she do?

'You owe the bank fifteen thousand pounds. Fifteen thousand pounds that you have no way of repaying. And, as you said, if you're made bankrupt, you'll lose your job as well as your home.'

He summed up the situation dispassionately, leaving her stomach churning with an intoxicating mixture of fear and lust, each one feeding the other until she was struggling to concentrate on anything except her body's increasingly urgent demand for sex.

'But if you do exactly as I say, I'll use my discretion.'

'And what does that mean?' she challenged, but she'd stopped with her hand on the door handle.

'It means that you've got a chance to save yourself as long as you're obedient. If not, then you've lost everything. Sit down, Amanda.'

When she'd come in she'd been Miss Morgan, but they both knew that she'd agree. The question was, what was she about to agree to?

'What would I have to do?' she asked, surprised how steady her voice sounded.

'Whatever I order you to.' When the manager smiled she knew that wouldn't be difficult.

She wanted to obey him. She didn't know or like him, but she wanted him to master her; and he knew it.

Somehow, he even knew about her deepest, darkest fantasy, and now he was giving her a chance to turn it into reality and save her bacon in the process.

'Undo your shirt,' he said, as if her answer was a foregone conclusion. 'It's your word against mine,' he went on silkily. 'And no one's ever complained about me before. While you . . .' He didn't bother to finish, but he didn't need to. His supercilious expression said it all.

She definitely had a reputation in this small town, where gossip spread like butter on hot toast. It wasn't a good one, so she knew who they'd believe as well as he did.

All right, she thought as she reached for the top button of her crisp, white shirt, you don't need to rub it in. I know I'm not a virgin, but I'm not a whore either, and that's what you want to make me. But he could make her bankrupt if she didn't give him what he seemed to want as much as she now did. Besides, it wasn't as if he could try anything too drastic. Not with the business of the bank going on just outside that closed door and his only protection the red 'no entry' light. If it got too bad all she'd have to do was scream. Better still, once she'd done whatever he wanted, he wouldn't be the only one who'd be able to blackmail. She didn't fancy the idea, but she didn't have enough choices to let her conscience stop her saving her home and career.

Slowly, deliberately, she unfastened the shirt that now felt tight against her swollen breasts, glad that she'd worn her confidence-building underwear. The white Wonderbra pushed her breasts up and together, as if offering them to him, and the matching thong would show off what she knew was a good bum, but somehow they didn't work their usual magic. Instead, she felt more helpless with each button she unfastened.

He didn't say a word, and that made her more nervous still. Instead, he kept watching her, his cold grey eyes curiously expressionless, and she wondered what he was planning. But she didn't ask. Why bother? It wouldn't make any difference, and the suspense was making it easier for her, as he must know. Her nipples thrust against the lace, blatantly advertising that she wasn't as unwilling as the sullen pout on her face tried to claim.

'Push the cups down.'

Was that a hint of excitement in his voice? It was hard to tell, but as she obeyed she swore that she'd break that control, no matter what it took.

'And don't say a word,' he ordered, then stood up, pushing his chair back from that enormous old-fashioned desk before walking slowly round to her.

Amanda bit her lip as the reality of what she was doing hit her like a brick, but she still didn't consider disobeying him. Instead, she concentrated on the perverse situation, using the pleasurable wickedness to help her do what she increasingly wanted to do. Here she was, in this most respectable of places, where anyone could walk in at any second, with her shirt hanging open and her boobs exposed. The underwiring cut into the sensitive skin, but the small pain only turned her on even more.

'Yes,' he murmured, running a finger down the side of her face. 'You'll do nicely. Crawl under the desk.'

She longed to scream that she wanted to be fucked, maybe even felt like laughing at this oldest of all the tired clichés. Mostly she felt relieved. If oral sex was all he wanted then this wouldn't be so bad after all.

'Crawl,' he repeated. 'I want to see your bum wiggle.'

She winced at the coarseness but still did as she was told, feeling almost as if she'd been hypnotised. She swung her hips as she moved, determined to turn him on as much as he was turning her on. Her knickers were wet and sticky now, clinging to her crack, and her skirt had ridden up so much that he'd know that too. But he didn't say anything. Instead, he waited until she was crouching in the footwell of the desk, then sat down again.

'Now unzip my flies.'

She did, then, unbidden, reached inside his boxer shorts to free his erection. It nestled among the wiry grey hair, but it wasn't an old man's cock. It was large, thick, firm, just waiting for her. And she was ready for it, but not for the sudden slap that landed on her breasts. She yelped, then shut her mouth as the second, more vicious slap hit home.

'I told you not to make a sound. If you do ...' He didn't finish; he didn't need to. He might have a lot to lose if they were caught, but so did she. Her employers would fire her if she were bankrupt, but they wouldn't fancy the scandal of having an employee caught in flagrante much either.

Besides, having to stay silent added to the dirty, degrading, thoroughly erotic thrill of what she was doing, so she waited, watching him, trying to work out what he'd want from her. For now, he seemed intent on her breasts, lifting first one, then the other, cupping them in long, firm fingers before turning his attention to her nipples.

Amanda gasped as he pinched them, but it was more from pleasure than pain. Normally, she didn't like it rough, but what she liked wasn't going to come into it today and knowing that made her wetter still. She stared up at him defiantly, and he smiled.

'When I've finished, you'll know who's in charge.'

I'll see you in hell first, she thought, but she obeyed

him and stayed silent while he played with her breasts, determined not to let him know how he was getting to her. Dammit, she wanted him. Right now, she wouldn't care if he jerked her to her feet, bent her double across the desk and thrust that long, firm cock up her without bothering with foreplay.

The phone rang – sharp staccato rings that brought her back to reality and shame, but he wasn't fazed. Instead, he put the phone on loudspeaker, leaving Amanda feeling eerily unnerved, as if she was being watched as they exchanged pleasantries. Then the manager gripped her breasts so hard that she felt as much pain as dark pleasure.

'Excuse me a moment,' he said urbanely, then pressed the 'hold' button. 'Suck me.'

She nodded as he gave her permission to do what she'd been aching to, and bent forward, running her tongue the length of that red erection that strained towards her, determined to get her revenge. Taking her time, she slid her tongue beneath his foreskin, then began to suck, tasting him, wanting him, revelling in the moment in a way she hadn't known she was capable of doing.

His breathing didn't change, he gave no signs to his caller that anything untoward was happening as he discussed a loan application, but his hands on her breasts and his cock in her mouth told a different story. He pummelled her breasts, kneading them viciously. With each squeeze his cock seemed to jerk until it thrust against the back of her throat, leaving her wanting to gag.

But she couldn't resist him, and she couldn't kid herself that it was only because she couldn't risk him taking her home and job away. The shameful truth was that she didn't want to resist him any more. She wanted sex so badly that she slid a hand cautiously down, reaching between her sticky thighs, feeling her hard clit pushing against the flimsy thong, knowing it wouldn't take much to let her come.

She'd been sure he couldn't see her, but suddenly he twisted her nipples so hard that if she hadn't been gagged by cock she'd have damned his rules, and the scandal she'd cause, and screamed. She took the hint and moved her hand away, closing her eyes as the enormity of what she was doing sunk in. She wasn't here to enjoy herself. She was here to service him like the cheapest of whores. What she wanted didn't matter and realising that, to her horror, made her feel hornier still. She'd never thought she was the submissive type. Far from it. Until now, she'd always called the shots in bed, but this was as good as it was different.

She tightened her mouth round his cock, reaching to caress his balls, feeling them tight with unshed sperm, willing him to take pleasure. She'd have liked to be able to convince herself that she was only obeying him to get it over with, but she knew that wasn't the truth. She was enjoying pleasuring him, and the very lack of passion in his voice added to her determination to break his control.

'I've got a slot free next Tuesday.' He still sounded unmoved by her ministrations, but she knew he was as much of a liar as she was. His cock was jerking constantly, weeping salty liquid. 'I'll see you then.'

He said goodbye and then gripped her head in both hands and began to drive himself into her. He used her mercilessly, pounding home, grunting with pleasure with each long stroke. She writhed against the carpet, pushing her sex down to feel the harsh nylon fibres stroke her aching clit, fighting for the orgasm that she was so maddeningly close to, but he didn't seem to notice, let alone care.

His cock jerked, then jerked again and again. He went rigid, then come flooded her mouth. For a second, he slumped forward. Then he released her hair, pushing her backwards until she was crushed against the back of the footwell, crumpled, dishevelled and needy.

But it was over, so she gathered her dignity and crawled forward.

'Well?' she asked, determined not to let him keep control. He might have touched something deep inside her that left her quiveringly anxious to please him, but she wasn't letting him realise that he'd done what she'd always sworn was impossible and mastered her. 'Will I do?'

'I don't know. I've only just begun to use you.' His urbane calm hadn't wavered, but the way he was watching her had changed frighteningly. 'Stand up.'

She stood, abandoning any pretence of being anything except obedient.

'Walk across to the coat rack.'

She walked, stopping in front of the old-fashioned rack with its polished wooden pole and eight arms that jutted out above her head. Unbidden, she reached up and gripped them, blushing as she imagined being tied like this and felt her breasts harden painfully.

'Good,' he purred, leaving her ridiculously thrilled to have pleased him.

Strong, smooth hands slid beneath her skirt, pushing it up until it was bunched round her waist and she began to tremble with excitement rather than fear. She wouldn't have stopped him now even if she could – and she couldn't. Not because she was scared of what he could do, but because she wanted it too badly.

Now he was satisfied, he moved with tantalising slowness, sliding a dry, cool finger beneath her thong, making a careful exploration between the crease of her buttocks. He'd know how wet she was now, know how she longed to grind herself back and encourage that finger between her thighs to fill the aching, wet emptiness. But what would he do about it?

For minutes that felt like forever, he did nothing at all. Just kept that finger pressing against her anus. Then, seconds before she'd have broken his rules and screamed at him to get on with it, the finger pushed down.

She swallowed back a whimper as he pressed against her tight entrance, dreading the intrusion. No one had ever done this to her. It wasn't her scene. She didn't want it now either, but she couldn't resist him, and part of her was curious about what it would feel like; whether pain really could turn to pleasure, the way it had in the erotic stories that she often read while she masturbated.

'That's good,' he murmured, and the finger withdrew, leaving her panting with relief.

He pulled her knickers down, leaving them round her knees, effectively hobbling her so that she couldn't escape him easily, let alone spread her legs to welcome him as she longed to.

'Now keep still,' he breathed, and knelt behind her. His hands were cool as they pulled her buttocks wide apart, then a long, firm tongue slid between her lower lips, tasting her, testing her.

She longed to jerk backwards towards him, and her nails dug into the wood as she forced herself not to move in case he carried out what now struck her as the worst punishment imaginable and stopped. His tongue slid maddeningly in and out of her wet, greedy cunt, as unhurried as if discovery and scandal wasn't a possibility.

Right then, she wouldn't have cared if someone did come in. Her world had shrunk to her wide-stretched buttocks and the incredible feelings he was generating in her. His tongue slid free, then forward. She gasped as it curled round her clit, teasing, tasting, taking her so close to the edge that another touch would send her screaming into orgasm. Then he stopped again, leaving her hanging impotently.

'Would you like me to gag you?' he asked solicitously.

She nodded, wondering what was happening to her. She knew she should be struggling, or, better still, running, not counting the seconds until he ripped the knickers away altogether.

'Turn round.'

She turned, feeling cool wood against her back, then gulped as she saw her reflection. God, she looked cheap! Her hair was hanging in sweaty strands round her face, her lipstick was smeared, her eyes wide, her face flushed. Her shirt hung open, her breasts thrust upwards by the underwiring that bit into them. Her black skirt was bunched up round her waist, an obscene counterpoint to the white flesh and blonde pubic hair beneath.

Her sex was so wet that it glistened, and to pile humiliation on humiliation he knew exactly how turned on she was by a man she should have been resisting. And he liked what he was seeing. His cock was stirring again as he forced her soiled knickers into her obediently opened mouth, fastening them in place with the torn side strings.

'Soon.' He made the word a promise that set her shuddering again.

If she could have spoken she'd have pleaded with

him to do whatever he wanted as long as it made her come, but she couldn't speak now, and the feeling that gave her was exhilarating. Thanks to that debt her boyfriend had run up, he owned her, body and soul, and she wanted to be owned. She wanted to be used, maybe even abused. Most of all, she wanted to come. No, it was more than want now. It was need; tearing, thought-obliterating and better than the most erotic thing she'd ever dreamed of, let alone experienced.

She tried to signal all that with her eyes, but if he understood he gave no sign of it. Instead, he gestured her over to that wide desk, pushing her shoulders down until she was lying with her head dangling over the edge, her wide-spread legs reaching to the corners.

She'd expected him to thrust into her. Instead, he moved in front of her and unlocked a drawer. The packet of heavy duty condoms he removed was both a promise of fresh depravities to come and a relief, but he didn't open them. Instead, he left them beside her head, almost as if he were taunting her, and moved to stand between her legs.

'You want this,' he murmured, waiting until she nodded before going on. 'You've always wanted it. And now I'm going to give it to you.'

She felt as if she were blushing all over, but she couldn't deny the truth. She did want it. Right now, if he'd wanted to use her arse she wouldn't have stopped him. But it was a relief that he didn't. Instead, two of those long, long fingers stroked along her thighs, then darted inside her, lacing together as he stretched her wide. She jerked convulsively, her body arching upwards, and he smiled as he knelt down in front of the desk.

His tongue darted out, snakelike, curving round her clit and she screamed against the gag as he began to work her body with the dispassionate control of a true expert. Her head lashed from side to side and she gripped the sides of the desk rather than move and risk breaking the spell.

She couldn't bear it if he stopped now. She wasn't sure she could bear this much longer either, but she knew protesting wouldn't have helped even if she could have spoken. Instead, she bit down hard on her gag, tasting herself on the thong and knowing she was far wetter now. His fingers squelched inside her as he thrust and withdrew, now lacing his fingers together, now scissoring wide and stretching her open, always, always, leaving her seconds away from the orgasm she craved.

She was moaning softly, constantly, her plans to keep control long abandoned, but he seemed in no hurry. His tongue caressed her clit like a cat lapping a saucer of milk, and she stared at him pleadingly, willing him to take her that last little step to orgasm. His dark business suit was as immaculate as ever, his grey hair as crisp. He was in control; and knowing that gave her back a tiny amount of control.

Her belly contracted, her stomach wrenching as she made it over the edge at last, and he didn't try to stop her. Instead, his fingers slid free from her, pulling back the hood that tried to protect her clit as his mouth ravaged her. She gasped, she whimpered and moaned against the gag that she now welcomed because it stopped her betraying them both. But she didn't consider moving, and he was smiling when he straightened up, his mouth still glistening with her juices, starting her stomach lurching all over again.

'Promising,' he whispered, then flipped her over.

She closed her eyes, exhausted now that the passion was fading, marvelling at his stamina. For a second she was scared as he slipped the condom on, then used that latex-sleeved cock to spread her juices back, working them round her sphincter muscles.

She tried to tense, then accepted the inevitable and relaxed. There was nothing that she could do to stop him doing whatever he wanted to with her; nothing she wanted to do either. He owned her now; and she wanted to be owned. She lay waiting passively, not arguing when he slid his hand beneath her, although the touch of his hand on her overused clit caused as much pleasure as pain.

Instead she waited, listening to his fast breathing and anticipating the moment when he broke through that barrier. She remembered the feel of him in her mouth, how big he'd been, knowing he was far bigger now, but she didn't even consider protesting.

'You've never done this before, have you?' he asked. She shook her head, wondering if he'd take pity on her; and if she wanted him to. 'Do you want me to?'

She knew she should shake her head, maybe push him away and bolt, just as she could have bolted all along, but she didn't move.

'Well?' he asked, and she found herself nodding.

'Don't worry, I'll break you in gently,' he soothed, and she cursed herself, not just for being stupid enough to believe him, but also for relaxing and making it easier for him.

This wouldn't change anything, and she'd been a fool to believe that it ever could. She'd still owe the money after it was over, and there was no way that she'd ever be able to face telling anyone what had happened, or stop him doing it again. How could she when it made her sound like the cheap little tart she'd always prided herself on not being? How could she explain that one look at this man and all her self-confidence vanished, leaving her wanting only to please him? Until she'd met him, she wouldn't have believed it herself, so there was no way that she could expect anyone else to.

All those thoughts shot through her mind in a second, then she abandoned thought and gave herself over to sensation again. His cock had slid inside her, but not where she'd dreaded it being. He was filling her cunt as she'd longed to be filled for what felt like forever, his fingers soft and gentle on her clit. She moved hopefully beneath him, stopping when she heard his soft laugh.

'Soon,' he promised.

Then there was a sucking sound, followed by a wet finger pressed against her arse. She tensed, ready for pain, but the finger didn't move. Instead, his cock flexed inside her, his other hand working her clit until pleasure began to drown out her ability to think again, and the idea of protesting was a faint, fading memory.

Then, as her body gathered itself for a second, stronger orgasm, it happened. There was a small, sharp pain as his finger drove where less than an hour before she'd have said no one would ever go. It stopped just inside her, giving her time to get used to the intruder. She whimpered softly, glad that the sound was muffled by the desk so he couldn't hear it and punish her for it, as she deserved to be punished.

'It's good,' he coaxed, and it was.

As her body adjusted, she was feeling something she'd never felt before. A raw, dirty pleasure that intensified when he began to move again, moving his finger in time with his thrusts. She lifted her arse to encourage him, revelling in his murmured praise, feeling her body tightening, tightening. She pressed her legs together, wanting even more, and he closed his legs around her, imprisoning her.

She was completely helpless now, she thought exultantly as he began to move frantically. Then she stopped thinking and let her body take over, jerking her buttocks up to meet his increasingly frenzied thrusts, their gasps for breath mingling as they coupled like rutting animals.

'Yess!' he grunted as he emptied himself inside her, but she didn't care. She remained silent, just as he'd ordered her to be, revelling in the pleasure of being mastered, focusing on her debasement to increase the sensations. Her pussy contracted, plunging her from one orgasm to the next with dizzying intensity and her arse welcomed the intruder as she came, triumphantly, again and again.

When she was next aware of what was going on he'd withdrawn and tucked his cock away, leaving him looking as immaculate as ever. If she hadn't looked and felt such a mess she'd have been sure she'd somehow imagined it all; that her aching cunt and arse couldn't have been caused by this charming middle-aged bank manager. No one would believe a word of what had happened if she told them; which she wasn't planning on doing any more than she reckoned he was.

'There's a toilet through there. Use it to clean yourself up,' he said, gesturing towards a door in the panelling.

She nodded, stood up and unfastened the gag, then looked at him. She'd expected some words of praise, but instead he was as intent on the computer as if she hadn't made him come twice in less than half an hour. Accepting her dismissal, she headed for the loo, feeling cheap and used, then saw what he was doing and stopped dead, too stunned to speak, let alone thank him.

That was her joint account called up on the screen, her overdraft that was being marked 'repaid in full'.

'Don't you think you earned it?' He swung round in the swivel chair and smiled at her, and all she could do was look at the floor.

Oh, she'd earned it all right! She'd paid that debt with her body; and with something far more important. Not only had the bastard mastered her, but he'd also given her something that she couldn't get anywhere else, and left her hungry for more. And he was the only one who could feed this sick new craving, so she'd swapped one disaster for another, greater one.

Or had she? She'd never felt so alive, or so sated. And the future was bright again, with no debt to haunt her and opportunities she'd never known existed before.

'Yes!' she said smugly, and had the satisfaction of seeing him look surprised as she tossed her soaking knickers into his lap and headed for his bathroom.

He might have won round one but there'd be other rounds, and she knew how to play now. And there was that scarlet convertible she fancied, almost as much as she fancied what her manager and master would do to her when she told him she couldn't repay the massive overdraft she was about to run up. Oh, yes, she thought exultantly, she couldn't wait for the next payback time.

The Cello Lesson Maria Lloyd

I was allowing my cello teacher to commit murder.

I had moved to a different part of London and he was the only teacher within easy distance, which is something to consider when you are as petite as I am. Carrying the cello case, swinging it into taxi cabs or on to the tube, can threaten to clip and chip your kneecap or ankle bone with every clumsy move. But this teacher was mediocre. Worse, he endeavoured to hide his incompetence with blustering rhetoric designed to destroy all confidence in any promising pupil, thus ensuring that the minimum work was involved for himself.

Nevertheless, I gritted my teeth and submitted for a whole windy spring. Work was demanding and this was the only way to continue to play. I would drag myself from my cramped bedsit and walk to my cello teacher's flat every Sunday afternoon. The acoustics of his practice room were dull and failed to inspire. His flat smelt of cardamom coffee and Italian pastries, along with the faint whiff of cat litter (he had two Persians that treated him and all humans with appropriate disdain).

He was a single man of the generation that rarely cook for themselves. Somehow I guessed he resented the fact that I did not present him with a clingfilm-covered bowl of macaroni cheese or lasagne as a tribute before I settled down to practise my scales.

But I persevered. Because I love music, and I love the cello. It does wonders for my soul, for my heart, to produce those deep intimate tones which soar through the room like the voice of raw grief or a lover's cry of orgasm. The strange alchemy produced by my rosined bow and those quivering strings across a curve of polished wood.

My job sent me abroad for a while and I had to leave my cello behind. My cello teacher admonished me to 'practise in my head as best I could'. I smiled politely, swinging the cello case gangster-style towards him as I hurried out of his hallway, imagining a spray of bullets peppering his chest.

I was surprised at my venom, and then amused. I felt my cello teacher was guilty of the supreme sin – putting pride and self before art. If I had fawned on him it would have been very different, but that is not required by all professional teachers, surely? I despised him and he sensed it, I suppose.

But I digress.

I returned home in autumn, when London is at its best. The twilight was full of lapis lazuli promise, arching above early evening shoppers and commuters. There was the acrid smell of roast chestnuts outside Tottenham Court Road station, the Christmas window displays glistened in the West End and there was a carpet of fallen leaves in Green Park – another season gave way to a rich and intimate promise as the nights drew in.

I was invited to a dinner party by my downstairs neighbour, whom I barely knew. Curious, I accepted.

Imagine my dismay when I discovered that my cello teacher had also been invited. I hoped to make the best of it and leave as early as possible. Fortunately he was seated at the other side of the room, regaling his entourage with tales of his glittering career as a composer which, alas, he had to supplement by teaching. Of course, he then wagged his finger at me to say, 'I do hope you practise a little before you return to your lessons. It is excruciating to listen to rusty playing and know that it will take three months to get you limber enough to play adequately again. *Mon dieu*, such a trial to my poor ears! Perhaps I should charge you double!'

A ripple of laughter around the table, a forced smile from me as the dessert was served and I bashed into my crème brûlée.

'So you play the cello?' A soft male voice spoke into my left ear. I turned to survey its owner.

Tall, fair hair, strong nose and jaw. A tilt to the head, a glint in light blue eyes which struck a chord. I smiled.

'Yes.'

'Do continue to play. It is an instrument of the gods.'

'One to mock us?'

'One to teach us love.'

I smiled again as I took a mouthful of crème brûlée. I glanced at his hands – short nails, callused finger pads, a musician's hands.

'I am afraid my muse despairs. She has been flogged at the altar of another man's pride,' I muttered as I took another generous gulp of Chablis from my wine glass.

'How very Alexander Pope.'

I laughed. 'How typically feminine. Every male teacher I have known, from my ex-driving instructor to that pratt at the end of the table, has disliked me more intently than they ever loved their subject. Why else discourage me from learning? Why else insist on belittling me rather than impart their knowledge?'

He shrugged. 'They are afraid of you. Afraid that you have more talent, can do the thing they teach you better than they ever could.'

I laughed. 'That's a stunning theory. Do you think that I am really that efficient or intimidating?'

He shrugged, took a spoonful of his own crème brûlée.

'Perhaps. But I do admire such qualities in a woman.'

I lowered my eyes, looked back at his merry blue gaze. I was as rusty at flirting as I was at my cello.

'I could teach you if you like,' he suggested abruptly, as if on impulse. I blinked at him, and took a while to register his meaning.

'You teach the cello?' I asked incredulously.

'I am a lecturer at the academy, mostly music theory but I still teach a few pupils privately. Would you be interested?'

'Oh yes.' I exhaled slowly and realised how elated I felt to find a teacher who actually chose me, who seemed on my wavelength.

'Here is my card.' He produced a small oblong of vellum from his jacket pocket.

Theo Kaminsky. Professor. An address in Hampstead.

'Thank you. Thank you very much.' How lucky was this? I thought to myself.

'Why not come across Sunday afternoon if you can?' he said gravely. 'We will put right everything that Jackass ever taught you.'

My new teacher's home was elegant, neat and fascinating, just like its owner. He taught in a large room at the rear of the house, where a French window overlooked a small, high-walled garden. The room was painted white and the walls and ceiling reflected the greenish light from the garden even on a dull autumn day. The floor was polished parquet. Shaker-style chests of drawers containing sheets of music, cupboards containing music stands and various instruments lined the walls. A stool and stand, with music already set out, were positioned in the centre of the room; a chair was placed beside the window.

He sat me on the stool facing the window, arranged

the stand to my perfect satisfaction and said simply, 'Play.'

It was one of my favourite pieces – a test of stamina with long sonorous notes. I chalked my bow, placed my freshly strung cello at an angle between my knees, leant forward to listen to its cadences and tried to play at my best.

Theo sat by the window, his lean body sheathed in T-shirt and chinos. He glanced at the garden, so I could not have read his expression even if I had dared look at him.

I was surprised to find that the insides of my thighs trembled slightly and my stomach fluttered and my hands shook minutely as I played. I had never felt this before, playing the cello. Yet now it seemed that I was indulging in a most lewd and flagrantly immoral act.

Why? All I was doing was performing a piece for my new cello teacher. Yet it seemed as though I was giving him a preview of my repertoire as a lover.

Only at the end of the piece did I dare look up.

Theo was looking at me intently, his pale blue eyes cool and detached, his mouth relaxed but firm, as though held in deep concentration. He was looking at me in such a veiled way that I could not read his expression. I was used to looks of lust, or superior dislike which disguised lust. As I explained earlier I am petite, blonde, people tell me I am pretty, and I have trouble with authority figures. But this look was something more vibrant and serious and erotic than anything else I had known.

'What do you think?' I asked at length in a hoarse odd voice, because I was uncertain what else to do.

I expected him to run through a spiel of greater control, softer tones and so on. Instead he approached me and with an index finger lightly pressed my chin so it was less tilted forward.

My defences melted, as did my anxiety.

Then he moved my shoulders further back ever so slightly. I could feel his breath on my neck as he made this fine adjustment.

Finally he knelt in front of me and carefully moved the cello until it was sitting more symmetrically between my legs, and the neck of the instrument was somehow easier to support because of it.

'Begin again,' he said.

It was almost impossible. I was still zinging from his touch and fired by his strange dispassionate gaze. Where he knelt he almost touched my knees and I could see his biceps ripple against his weight as he leant on his hands and cocked his head to check the line of the cello as I began to play.

Satisfied, he retreated to the chair by the window. The calm acoustics of the room reverberated with another version of the piece – this one much more measured, powerful with suppressed passion which I had never injected into the music before.

'Good,' Theo said when I had finished. He even broke into a grin. 'We are really making progress.'

'After a year of sawing wood, it's a miracle to hear music at last,' I said. 'You are a magician.'

He looked away and I was touched by his sudden modesty.

'I am merely permitting your body to sing in harmony with your cello,' he explained. 'After that the rest will come.'

It was the first of many Sunday afternoon lessons in that elegant room. I used to peek at the rest of the house when I went to the loo and soon realised he lived alone. There were still boxes to be unpacked from his recent move – books, mostly; if he had a wife, these would already be sitting neatly on the shelves. But the house was tidy, polished, well cared for – so he had a part-time help to do the impersonal housework.

I must confess that I loved visiting his bathroom. It was so male, and it had been many years since I had known a man's intimate space. I sniffed his bottles of aftershave, squirted little gobbets of shaving foam to feel its smooth texture between my fingers and handled his heavy chrome razor. I stroked his striped bath towel, hanging to air from his morning shower across the shower curtain rail and weighed myself upon his bathroom scales.

Foolish teenage stuff, I know. But it somehow compensated for the subtle assault he had begun on my senses during our cello lessons. The way he made me sit just so and repeat a piece of music again and again to his impassive silence – and yet within that silence was an electricity, a concentration that inspired me to try harder and play more professionally, more beautifully than I had ever managed before. It was as heavenly as flying, as dangerous as thin ice. It became a paraphrase of sexual exhibitionism to me, to lay my soul bare for him in this way for his avid attention, his expert tutoring. I submitted, I burned. I grew feverish to improve and earn his approval.

Even to earn his sexual favour.

Not that he ever tried it on, even when he took hold of my ankle, my calf, and moved my leg a little wider so the upper curve of the cello skirted my soft inside thigh, just above the knee.

But afterwards, at home, I would suddenly tremble at the recollection of his tender yet professional touch and ache to feel his fingers higher up my thigh, against my sex.

I took to wearing flimsy French knickers, of the softest most expensive lace I could afford, silk bras and short flared skirts. Stockings and high-heeled lace-up shoes. My lambswool sweaters or cotton shirts were tight over my breasts, which rose and fell in time to the music. I became a quivering instrument, like my cello. Just as I strummed its strings and engendered musical notes, my teacher softly handled my limbs and rearranged my posture until I thrummed with passion.

I was his floor show. I was the object of his subtle design. An instrument of mind and body, bent in harmony with the smooth curved belly of my cello until I was symbiotic with its beauty, its contralto. And, at the same time, I grew to know the man who altered my breath with his breath, my posture with his posture, imbued me with some tantric meditation of poise and silence that engendered sound of great timbre from my cello.

He was training me. Taming me. In more ways than one. And I loved it.

It was a slow and steady taming, a testing of my submission and my resolve. I was shocked to find that I succumbed gradually, by smooth degrees, each week, no matter how I rebelled and regrew my feminist agenda during the intervening days. The age-old dance of pheromones and power is hard to tackle with cold reason. Especially when one's body aches to join the waltz.

I lived for that hour on Sunday afternoons when I bowed my head and played heavenly music for the maestro who had adapted my body to his will.

Many such weeks passed. I longed for him to complete the seduction. I thought about making a pass at him myself, just to ease the sexual tension. But I knew he would find this distasteful and I was enjoying being led along another's path of desire. I wanted to see where it ended. And so I endured my sensual purgatory for some months.

Until finally he told me I was at the stage when I could perform in public.

'There is a charity concert at the Academy. I would like you to perform one of my own compositions. Would you?'

'Yes,' I said simply. How could I refuse?

The composition was as simple as it was beautiful. Yet it was challenging in the demands it placed upon the performer. Simple art always belies greater complexity. I enjoyed struggling to learn it well and play it with feeling. It was as though playing Theo's own composition could bring me closer to him – that he had positioned my body thus, made me play this succession of precise and sombre notes, to prepare me for his final seduction.

It was the final practice before my performance and I was so desperate I wanted to rebel, walk away, forget the whole thing. I had begun to think that I had imagined it all, that I was gross in my sexual hankering, that I was ugly and no longer attractive to anyone, let alone Theo. What was I, chopped liver, in my flimsy blouses, silken stockings, French knickers?

Nevertheless, I played my best for him because I wanted to stun him with my art. Prove that I could be a consummate musician for the teacher, before I walked away from the man. If I could manage to walk away, that is. I feared he held me on a skein that he could ravel in at will.

As the final note of the piece shivered into the room, I felt him approach from behind and softly stroke the base of my left ear.

'Exemplary,' he whispered. 'You deserve a reward.'

He bent and kissed me chastely on the cheek.

To feel his lips against my skin sent me wild. I let the cello slide to the ground, placed the bow beside it and arched back in my stool to allow him to kiss me full on the lips.

He bestowed a slow, subtle, arousingly sadistic kiss. Tracing and teasing and nipping and only permitting the most chaste response on my part – if I tried to French kiss, he backed away until I surrendered all control to his probing, cruel kisses once more.

I was trembling, almost weeping with desire. And he knew it.

'This is what I have wanted,' he whispered, 'since I saw you take that mouthful of crème brûlée the first time we met.'

I was suddenly shy. I looked down at the parquet floor, bent my neck in mute submission, almost shamed by my complete abandonment to him. I had never been so slowly and completely enslaved by any man.

I wondered what he would do.

'Continue to look down,' he said approvingly, 'and take off your blouse.'

Staring at the floor, I was shocked to find myself blush at his first strident command. Yet I also felt a leap of excitement in my groin that the ritual had finally begun. Slowly I unbuttoned my blouse and shrugged out of it as shyly as any reluctant virgin. My bra of raw silk barely contained my swelling breasts, my darkening nipples. I could feel a faint flush on my exposed cleavage, my arms, my abdomen, as they were exhibited naked beneath his gaze. I wanted to cover up and yet his eyes compelled me to sit silently, demurely, in this manner for what seemed like an age.

Finally he cleared his throat.

'Now,' he said, 'spread your legs like you would for your cello, and hike up your skirt.'

Slowly I obeyed, my high heels scraping across the parquet floor as I did so. My stocking tops and French knickers were now fully exposed for his idle predilection. My legs trembled gently with excitement as I held the pose, my eyes still downcast modestly.

'Now,' he said carefully, 'I want you to play with yourself. Stroke your skin, your breasts, fondle between your legs. Slowly. Without moving your torso or bottom or legs one muscle. Just use your hands, playing upon your body as if it were as inert as your cello. This is what I want to see. And I want to hear the music it produces within you. Be vocal.'

With trembling fingers I traced the contours of my own body while my teacher watched my every move. I stroked my neck and shoulders, my flat tense stomach, my bare wrists and arms. Slowly I rolled and pinched my aching nipples through the soft silk of my bra. I stroked the moist mound of my sex through the lace of my French knickers, rubbing the hard nub of my clit until my eyes closed tight and my sex unfurled like a lotus. I took my time. Elaborate in my caresses, I teased myself to full and aching arousal, while holding as still as I possibly could.

All the while I felt his blue eyes burn me and note every flutter of pleasure in my stomach, every slight tremor in my parted thighs.

Soon I found that I was uttering sounds that I had never made before. Little soft whimpers of yielding ecstasy reflected the waves of heat and need that coursed through my sex, my nipples, my parted lips to shudder through my nervous system. I bent my neck ever so slightly to one side, tried to stop myself arching back to accentuate this strange submissive abandonment. Juices oozed copiously from my musky sex and I spread the juices from within the confines of the lace along my bare flesh, my thighs, my breasts, so that my pale skin glistened like a pearl. My body opened like an oyster before him to display the pearl of my feminine need. Time did not exist; the world beyond this room did not exist. All that mattered was the man who sat opposite me and watched with such close attention the ballet of self-pleasuring he had put in motion.

I felt that I would faint. All those Victorian clichés of maidens overcome with their own sexuality suddenly made sense to my twenty-first-century body and brain. The months of longing had translated into this slow languorous turn-on, allowing every cell of my body to ache and hunger for sex. Sex with the man who was watching my performance as carefully, as impassively, as he had watched me play cello.

I wanted him so fiercely I could scream. And yet I almost feared what he wanted from me. Despite this apprehension I decided to take the risk and was totally open and submissive without realising what the final movement would be. That would be in the hands of my teacher.

Finally he said softly, 'Go down on all fours, with your back towards me.'

Slowly, with all the grace I could muster, I obeyed. I looked down at the parquet floor. My lace-sheathed buttocks rode high and tender and my stockinged knees slid silkily on the polished wood. My palms were slicked with fine sweat and pressed gratefully against the unyielding surface. I knew I was desperate for him to use me in the most unspeakable ways and marvelled at my own abasement as I waited in silent supplication.

I felt the rustle of his clothing as he knelt behind me. His arms encircled my waist with unhurried possession.

One palm pressed flat against my stomach, while his other hand delved past the waistband of my French knickers and sought out my swollen pussy.

He pressed his hand against the full length of my sex and I gave a long low moan of satisfaction. Then I gasped as he eased three fingers knuckle deep into my waiting cunt with consummate grace and began to frig me back and forth, side to side, in an undulating motion that encircled my clit with every other pass and jolted me with extreme, almost tantric bliss. His expert fingering sent ripples of molten joy through my stomach to my tight breasts, and across my buttocks and down my legs. I had been aching for this so much and for so long that I could not stop trembling reflexes I did not even know I had possessed until this man had triggered them. Images ricocheted within my brain, swayed my torso, forced my head up and back in surrender to his touch. Now I was his instrument and I sang my pleasure in perfect pitch to the acoustics of his elegant room as I trembled with the orgasm that had been six months in coming. Even this he controlled, by pressing his palm against my stomach and leaning against my lower back, positioning me just so, crouched beneath him, and bidding me to stay still so he could have absolute control over motion and tempo. Blind with tears, I humbly obeyed. Slowly, with impossible stealth and subtlety, he brought me to an extended brain-splitting climax that made me whimper in pleasure and pain, wilting on the edge of the most exquisite experience of my life, even as he continued to touch, stroke and press just the right spots to allow total release.

Afterwards, as I lay in a collapsed heap beside my supine cello, he cradled me to him. I kissed him and thanked him, expected him to begin to make love to me, penetrate me with the stiff cock I felt resting against my buttocks. Sensing my thoughts, he chuckled, stroked my hair back from my forehead. His fingers, still moist with my juices, traced the contours of my parted lips and I could taste my own musk upon them.

'This is only the beginning,' he murmured. 'Perhaps if you consent to another six months of cello lessons, you may be ready to sing while you take my cock inside you.'

My first public performance was a great success. Now I am learning more difficult music from my maestro, and my cello playing has never sounded so heavenly.

I'll let you know how the final version sounds in another six months' time.

The Special Wine Mini Lee

He was handsome. Vince hired me the summer before my second year of university. I only had a couple of months to make rent and tuition money. He'd just opened the restaurant. It was all redone, cheaply, and I wondered about the food which the customers frequently complained about. Cartons of powdered gelati along the back steps spoke volumes about the authenticity of an Italian restaurant.

This was the first restaurant I'd worked in and I didn't know anything about the restaurant biz. I got the feeling Vince wasn't exactly above board, but he hired me, I had a job, and that was all I knew or cared about at the time.

He wanted me to wear short skirts and that wasn't so unusual, I thought. At first, I wore leggings underneath. But he kept urging me to go bare legged. A part of me was excited by this; I mean, there was something very attractive about him, and dangerous, and the regulars that came in, his friends. I suspected excitedly that they were all mafiosi. They could well be – they seemed dangerous and no one fooled with them. They always talked provocatively to me. On the other hand, I felt a bit like the prosciutto I brought raw on their appetiser plates.

I mostly kept them at bay and daydreamed some dirty scenarios about them; all innocent enough. Scenarios where I wore nothing underneath and I would toss my skirts about for them all. But ultimately I was shy of them and Vince's instructions about my job were always changing; I was disconcerted and felt I was always making mistakes. I was worried that he would fire me. But then, when he'd take the occasional liberty with me, it was oddly titillating. He'd slap my bum as I passed with a loaded tray. I wanted him to do more than that – I wanted him and all his cohorts to do more than that, all together, if you know what I mean.

I found myself going to work without my tights on, just panties under my short skirt. This is what Vince had always wanted and my tips did improve. I was really playing the part of a kind of bad girl waitress. And in order to provoke him further, to move him to further indecencies with me, I'd secretly cheat Vince here and there, giving his associates breaks on the tab, and accepting bigger tips for it. I was a bad girl. It was fun. Vince and I both knew I needed to be spanked. And when he'd catch me in my miscalculations on the bills he'd give me sharp stinging slaps on my ass. He'd pursue me as I tried to escape and he'd raise my skirts, asking if I'd hidden any money in my panties. Sometimes he'd pull on my satin underwear and I'd withdraw shyly, and he'd warn me not to cheat him. I'd deny any mishandling of cash, but we both knew the truth. He wasn't going to fire me. I knew this was the beginning of a special little game we had.

One night he blamed me for the shortage on the register, and then he threatened my job and took me downstairs to his office.

He sat me down on the couch and he sat opposite me in his chair. He told me how the restaurant was everything and that I must be loyal to the nth degree to it. He explained how he'd gotten ahead in the business by slicing the bread so thin so as to get the extra mileage from this, the soul of life, bread.

'What else is the soul of life?' he asked, smiling. 'Are you wearing panties?' His handsome head leaned forward. 'You are?'

I looked away, wanting to part my thighs for him to see my soft in-between. It was an involuntary thought; I couldn't truly be a bad girl for him, could I?

He pulled on the hem of my skirt, lifting it up. 'Do you hide some of my money in here?' he said. 'What is this?' He pulled up my skirt.

'Do you hide money up in here?'

'I don't steal. You make me cold when you do that,' I said. 'It's chilly down here in the basement.'

'Are your nipples hard? Are your little skirts up?' He smiled and yanked at my panties roughly. 'You can't hide anywhere and bad girls must hide.' He pulled my underwear down a little. 'What's under here?' My thighs were slightly parted now and he pulled my panties away so he could see my satin lips underneath. Next, I tried to move away. This only served to expose my pussy more fully. I couldn't help myself as I released a gush of wetness between my legs. He took it upon himself to feel the wet spot and, as he touched it, feeling my protruding clit through my panties, he said, 'You're wet, aren't you?'

We heard sounds out in the stairwell. Vince pulled his hand back from my pussy. Suddenly the door opened and Vince's wife entered. My skirts were down and nothing was amiss to her and she proceeded to tell Vince that she would be away tomorrow.

The next day at work, I naughtily didn't wear any panties underneath my short skirt. I don't know what possessed me. I was a little nervous on the outdoor deck – it was a windy day. Some of Vince's friends were waiting to be served. They were the hot boys, with lots of verve and illicit money to back it. I approached the table and they asked for wine. They were all looking at my bare legs and short skirt. 'Vince has her wearing the uniform the right way now,' Luc said. 'This calls for the special wine – bring the special wine, beautiful, for the special guests.'

'The special wine?' I asked as the wind rose up a little around my skirts. The anxious prospect of them seeing my lack of underwear cause me to release a gush of pee. Embarrassed, I couldn't handle the way they were all looking at me and could barely resist the urge to go in, now scared, put on my tights and go home.

'The special wine, ma bella,' one said, heavy with an Italian accent, 'you ask Vince for it.' There was something conspiratorial about the way they laughed together about this special wine. One of them fondled my bum under my skirts. They tried this every night, but tonight, I was underdressed. I jumped away, flushed.

'He's not here yet, but I'm sure Gino can find the wine.'

I went in. It was warmer inside the restaurant. Gino would be in the kitchen, cooking for his father while he was out. Gino always gave me a strange feeling. It wasn't like his dad did, though. This was a guardianship in a sense. I'd catch him sneaking around the restaurant, checking on me. He was my age but had a different social scene from my own friends or boyfriends. He was into muscle cars, like the rest of his friends. He worked for his dad; that's what he would do for the rest of his life. I was going into second year university next fall. We had nothing in common. This is a waitressing job. I was just a waitress there and I didn't want any complications; I was glad to have a job. It shouldn't have bothered me that Gino seemed to disapprove of me. Although he was very handsome, like his father, he was somehow threatening to the bad girl.

I went into the kitchen, thinking nervously about how I'd like to get my tights on and stay warm and safe. Gino stopped what he was doing on the stove to look at me in the way he always did. He never looked right at me – he'd see my legs, the short length of my skirt, he'd check my bosom. He'd give me his usual cursory, reproachful look. Tonight, when he saw me, his looks were very dark indeed. He turned his back without saying a word and went back to cooking before I could ask my question about the special wine. I didn't need to ask him anything for, as it turned out, Vince arrived and came into the kitchen. He stopped in his tracks to look at how I'd dressed for my shift. Suppressing a smile, he cleaned his teeth with his tongue.

'Vince, Luc asked for something called the special wine,' I said nervously. Gino dropped a metal spoon on the stovetop.

'Come out to the bar,' Vince ordered me sternly. I moved quickly past him, out to the long-countered bar, which blocked his view of me when I went behind it.

'How much did you steal tonight?' he asked, coming behind the counter. 'Is the bad girl being a good girl now?'

I knew he meant that he approved of my attire and, as he came around the bar, I could see he was intent on investigating closer. I wished I'd worn the leggings – tonight it would be too easy for him. I felt my pussy getting wet. I was bad, I'd mishandled a little money from his restaurant, yes, and now I had to repress the uncontrollable urge to pull my skirts up and show him my swelled clit to atone for it.

'The special wine is under the register,' he said, 'and don't keep the customer waiting.'

I leaned over, nervously feeling his shadow creep over me in my ludicrous position, which he could plainly see.

And yet I still leaned over without bending my knees, knowing the wetness between my legs could be detected by him. As I bent over, the wetness got wetter. I wanted him to spank me, punish me for being a bad girl, for my dishonesty to him. I squatted now, modestly, my heart actually racing. I found the wine bottle and produced it, held it out to him and took a step back.

'Hmm,' he moaned. 'Don't get too near the till there, little girl.' I backed into it and he spanked me with two rapid slaps across the front of my skirts. I gasped. He lifted my skirts up just as his friend, Luc, was coming into the restaurant from the terrace.

'Is she stealing again?'

Behind the bar, Vince was pulling up my skirts, exposing me for Luc to see. I breathed rapidly. I had nowhere to move.

'See this girl, Luc? I hired her and I could fire her. You know how much money she steals from me?' His finger roughly tilled my slit in front of Luc. I couldn't help but release my juices and there were wet sounds coming from between my legs. I turned away as best I could and moaned in spite of myself.

'She's a dirty girl; she likes me,' Vince said. 'Look how wet she is.'

'Let's uncork the wine,' Luc suggested as he helped Vince pull up my skirts further. I tried to squirm away but they only took further liberties with me as their hands roamed all over my body.

'The special wine now,' Vince said. Vince took the wine bottle and brought it near my naked crotch.

'She's ready,' Luc said. Together, they spread my legs up and apart.

'Oh please!' I moaned.

Vince slowly rubbed the neck of the bottle backwards and forwards over my sex. While Luc held me up, Vince moved the bottle gently in and out. It slid in tightly and smoothly. I tried not to groan for the inexplicable pleasure of it.

'Now the wine is ready,' Vince cooed. He handed it to Luc. With evil ceremony, Luc took the bottle and licked my juices off it. I felt flushed with shame.

'Bring it to the boys, Luc.'

'You get ready to come take our order, sweet lips,' Luc said, pointing at me. Then he left with the prized bottle. Vince was looking down on me.

'I only took a little money one night.'

'Every night!'

'I can give it back,' I pleaded.

'You will. Get up.' I rose and tried to get past him just as Gino came out into the bar area. He looked at us both, his expression hardening. I felt that he knew his father had just seen my bare cunt. Had he been watching?

'Take care of the front, Gino.' Vince guided me by the arm to the stairs to the basement. Would Gino save me somehow? Save me from my own lust? Did I want a white knight? Did he care I was going to the office with the black knight?

I had no panties on and Vince lifted my skirts at the top of the stairs. I stumbled down a couple of steps. 'Let me support you,' he said, slipping his hand in between my legs from behind. This he did all the way downstairs, his fingers probing.

At the bottom of the stairs, he whispered, 'We have to get you ready for your shift, the one where you work off your debt to me.' He opened the office door and took me in. He gently pushed me over to the couch beside the desk while he turned to lock the door. I sat down and stared at him. Nervous, I started to rummage in my blouse pocket for my tip money.

'Here it is, Vince. I'm sorry. I think this should cover it.' It was all in vain.

'You're a criminal. Do you know what could happen to you?' He sat down on a chair by the desk. 'I could send you to jail. Now, take off your top.'

I obeyed, shyly opening my shirt and letting it fall off my shoulders. I crossed my arms over my small breasts, I felt the hardness of my nipples against my upper arm.

'Let me see them, stand up,' he ordered. I kept my arms crossed and stood up. He firmly took my wrists and spread my arms out. 'Oh, little dark ones.' Holding my arms out, he guided me to the front of his desk, in front of his chair. 'Sit down here.'

I sat down on the edge of his desk. He leaned me back slightly, directing my arms behind me in order for me to hold myself up. He brought his desk lamp up close to my breasts; the light was warm and my nipples were sensitive. Involuntarily, I stretched myself towards the light. 'Mmm, you like that.' He squeezed my nipple. 'I'll get you all ready for your naughty shift, don't you worry.' His finger circled my small nipple. 'Such dark buds, these nipples.' He pulled out some tweezers from inside his left-hand top drawer. 'Any stray hairs?' He pinched my nipples. He looked closely at them with the light. 'We don't like hairs, anywhere – bad girls should have no hair. At first, they always do.' He plucked one or two fine hairs from around my nipple and then, when he was satisfied, he squeezed my nipples with the tweezers, giving me a sharpish pain that went straight down to my clit. 'Not many there, but that doesn't mean you're not a bad girl. There's somewhere else you have hair.'

He urged me to lean further back, lifting my skirts away from my naked sex underneath. 'Lean all the way back.' I reclined back. I was lying on his desk, with my legs dangling over and my naked cunt arching into the air. My pelvis has always protruded higher than most and my clit stood out even with my legs closed. Vince inhaled and began to spank my protruding clit and pussy lips. 'Dirty girl, you masturbated from just a little girl. Look at how you're formed.' He clasped a hand over my wet mound and moved it in a circle. He was right, I did masturbate a lot, and from when I was very little. That's why I had an overdeveloped pelvic tilt, I thought. I knew my clit was so inflamed that it protruded. How wet I was; I felt I might come with his rubbing. I reached upwards with my crotch towards the rapid hand slaps. 'Open your legs.' He spread my dangling legs upwards and placed my heels on the edge of the desk. He pushed my legs apart as wide as they would physically go.

From his desk drawer, he took out his razor and some shaving foam. His first stroke was a slow one above my clit. The nakedness underneath was revealed in multiple folds, with my clitoris sticking out well beyond. I gushed more juices; I felt like I was peeing. I closed my legs. Vince pushed my legs to the side and gave me three sharp slaps on my bum. 'Bad girl in every way.' He moaned, fondling my arse, which was hot from his spankings. He spread my legs open again as he plunged his finger into me, deeply, saying, 'Now we'll have to wipe you up.' He pulled his finger out of my wet pussy and wiped it on my skirt.

His razor now ran along the inside of my cunt lips, which he spread apart, making sure not a single hair would be remaining. Then he wiped the razor clean on my skirt and, in short order, I was completely shaven. He patted my shaven pussy lips and it made a wet sound. 'Hmm, all the boys will see this.' His finger went inside me. 'You must get dressed for your shift.'

Into his desk drawer he went, pulling out the leather braided harness to put on me. He dressed me in it. The rope went in between my legs and separated into two cords that went around my clit, making it stick out as the folds around it were pressed down by the rope. I was lying back on the desk. 'I have to pee,' I said.

'Yes, pee then.' He placed his mouth over my peepee. His tongue circled my clit. Then he sucked gently on it.

'No. Let me go to the bathroom,' I suggested desperately.

'Give me just a little, but save some for Luc.' He smiled at me as he pressed back down on my pussy with his mouth, whereupon I let out a few short spurts of pee. 'Hmm,' he groaned, pulling his mouth away. Next, out of his drawer, he pulled out my evening attire, which consisted of a shorter skirt than I had before and a demi-length transparent top. He dressed me, the sheer blouse draping across the clips on my nipples and the miniskirt that barely covered the straps between my legs. I looked down and could see my clit protruding from under the hem of my skirt. He stood back to admire the costume and then he roughly pulled me off the desk and on to my knees. He was stroking his hot hard cock, which he edged towards my mouth, using the hair on my head to guide me towards it. His cock charged into my mouth and I sucked greedily as he moved in and out of me but half a dozen times before he came. I hoped that this ultimate release for him would spare me from the boys, and yet I knew it would be my ultimate satisfaction. If Vince was pleasured, he would be rewarded further by the pleasure of his friends. How I wanted to satisfy his friends too, and so myself.

Pleased with me, Vince stood me up. He then motioned me to the door. As I went slowly through, he slapped my bum, barely covered by my new skirt. 'You'll do everything I say,' he warned. I went ahead of him, up the stairs, with him following below and looking up at the new nakedness between my legs.

Upstairs, Vince led me to the private dining room. We passed Gino along the way. I inhaled nervously as Gino looked me over. Something crossed over his eyes and I realised then what it was I saw in them when he looked over at his father. It was a look of complete possession.

Vince stopped and smiled. 'Do you like her? I think she looks very nice.' He brought me closer to Gino. 'Don't worry, you'll get your chance.' Then he flicked my erect clit back and forth in front of him. I closed my eyes and imagined Gino sucking it. I didn't know what was happening to me; I was orgasming now. Vince was chuckling, still flicking my clit back and forth lightly with his finger. I turned my face away, unable to stop my body's reaction to this. When my orgasm subsided, I looked ashamedly at Gino, who stood there silently intent. 'See what a bad girl she is? Steals from the till and shows us her pussy for it,' Vince explained. 'You can make love to her.' Gino looked away. 'Now, my dear, you have a table to serve.' Vince moved me to the door and turned the knob.

Inside, the men were seated around the large table, waiting for me.

John Stone

Lois Phoenix

Shelley climbed out of her car and soaked up a little sunshine as she waited for one of the boys from the station to arrive. One last check that she had everything to hand: camera, spare rolls of film. She just wanted a feel of the place; forensics had removed anything there was to see days ago.

She knew she had a downright cheek expecting a police officer to escort her on what Sheriff John Stone would call one of her Nosy Parker missions, but what the hell, the good folks of New Orleans liked to read all about the gory details of a good drugs haul and who was she to deprive them of it? And, as for cheek, well you don't get to be a good journalist without a good dollop of that. She bet John Stone was turning the air blue down at the station about now. Shelley smiled to herself; she had to admit that it brought her a frisson of pleasure each time she riled him.

After covering crime for the *New Orleans Herald* for over two years, nothing much surprised Shelley McMann any more, but the sight of Sheriff Stone arriving in his jeep to take her over to Cat Island that morning sure did. Shelley steadied herself for a fight, willing the excited acceleration of her heart rate to slow as she watched Stone swing his solid build down from the cab.

'Ms McMann.' The ms was an insult and she knew it.

'Sheriff.' Shelley removed her shades and smiled her prettiest smile. 'This is an honour.'

'Damage limitation, ms, that's all there is to it. The youngsters down the station listen to their peckers too much, but when you get to my age . . .' Stone removed his shades to face her down, revealing blue, blue eyes surrounded by laughter lines. 'Let's just say I'm a little more discerning about what I tell the press. Hell, you'll make the rest up anyway.'

'I do not fabricate copy, Sheriff, and you know it.' Shelley allowed herself to be helped into the boat. Stone's hand was large and square and she noticed a scar running across three of his fingers – the sight of it sent a primitive sexy thrill running right through her.

Stone turned his back to her as he stooped to start the engine. His shoulder holster cut a ridge in his immaculately ironed shirt. He steadied the boat as the engine began its persistent thrum. Shelley shifted slightly on the wooden seat, the vibrations sending a shiver from her toes all the way up to her quim.

John Stone was one miserable son of a bitch. Solid as a rock in character as well as build; men treated him with respect and women tolerated his chauvinistic attitude because they believed that deep down he was just an old-fashioned teddy bear.

Nevertheless, he irritated the fuck out of Shelley, not least because his arrogant, patronising manner completely turned her on. The harder they come, Shelley thought to herself, the harder they fall.

Shelley turned her face up towards the sunlight filtering through the overhanging branches, blazing hot one second and shadow the next, and listened to the toads calling each other across the bayou. Shelley arched her back, feeling her nipples push against the thin cotton of her T-shirt and, from the corner of her eye caught John

Stone staring at her. She turned to look at him and Stone swerved the boat dangerously as he looked away. Shelley felt an immediate swelling in her clit. Well, well. Shelley sensed weakness and suppressed a smile, running her tongue over her bottom lip.

'I must thank you, Sheriff, for bringing me out on such a beautiful day.'

Stone cleared his throat, resolutely scanning the water in front of them. 'Just saving myself a whole load of trouble, lady. A little missy like yourself could fall into the water and the 'gators would make sure no pathologist ever got to determine cause of death. Could do without the paperwork, that's all.'

Shelley bit her tongue and wondered why he'd really chosen to take her to the island himself. A widower of fifty, John Stone had a brood of grown-up kids who took care of him. Shelley guessed that his maternal, homely daughters were Stone's idea of perfect womanhood. Shelley had done some digging and discovered that he'd never remarried, despite the fact that there were a few middle-aged women in town who positively glowed whenever he was near. The boys in the station pulled his leg about the fact that he was often asked for personally by lonely divorcees convinced that they'd seen a prowler in their back yard.

Shelley admired the back on him – it had to be at least six hands across – and wondered why he hadn't settled back down with someone. The man had to have urges. She bet the only sex he'd ever had was straight vanilla, and not even that for a good while. Shelley crossed her legs and tensed her thighs against her clit, imagining what she could teach him. It would be like lassoing a bull.

'Here we are, lady.' Ever the gentleman, Stone tied up the boat and held his hand out. Shelley took it but slipped and was forced to grab on to his shoulders. She was amazed by the strength in him; he felt like a solid slab of granite. Shelley dared to look up. Stone's jaw was clenched tight but he didn't flinch. He looked her straight in the eye. Neither spoke. His hands were warm on her waist where he had steadied her. Shelley saw all the living he had done etched into the lines on his face. There were deep grooves when he frowned and Shelley had seen grown men cower when he lost his temper. Stone's nostrils dilated slightly as he smelt her expensive scent and he backed off. As Shelley let go she ran her hands over his enormous pecs. If she didn't fuck this man soon, she was going to explode.

Shelley wished she still smoked, it would have been something to do with her shaking hands. As she watched him secure the boat, sensing that he too was playing for time, she wondered if his erection was as stout as the rest of him and how many moves it would take to get his pants round his ankles and his cock in her mouth.

Stone reached into the boat and pulled a rucksack out of the hull. 'Provisions,' he muttered.

'How sweet.'

'My daughter insisted,' Stone strode off through the trees. 'She guessed you wouldn't have the homely instinct to prepare one.'

Fuck you, Shelley thought, but said instead, 'I didn't want you to think I was setting up some kind of seduction.' She was gratified to see Stone's thick neck turn pink all the way up to his grey crew-cut.

He gave himself away by his lack of response.

It took them about half an hour to reach the old house which the gang had used for a hideout. Shelley followed in Stone's wake; he used the path that the smugglers had beaten through the undergrowth. The sun was high in the sky and they were both glad of the shade by the time they got there. Stone used his weight to test the strength on the porch and handed Shelley a bottle of water. She leant against the railing and watched him, her face hidden in shade. Stone had removed his hat and had one leg up on the wooden step, his massive thigh straining the cotton of his uniform pants. She was amazed that he didn't have sweat stains in this heat. He slugged from a bottle of water and wiped his mouth with the back of his hand, leaning an elbow on the raised knee as he fiddled with the bottle cap with huge blunt fingers. Shelley watched him in silence, imagining his hairy forearms hooked beneath her knees, spreading them. No woman alive would be able to fight off a man of John Stone's weight. Jeez, she couldn't imagine anyone would want to, despite him being an uptight, miserable old grouch.

'Finished?' Stone's big boots sounded loud on the dried-out wood.

Shelley nodded and took a last pull on the bottle of water. A trickle of water ran down her chin and into her top. Without thinking, Stone reached out one callused finger to scoop it up, touching the skin just above her cleavage. He snatched it back as if burnt. Shelley lowered the bottle and took his finger, raising it to her lips to wipe away the droplets around her mouth. When she had done this, she pushed it into her mouth and sucked it, hard.

Stone looked dumbfounded. He stood in front her, as solid as a bull, a nervous tick beginning to throb in his temple. Shelley reached for his rough hands and slowly placed them on her belly, pulling them up under her T-shirt until they were covering her breasts. God that felt good. Her nipples were like pebbles under his palms. Stone just stood there, his hands limp under hers, making her feel like a complete idiot. She let go of his hands and they dropped back to his sides. She jerked down her top and spun away from him. 'Fuck you, Sheriff,' she spat.

In a split second, he had virtually lifted her off her feet in a vice-like grip. The bottle skittered over the floor. 'What the hell do you think you're doing?' He was right in her face now, his eyes glinting dangerously.

'Trying to get you to fuck me, you dumb prick.'

'My, my.' John Stone released one arm and ran his thumb over her bottom lip. 'You talk just like a whore, lady.'

'It's the only thing that gets me noticed with Captain America here,' Shelley bit his thumb, hard.

Stone flinched but held her tight. 'Not the only thing, lady,' he muttered, pushing his hand up under her T-shirt. 'Not by a long chalk.'

'Get your fucking hands off me,' Shelley snarled as his huge hand kneaded her breast.

'Too late now,' Stone nuzzled into her neck. 'You've convinced me.' He had her in exactly the position she had been hoping for, for months now: T-shirt up under her neck, his huge rough hands all over her breasts, his mouth on her shoulder and those granite thighs stuck hard between hers. Shelley's clit thrummed as she struggled against him, but she felt like a fool.

'Get the fuck off me!' Shelley pushed uselessly against his huge frame, her exposed breasts bouncing with each effort.

And suddenly she was released. She tugged down her T-shirt. It was her turn to blush now.

Stone was busy catching his breath. 'I've never forced myself on anyone in my life, lady, but you sure get a man confused.'

Shelley watched him out of the corner of her eye. He

was running a hand over his hair and also, she noticed, failing to hide a massive boner that was trying its best to escape from the front of his pants.

She just couldn't dampen that thrum. 'Sorry.'

'Pardon me?'

'I said sorry, OK? I guess I'm a bit of a control freak.'

'I've put away guys for less than I've just done to you.'

Shelley let out a peal of laughter. 'Oh come on!'

He held up his hands in a gesture of surrender. 'You just stay away from me now, you hear. There are dozens of guys down the station who'd just love to give you what you want, lady, it's just about all they talk about. Frontwards, backwards, things I never heard about. The last time I courted a girl there were rules and limits, you know . . .' Stone choked to a halt.

But Shelley wasn't about to leave him alone, no way. Her quim was damp and heavy and she was damn well gonna make sure that Stone did something about it. 'I don't want courting, Sheriff.' Shelley slipped one of his shirt buttons through its buttonhole. 'There are no rules and no limits. A big bull of a man like you makes a girl go all damp between the thighs.'

Stone made a small noise in his throat. He didn't touch her but his erection was straining out for her. Shelley released another button, then another. She slipped her hands inside his shirt and felt the crinkly mass of slightly greying hair.

'I'm a grouchy old widower with no time for . . . aaargh, Jesus, I'd forgotten how good it feels.' Stone's Adam's apple bobbed in his throat.

Shelley liked him like this. His shirt was spread open to reveal his broad muscular chest. His flies were undone and Shelley stroked his massive dick, which ran like velvet through her palm.

Shelley ran her tongue over the underside of his chin. 'You know, Sheriff, you really are the most arrogant, anally retentive son of a bitch I've ever met and I'm going to have to fuck the living daylights out of you.'

Stone grabbed her wrist and pulled her up against him so sharply that her head flicked back. He grabbed her tush with his other hand so that his boner dug into her belly. 'Not if I fuck you first, Ms Shelley McCann.'

Shelley opened her mouth in shock; she had never once heard Sheriff Stone curse, but his mouth stopped her. 'Just shut the fuck up, now, lady.' His huge hands moved up to hold her head and dug into her hair. John Stone kissed her, carefully at first, but Shelley was having none of it – she ran her tongue over his lips until they were both open mouthed, uninhibited, wet tonguing each other. Stone pressed her back against the railings and, standing back a second, took her vest in both hands and ripped it straight down the middle.

'I'll show you anally retentive, lady.' He lowered his head and sucked each nipple in turn. Shelley ran her hands over his crew-cut and pulled him tighter until he had no choice but to suck her nipples harder. Shelley arched backwards over the railings.

'Fuck me with your tongue, Sheriff,' she groaned.

Billy Ray froze in the dark cellar and the hair on the back of his neck bristled. Intuition told him there was someone else in the house. He knew he'd taken a huge risk coming back here but greed had got the better of him. He'd lost track of the hours he'd spent digging for the lost bag of heroin, convinced it was still buried beneath the soil on the cellar floor. Something wasn't right. Billy Ray propped his shovel in the corner and slowly opened the cellar door. Sunlight assaulted him and Billy Ray took a firm hold on his .45, grimacing in the daylight as he crept up the old stairs. He was a fool for coming back and he knew it. He crept over to the tattered screen and craned his neck to check out who was there. His free hand flew to the puckered scar on his shoulder in reflex when he saw who it was. Sheriff Stone. Trust that sanctimonious old prick to come back round for another sniff.

Looked like the crime scene wasn't the only thing the Sheriff was sniffing around. Billy Ray felt his pecker harden when he caught sight of the brunette. She was some classy piece. Billy Ray ducked and moved slowly over to the other side of the screen for a better look before he decided whether to blow that prick away. If he'd found the heroin, maybe, but otherwise ... Unconsciously, Billy Ray gripped the handle of his .45 tighter in his grubby, sweaty palm. Pressed tight against the wall, Billy Ray strained to hear what they were saying.

He had to stop himself from whistling through his teeth when he saw the Sheriff reach out and tear the broad's T-shirt open. Billy Ray scanned her face for fear but the brunette just smiled and licked her lips. He bet she had one hot pussy. Billy Ray slipped his .45 into the well-worn belt that he wore slung low over his bony hips. The brunette's tits were small and high with tight rosy nipples. Billy Ray wiped at a dribble of saliva that had escaped the corner of his mouth. The whores down at Martha's mainly had huge pendulous lalas like saddle-bags. But he wasn't looking at a whore now, no siree.

Billy Ray undid his jeans buckle as he watched the Sheriff sucking on the classy piece's titties. His pecker felt like it had grown four times too big for it's skin. With a grunt, Billy Ray released it.

The Sheriff was kneeling now and slipping the lady's panties down to her ankles. Oh she was loving that all right. Billy Ray stroked himself in the shadows and dribbled some more at the sight of her pretty little pussy. The Sheriff was obviously liking it too because he was just kneeling there having a good old look.

Billy Ray hadn't had himself an expensive piece of pussy pie since he used to spy on Rita La Salle when he was fourteen years old. What that lady couldn't do with her expensive body cream and the thick ivory handle of her hairbrush wasn't worth knowing. Those classy bitches certainly knew what they liked, and it was usually dirtier than anything you could pay for. Billy Ray rubbed himself a little faster, not taking his eyes off the shiny dark pelt that ran in a neat line down the cleft of her pretty little cunt.

Billy Ray felt his balls harden like pomegranates as he watched her run one well-manicured finger down between her pussy lips and spread them wide. He could see her bud all puffed up and glistening with pussy juice in the sunlight. Billy Ray stuck his free hand inside his jeans to finger his balls. In his state of arousal it never occurred to him that he could have taken John Stone out with one bullet and then he and the brunette could have had the whole island to themselves . . .

Shelley revelled in the power she had over the arrogant giant of a man who was now on his knees in front of her. Any other man would have had his tongue out panting for it by now but the only giveaway, apart from Stone's huge erection, was a nerve pounding at his temple as he tried to feign control.

'I can't believe you've never gone down on a woman before, Sheriff.' John Stone's eyebrows lowered a fraction. 'Given head, tongued her slit, licked her out, never tasted a woman's love juice. Where have you been for the last twenty years?'

Shelley reached down and parted her quim lips for

Stone to see. Her clit was agony, all slick and pouting for some attention. 'I need you, Sheriff, here.' She rubbed her bud with one finger. 'And here.' Reaching down, Shelley dipped her fingers inside herself, feeling her own heat, her own juices. She was hungry for it all right, but she wanted the job done properly. To have him rutting at her like some schoolboy would be worse than no fuck at all.

Shelley traced Stone's thin lips with one moist finger and pushed it into his mouth. Stone sucked it, hard. With her other hand, Shelley reached over into Stone's shoulder holster and smoothly lifted out his gun. Stone tensed, one thick arm shot up and he gripped her wrist, his eyes narrow.

'Relax, Sheriff. You can have the bullets, it's the metal I want.' That, and the fact that he'd never look at his gun again without thinking of her. Awkwardly, her wrist still held, Shelley emptied the chamber of its bullets and poured then into Stone's shirt pocket. Reluctantly, Stone let her go, but he was tense; muscle and sinew stood in hard relief on his arms.

Lifting a leg, Shelley placed one foot on Stone's shoulder so he had a full view of her tight cunt as it gaped for him. Shelley dipped the barrel of the gun just inside her opening. It was cold and unyielding. Shelley's eyelids lowered in ecstasy. She withdrew it and stroked the barrel over her clit, then back down and up inside her again. She wasn't sure which was turning her on more, the cold hard metal inside her or the fact that Sheriff Stone was on his knees watching her frig herself with his gun.

'Enough!' The word was barely audible. 'I want to taste you.' Stone snatched the gun away from her and dropped it on the floor.

Shelley moved her hands over the rocks of his

shoulders, pushing his shirt and shoulder holster on to the ground. Stone grabbed her buttocks and pulled her toward him, running a tongue from her belly button to her clit. Shelley hung on to the railings and spread her legs for John Stone, the arrogant son of a bitch, to lap at her clit with his tongue.

The contrast to the metal of the gun was exquisite. Shelley moaned and pressed herself against him harder. Bringing one leg up over his shoulder, she opened her quim up completely to him as he stuck his tongue up inside her. She could hear him lapping and sucking at her lips, pressing his face in her juices.

'Now, John. Fuck me now.' Suddenly it wasn't enough. She wanted him high and hard inside her.

Stone stood over her, panting. Shelley reached up and wiped her own love juices, that were smeared over his face.

'That's the first time you've called me by my name,' Stone reached under her and hooked her knees over his massive arms. He manoeuvred her slightly until her back was pressed against an upright post. She reached above her head to hold it for balance. She was totally at his mercy now, legs spread wide, it was only his sheer strength that kept her aloft. Tree trunks of legs planted firmly on the deck, every muscle in his body quivering, Stone entered her. Despite her slickness, Shelley had to stretch to accommodate him. Her cry startled a flock of birds out of a nearby tree.

Stone's face was buried in her neck. 'You tell me if I'm not doing this right, you hear?'

Shelley did hear but she couldn't answer. All she could do was hang in there as Stone entered her, over and over, each time a little higher. Shelley pressed her clit hard against him as he pushed deep inside her, his heavy balls banging against her with each thrust.

She was nearly there, teetering on the brink. Out of the corner of her eye, Shelley saw Billy Ray, a dark, eagle-faced man in the shadows of the house. Stone mistook her cry of surprise for one of pleasure and groaned as he held her on to him. The man was wanking as he watched them, his mouth slack with lust. One filthy hand was pulling fast on his cock while the other fingered his balls. As Shelley clung to Stone, she saw herself as the man must see her: breasts bouncing with each thrust, legs splayed wide open, Stone's big hands gripping her arse so that her cheeks were parted, and wondered if he'd seen her sex splayed open as well. The thought sent an extra shock of pleasure through her. The man's eyes were all over her; he couldn't get enough of her. His hand worked faster, working the foreskin harder until he came, spurting jets of jism on to his muddy boots. Shelley moaned, the sight of him tipping her over the edge of her orgasm. She dug her nails into Stone's back and held herself down on him as he pumped his own orgasm into her. Sated, Shelley looked up over Stone's shoulder, but the man had gone.

Shelley and John Stone ate his daughter's picnic in the shade of an old tree. Stone grinned and said he'd never worked up such an appetite. Shelley had washed the Sheriff's come off her legs at the edge of the river, while Stone reloaded his gun which still smelt of her pussy and laughingly watched out for 'gators. He wore his gun and holster but no shirt, the leather straps accentuating his greying chest hair and work-honed muscles. Shelley's T-shirt was ruined, so Stone leant her his uniform shirt. The sight of her pussy hair peeking out at him from beneath his own shirt gave him one massive hard-on, but he didn't think a man of his age would be able to fuck twice in one afternoon. Shelley stretched a foot out at him across the picnic blanket and smiled knowingly. 'You've got a lot of time to make up for, Sheriff.'

Hours later, when two boys from the station came looking for them, worried that a man called Billy Ray, whom they'd arrested for suspected narcotics possession, had done them some harm, Stone was on his back, with the journalist from the *Herald* sitting on his face and eating pineapple rings off his cock. The officers were purple with shock and not a little jealous. One thing was certain, they were damn well sure that his daughter hadn't had that in mind when she packed the picnic that morning.

Shaken and Stirred

Fransiska Sherwood

I know it's William before he turns round. The controlled way he stands there, the set of his shoulders, even how his jeans hug the crease of his bum. Although serving behind the college bar is the last place I'd expected to see him.

'Samantha!' He almost drops the glasses he's just picked off the shelf when he notices me standing here – rooted to the spot, horrified at coming upon him.

For a few moments all we can do is stare, our faculties temporarily out of action. Then our brains begin to work double speed as we try to comprehend the metamorphosis that's taken place over the last few years.

William averts his eyes, breaking the spell cast upon us, and puts down the glasses. He smiles with a trace of embarrassment as he seems to grasp it really is me. Words tumble into my mouth in haste to apologise for my being here. I'd no idea I'd come to the same college. But before I can say anything he looks up at me and grins, and my anxiousness evaporates, the half-formed words seeping from me as a sigh.

We look at each other for a split second, then he comes round the side of the bar and takes both of my hands in his. He remains standing a couple of paces away, his eyes travelling the length of my body. I can't believe it – he's sizing me up! And long before that fluorescent smile cracks across his face, I can see from the twinkle in his blue-grey eyes that he approves of what I've turned into. And what he's turned into isn't bad either – with the hint of a beard, an ear-ring and a coarse linen shirt undone at the neck, there's something of the pirate about him.

He pulls me to him and crushes me in a great enthusiastic bear-hug.

William – so familiar, yet so new and different. An odd shiver runs through me as I realise how much I still want him. But to someone that attractive, I can't expect to be more than a fond memory. We've known each other too long for there now to be anything more anyway.

Funny to think that at first we hated each other.

'You mean I've now got a sister!' were William's words of disgust that fateful afternoon we were introduced. His father, Peter, had just sprung on us the surprise news that he and my mother were to be married.

I was twelve at the time, William fourteen. He went to a posh school and thought he was better than me. At home all we ever did was fight. A never-ending round of bickering and scratching, quarrelling over supremacy.

I marvel now – as I discover him looking like Brad Pitt with his goatie beard – how I could have been so blind to his charms. Yet I only started to take proper notice of William when I realised how gorgeous my friends found him. They were gobsmacked when he joined the Lower Sixth.

It was when William and I stopped arguing that my mother and Peter started and, after about a year, they separated. When William left, a great chasm of want opened up inside me. A need barely alleviated by the sensations aroused by pretending my fingers were his exploring my body – a need not even a bad conscience could extinguish. He was always on my mind, and in my bed.

Yet I hardly saw anything of him until the school leavers' party at the end of the year, which incorporated the two leaving year groups: mine and his. I fevered towards that evening, the chance to be near him again. And when he grinned at me as I arrived, it sent a tingle of excitement through my stomach I'd never known before. I was high on adrenaline and anticipation and, with my adolescent notions of love and destiny, would have gone to bed with him eagerly, had he asked me to. But my secret desire for him remained a secret, and it was the last time we saw each other.

I'm jolted back into the present as William releases me and looks straight into my face. There's a smile on his lips and I wonder what he's been remembering, if his thoughts are akin to mine. Gently he takes my head in his hands and plants a kiss on my mouth. We pause, catch our breath, caught in the instant. Then our lips reach for each other, their yearning finally perceived.

The noise of the bar retreats into the background, a mere hum to lull the turmoil inside. My feelings are running riot and a spasm shoots through my stomach which I'm sure he must have been able to feel.

Why does he still stir up such excitement in me? Surely it's all over and done with – a teenage crush on my older step-brother that came to nothing.

But my panties are damp and firmly clamped between my legs, my stomach is aflutter and my pulse rate soaring. I ache with want, and a flood of jealousy washes over me as I think of the other girls who've known him. Tears sting into my eyes and I blink them away – what if he's got a girlfriend waiting for him at their flat? What shall I do then? I wish we'd never met!

I bury my face in his neck, trying not to let conflicting emotions get the better of me. He holds me close, sniffs my hair, plants little kisses on my ear. I breathe him up: a uniquely concocted scent of sweat, aftershave and his own smell. He'd had it as a boy, but now it's much more masculine and compelling.

He laughs. 'Are you testing whether I showered?'

I redden – and something changes in his expression. He shifts his grip on me and looks uncomfortable for a moment. On impulse I run my hands down over his body, so firm and muscular, and pull his denim-clad buttocks towards me. A wave of heat surges through both of us and, as we stand locked together, I become aware how hard he's grown.

'I get off here at midnight,' he whispers. 'Can we meet up afterwards?' His words are urgent, breathless, insistent.

For a second or two I feel as if the wind has been knocked out of me. I nod dumbly.

He smiles – a smile full of promises.

Elation sweeps through my body: he doesn't just think me a stupid kid, a mere embarrassment from his past. I'm a viable prospect.

'What can I get you?' he asks, abruptly turning towards the bar.

I stand there like an idiot, giddy with excitement, while he goes and hides his erection behind the counter. He pulls a ritzy, blue glass bottle of prosecco out of the cooler. 'Let's pretend it's champagne,' he says. 'To celebrate the return of my long-lost sister.'

I wish he hadn't said that.

I hear the cork plop and, before I can protest, he's already filling two flute glasses. 'It's on the house.' He grins, anticipating my worried query.

Our glasses chink and I take a sip. The taste is

disappointingly tinny and I almost choke as the bubbles break on to the back of my throat.

A noisy crowd have just entered and William immediately turns to serve them, claimed by his duties, too busy to deal with me, spluttering as if I've just received a ducking. I feel like a silly young girl enticed by her brother to try her first illicit mouthful of drink, and curse myself for appearing so unworldly. What's the matter with me?

The group surge round the bar and William leans across and kisses two of the girls on the cheek. I note with dismay the way both cling to his neck for a second too long, lingering at his face with their lips.

I slink off with my glass to a free seat by the far wall, feeling *de trop* and not wishing to be introduced to them as his little sister. My high spirits are sadly deflated. The magic of our encounter has passed; if I stick around, all it will be reduced to is reminiscences and questions about the family.

William falls back into his role as barman – the patter comes easily, he's in his element. I bet he's forgotten I'm even here, a momentary apparition already out of mind.

But as the group wander over to a table, I see William scan the room until his eyes come to rest on mine. He raises his glass and knocks back the last of its contents.

Hesitantly I raise mine, no longer sure what's going on. Am I just his kid sister? Did I read too much into his erection, imagine it even? Or am I getting cold feet, afraid that something I only ever acknowledged in untamed dreams might be about to become reality?

A girl with a long white apron comes by, collecting up empties and wiping tables. Although my glass is still half full, I'm starting to feel the effects of alcohol on an empty stomach. As she rattles off the list of sandwiches I order a salad baguette.

I wonder if she might be William's girlfriend, but her face seems too plain and boyish for it to be likely. The other two girls looked more his type. But which one? They seemed so interchangeable. Or were they perhaps previous conquests, ex-girlfriends who now enjoy an intimately amiable relationship with him in the knowledge of something shared. Or were they maybe prospective candidates? I'm sure there's no shortage of girls just dying to fuck him.

I throw back a quick mouthful as bitterness begins to clog my throat.

The two or so hours drag. I eat my baguette, drink the rest of the prosecco, which William sends over clad in a cooling sleeve, and watch the people around me.

Do I still like him? He's not the boy I used to know, and I'm not the silly teenager I once was. He now has something of a roguish air, flaunts his good looks, flirts. He has them all lying at his feet, but surely I can't be taken in as easily as the rest of his female clientele by the aura of adventures untold which he emanates? And isn't he taboo anyway?

Finally the place empties and, apart from a couple obliviously entwined, I'm the only person left. 'My sister, Sam,' says William, motioning in my direction, as the bargirl comes to collect up the last of the glasses. She gives a cursory nod. Did she buy that line from him – after all, I'm not really his sister – or has she heard it a hundred times before?

William starts to wipe down the tables and stack the chairs and, for want of some other reason to justify my presence there, I help him. We leave the couple on the back bench to it; sooner or later they'll notice everyone else has gone home. We return to the bar and he begins to clean up and arrange the bottles and glasses on the shelves behind. I wish he'd say something, even if it's only 'How's your mum?' Instead, he keeps turning to look at me with a bemused smile on his lips and that particular twinkle in his eye. The more he looks at me, the more uncomfortable I feel. If only I could think of something to say! I've never felt so awkward with him in my life.

'Shall we go someplace else?' he eventually asks.

I shrug my shoulders and look in the direction of the dopey pair still only aware of each other. How must it feel to be so in love that everything else fades from consciousness?

'Or I could make you a cocktail?' he suggests. He looks at me with a long sideways glance. 'What's the matter? You're very quiet all of a sudden.'

'It's nothing. Just ... everything's changed. You're so different.'

'So are you,' he says with a wicked grin, eyeing me up and down again, sending hot prickles up under my skin. 'The Sam I remember was a bit of a tomboy. She gave as good as she got. And now look at you! A proper little lady, and sexy with it! I just can't get over it.' He grasps me by the waist and pulls me towards him, ready to engulf me in a kiss.

'No, William. Look ...' I start to say, as I shrug him off.

'What's the matter?' he demands, his brow puckering and eyebrows near meeting in the middle.

'What would our parents think?'

'God, what have they got to do with anything?'

'It just doesn't seem right, you and me, that's all.'

He breathes out hard and gives me an unfriendly stare. I realise he probably had better prospects for tonight; I've just been a waste of his time. I feel I've let the side down, am being pathetic ... inventing excuses, afraid to cross the line. But aren't we heading somewhere brother and sister shouldn't go?

We look at each other cagily. Then William reaches for a bottle of Bacardi. 'Want one?' he asks, mixing it with cola. I nod.

We sip at our drinks in silence.

'Remember when you filled my straw boater with stones and submerged it in the pond?' He suddenly laughs, never one to be angry for long.

I redden. Why did he have to bring that up, didn't I suffer enough retribution at the time?

'You could be a spiteful little beast if things didn't go your way.'

I thump him in the arm, the rapport we used to have gradually being reinstated. 'It was your own fault. You shouldn't have teased me about my awful school uniform.'

'That green and maroon was pretty dire.'

'And you ended up having to wear it too,' I say with satisfaction.

A broad grin cracks across his face. 'That's more like the Sam I know.'

I scowl at him. 'How come you always have to have the last word?'

He's laughing at me now, and that makes me more annoyed with him than ever. And, seized by an impulse – fuelled by some obscure frustration – I throw my remaining Bacardi and Coke into his face.

He gasps as it stings his eyes, blinking in surprise. But before I've time to feel any real remorse, he goes for me, diving at my waist to fetch me down. I squeal and try to dodge out of the way. But he's too quick. His body is lithe and athletic and he catches me and brings me to the floor, pinning me there with his weight.

We writhe and thrash, transported back to the heyday of our fights, where I'd retaliate with ferocity and all the power my limbs could muster.

But we no longer seem so equally matched. He has a strength that easily outdoes mine, and I soon tire and lay helpless and panting, my arms shackled to the ground by his hands, my body flattened by his, our hearts beating against each other far more strongly than the exertion would imply.

Rogue that he is, he now steals that kiss. A rum and cola flavoured one that smacks of piracy and distant shores. Again I'm flooded by desire for him, my scruples battling with my secret, innermost longing. I hunger to taste him again, taste the sweet, exotic mix of rum, cola and William.

I begin to kiss him and lick his lips, unsatiated after wasting half my drink. I can't get enough of the taste and soon my tongue is travelling over his face. I lick his nose, and then, playfully, my teeth close round it and gently I bite him. He yelps and begins poking and prodding me in protest like he used to. So he wants to play, does he? And the fighting starts up all over again.

I eventually collapse in a heap of exhaustion, helpless with laughter and in complete submission. William's face is flushed, his eyes bright with excitement and mischief. I don't think we've ever had so much fun. For years we'd been denied this very particular pleasure, so that now it seems all the more potent. Never have our bodies done battle so intensely, rolled the floor with such a need to be pressed against each other.

As William buries his face in my neck I see a man's hand place a beer glass on the bar top. Behind him I hear the stifled giggles of a girl. Aha, the couple have returned to the here and now and are leaving. We must have been making so much noise that we woke the dead. Whatever did they think was going on?

The door creaks open and then falls shut. Apart from the bargirl clanking around in the kitchen, we're alone.

William grins, ashamed. When he pulls away from me, the straining crotch of his trousers is plainly visible.

'Fighting you always did turn me on,' he apologises.

The revelation shocks me. Even when we were children he was aroused by our scuffles? How could that be? Why hadn't I ever noticed he was physically attracted to me? I must still have been more of a child than William. And he was more of a man than I'd ever guessed. A naughty ripple of excitement runs through me as I imagine what might have been. What if one day we'd carried on the game, right through to the end?

I shake off the thoughts planted in my brain by love's phantoms and scramble to the cooler for a handful of ice. Before William has the chance to fathom my intent, I've zipped open his fly and thrust the freezing cubes inside.

'That should cool you down,' I say, not sure who needs cooling down – or hotting up – the most.

I've never seen him move so fast in his life. With the alacrity of someone just stung by a wasp, he whisks down his jeans. The darker-coloured stain on his blue underpants where the melted ice cubes have wet him makes me roll about with laughter.

'Now you're really in for it!' he threatens, crawling after me as I squirm away, his jeans round his ankles.

But I'm laughing too much to escape and soon he's stuffing melting pieces of ice underneath my T-shirt. The clingy, ribbed material gloves his hand, holding it there while the ice turns to water in his fingers. And, finding himself holding on to nothing, his hand opens and travels tentatively over my midriff, tickling my skin. There it hovers for an instant, as if awaiting permission or rebuff, before reaching up over my breast and closing round it.

I gasp with the thrill, at the same time my conscience bludgeoning me with thoughts that this isn't allowed. But my horror at what he's doing pales almost immediately, receding to let excitement take its place. Beneath his hand my heart's having palpitations. I'm too overwhelmed, too aroused to say anything – and too afraid of spoiling the moment by speaking.

As he touches the lacy material of my bra, tests the firmness of my flesh, William's nostrils flare. I can tell he's as enflamed with pent-up passion as I am. But how far can we go?

Gently he begins to peel back the T-shirt, revealing inch after inch of my skin. 'It's not healthy to wear wet clothes,' he says with his crafty, pirate's twinkle. 'I wouldn't want you to catch cold.'

There's little fear of that – I've never felt so hot in my life.

When he gets to my bra, he pauses and looks at what I've got to offer. He smiles, and I know he's well satisfied with his little sister's development.

He continues to lift the T-shirt higher, and pulls it over my head. He drops the wet black heap of material somewhere behind me. Then, without warning, he pinches open the hooks to my bra and whips its lacy camouflage from me.

I swallow, suddenly very serious. The childish games are over. We've now entered a different sphere. And I've never seen William so earnest, so intent on what he's about to do.

He lowers his head and, as his lips lightly skim over

my nipples, I tremble. A tentative tongue starts to trace circles round their points, before his mouth finally closes over one of them and he begins to suck.

It's a sensation that seems to pull right through me, reaching far down into the pit of my stomach. I've never been aroused like this before, never knew it was possible.

When he's finished sucking, the nipple stands out proud and swelling with hot anticipation. He toys with it, coaxing it to grow even larger. Then he reaches over for a piece of ice and makes the other nipple stand out from the cold. Contrary sensations, yet both have the same effect and only heighten my desire.

William kneels back and lifts his shirt over his head. The sleeves seem to be made of yards of material, like the kind worn in period films. A leather thong laces up the front, the ties hanging loosely across his chest. Silky brown hairs with a hint of gold curl round the leather cords. Hairs that weren't there the last time I saw him. And, as he pulls the shirt from his body, I see a whole mass of curls covering his chest and descending in a tapering line down over his stomach. The stripe disappears intriguingly into the waistband of his underpants, and I ache to find out where it leads.

There's a mischievous grin on his face and I know he's up to no good. Yet I yearn for whatever escapade he's got planned next. Don't let the game stop yet!

He reaches for the jar of cocktail cherries, the ready-stoned kind, and, chuckling, begins to fit one over the top of my nipple. It now looks huge and pinkish-red, and he seems to find its appearance amusing. Overtaken by his own laughter, he fits one on the other side, and pops a third into my belly-button.

Then he eats them.

Suddenly the playfulness in his mood evaporates and,

very solemn, he reaches inside the fly of my sloppy, button-down jeans. Something inside me is startled. I shouldn't let him carry on with this.

Yet, paralysed with indecision, I do nothing to stop him. One half of me wants William to carry on doing whatever he wants to do, the other is screaming at me to make him stop. It's the rational half telling me this is wrong, the irrational half it's so right.

And which voice should I obey? The tight-laced voice of decorum that forbids the fulfilment of my love for William, labelling it kinky, unwholesome, incestuous? Or the unleashed whisper of desire?

He begins to ease undone the metal studs while his other hand caresses the flesh of my buttock through the gaping slit in the seat of my pants. The hole was meant to be a window, not a doorway. Gently he pulls me out of my jeans, revealing the snow-white briefs beneath. He smiles. Then he begins to slip me out of them.

'William!'

'I always wanted to get inside your knickers. Whenever I saw you wandering about at home half-undressed, I had to go and lock myself in my room and turn my music up loud so no one would hear what I was up to. I don't think you ever realised what it did to me. God, the hours I spent fantasising about you!'

And the hours I've spent fantasising about him!

I let William part my legs and survey what's displayed before him. For a long time he just looks, then his thumbs begin to separate the hairs framing my pussy, already glistening with the honeyed moisture of anticipated pleasure.

My body knows what I want, even if my head is trying to tell me otherwise.

Tired of merely looking, his head now dips between my legs and, as my senses begin to reel, I feel the delicious caress of his tongue stroking over the tender skin of my sex.

This is a place I've never been before, and a frisson of excitement runs through me, like the feeling I used to get as a little girl when I was doing something I knew was naughty. I've entered a new realm, consented to partake in the ultimate forbidden experience. I've crossed the threshold. Am undergoing my initiation. And the rites to come promise to be of a kind barely imagined. I only have to prove myself worthy. Yet the touch of William's tongue is so delicate and exquisite I begin to wonder how ever I've come to deserve this. Surely a feeling so ethereal is reserved for heaven?

And now his tongue has found my clit and is weaving little circles around it, the way it earlier traced a pattern round my nipples. And very gently his mouth closes over it and he begins to suck.

As he sucks, he inserts a finger inside me and massages my inner walls until spasms shoot through me. I arch my back, squirm beneath him, the sensation almost too exquisite to bear. Yet I want it to go on forever. And the harder he sucks, the more intense the spasms, until the contractions in my pussy send ripples of pleasure radiating through me.

I've never thought I'd reach orgasm so easily. And the tears start to flood my eyes as the waves of pleasure flood my body.

William comes up and wipes the sobs out of my face, his expression tender and concerned at the same time. He kisses me lightly, tasting slightly perfumed, slightly salty, slightly acrid. 'Are you ready for more?' he asks in a whisper.

Yes, I'm ready to go the whole way.

Slowly William starts to prise himself out of his underpants, careful not to disturb the rigidness of his cock. My heart is beating like a percussion hammer: what will it look like? It's funny, I never once saw him completely naked when we lived in the same house despite our claustrophobic proximity.

I'm not disappointed. His cock stands proud and erect as soon as he frees it from the confines of his underpants. Good and strong, the instrument of a man, not some child's plaything. The sight of it alone is enough to send giddy little shivers of anticipation running through me.

William takes me in his arms, searching my eyes, verifying we both want this. He's very careful when he penetrates not to hurt me.

'Oh, you're tight,' he murmurs.

Slowly his hips set into a motion all of their own, gradually picking up speed, increasing the friction. Instinctively I push against him, rocking with his rhythm. He seems to guide me with the motions of his body, without having to tell me what to do. With William everything falls into place – there's no awkward fumbling, no embarrassed shyness. Our bodies just seem to fit together as if they were made for each other.

The thrusting of his hips gets stronger, sending shockwaves through me. And the harder our bodies come together, the greater the friction and the more intense the contractions that again echo through my sex, still humming from the first experience. The see-saw motion of his cock sliding in and out of me soon brings me to a renewed climax, the spasms rocking through me once more, the ripples of pleasure even more intense than the first time I came.

And as the sensations of pure ecstasy rebound through my body, feelings so powerful I fear they'll rob me of my senses, I'm vaguely aware of a face in the background. How long has she been standing there watching?

As he reaches his climax William abruptly pulls out of me and rolls to the side. His eyelids flutter, and I can see he's lost in a world of pleasure all his own. For a few moments he lies limp on the floor, arms splayed at his side, hands palm upwards, seeped of all energy. Then his eyes blink open and he catches sight of the bargirl. He smiles.

'Is that what turns you on, Janice, watching me fuck my sister?'

She doesn't answer, but after a second or two kneels between us. She seems to be studying me more than William. 'Three can play at this game,' she finally says.

I look at William and he grins.

'How game are you?' he asks me. 'Really ready to go the whole way?'

I can't believe what he's asking me. I look at Janice and the gleam in her eyes. I look back at William and see his deflated cock give a twitch, already anticipating more.

He reaches over and wipes the hair out of my face, fondly stroking over my ear. 'Only if you want to,' he whispers.

I don't know if I want to. I don't want to share William with anyone.

Janice bends closer and kisses me. Just a light peck – but it sends spasms of horror and excitement through me: I'm the one they'll be sharing!

William strains for the cherries and inserts one inside me. He retrieves it with his tongue, licking and stroking me long after it's been eaten.

'My secret hideaway,' he murmurs. And I know this pirate and his mate have plenty more games of treasure troves and hide-and-seek in store for me tonight.

How infinite the possibilities for pleasure with two lovers! But I've never been made love to by a woman before. Am I ready to walk the gangplank, dive headlong into this pool of unknown sensations?

I let William caress the nub of my clit while Janice begins to trace spiralling patterns over my skin. I feel a delicious tickling all over. I want it to go on all night. Soon the circles she draws come to concentrate round my nipples, making them stand out hard and greedy to be sucked. I'm again humming with desire. And I'm so aroused, I don't mind who does what to me – just don't stop now!

Father of the Groom

Sara Jane Fox

I have to say that the most exciting sex I ever had was on the day before my wedding. Unfortunately, my trusting fiancé Paul did not play a part in the experience.

There had always been an unspoken attraction between Paul's father, Michael, and myself. Michael was a successful middle-class businessman. He always dressed in smart suits, played golf at the weekends, and probably only shagged his respectable plump wife whenever he absolutely had to.

It all started at the breakfast table, the day before I was due to get married. The Grants had become my adopted family. Michael especially had welcomed me with open arms the very first night that Paul had taken me home for the obligatory meet-the-parents session. I had been shocked even back then to feel a firm erection digging into my abdomen as the tall, broad man embraced me. Drawing back, Michael had smiled at me with enigmatic steel-grey eyes and, unable to help myself, I had smiled back. And although I did love my romantic, sensible Paul, I knew that it would only be a matter of time before something snapped between his father and I. Many times, while Paul eagerly thrust into me, I would close my eyes and imagine that I was gripping his father's buttocks, shoving his dick into me as deep and hard as it could go.

So when Michael sat next to me at the breakfast table

that morning – with Paul loyally at my other side – I bristled with sexual tension.

'Good morning, Julie,' he said, in his deep, authoritative voice. 'Paul, Annabel.'

'Good morning, Michael,' I replied politely. Our eyes locked.

'Hi, Dad,' Paul mumbled, munching on his toast and marmalade, not bothering to look up. His wife, Annabel, had not even heard the greeting and she continued to keep busy with her breakfast tasks. So help me, God, I will never turn into that, I thought.

Then, just as I was pouring myself a coffee, I felt a hand graze my leg. I glanced left. Paul was still chewing his toast, engrossed in his morning paper. That meant ... Paul's father's small grin was wickedly delicious. I bit my lip to prevent a smile and averted my gaze, pretending to concentrate on stirring my hot drink. But my cup of coffee was not the only thing that was steaming. My pussy was hot, and aching to be touched. I could feel my juices staining my knickers damp and the top of my thigh was sticky.

Still keeping myself composed, I opened my legs wider as an invitation to Michael. As of yet, his large, strong hand rested on my knee, massaging gently. Yet even that small touch was enough to make my heart thump. My eyes darted around the room. Paul had not noticed and Annabel still had her back to us as she clattered about in the sink. The fact that we were possibly about to indulge in something extremely sexual, and everybody else was completely oblivious, made me shiver with desire. I longed to reach up and release my small breasts from their satin cage; to have their nipples sucked by this man's hot, hungry mouth.

Casually I reached my hand beneath the lace tablecloth and placed it over Michael's. I traced the smooth bump of his wedding ring, noting vaguely that it was loose – the metaphor did not go unnoticed. Taking the initiative, I bravely moved his hand over my bare leg and up towards my pussy. My stomach muscles clenched in anticipation. The feeling of his coarse palm against the smooth skin of my thigh gave me goose bumps. Thank God I had worn a skirt today!

'Some tea, darling,' Annabel enquired abruptly.

I bit my lip harder, nervous at the possibility of being caught. I cleared my throat while I wracked my brain to think of a suitable answer. But my head was stuffed with naughty images and dirty thoughts. Thankfully, Michael stepped in. He was completely composed as he said, 'No, it's all right, thanks, Annabel. Julie still has some coffee.'

And then one of his fingers delved under the fabric of my silk knickers. I let out a gasp.

'Are you OK, hon?' Paul asked, perturbed. Annabel was looking at me also, her face a picture of motherly concern.

I stifled a nasty urge to laugh. Instead I licked my lips and swallowed. 'Yes, yes, I'm fine. The coffee was just a little hotter than I expected, that's all.'

'Just give it a good blow,' Michael suggested. I nearly choked. 'That should cool it down.'

'Good idea, darling,' Annabel said, bringing her husband a steaming mug of tea, then retreating back to the kitchen area. 'You won't be wanting sore lips tomorrow now, will you?' she sang. 'Especially not for the you-may-now-kiss-the-bride part.'

'Of course not,' I managed. Paul gave me a peck on the cheek and went back to his paper. At the same time, Michael slid a thick finger into my slippery pussy. It was shockingly cool. My eyes grew sleepy with desire. But his finger was no contest for a big, hard, solid cock. And that is what I wanted now more than ever. As if he sensed my need, Michael pushed in another finger, then another. I rolled my hips into them, needing more. By now, my breasts had grown so tender they were almost painful.

In an attempt to maintain some semblance of normality, I picked up my cup of coffee and started to blow gently. My heart pulsed anxiously when Paul raised his head. But this action was accompanied by a noisy rustling as he turned the page of the huge broadsheet and went back to his reading. Then, Michael started to use his large thumb to tease my clit. This only made me crave his cock even more, wishing that it were his hard knob that was creating the waves of pleasure that flushed through my pussy instead of his fingers.

The phone shrilled. Startled, I jerked, causing my coffee to spill all over my nice, white skirt. I yelped. The hot liquid seared my flesh.

'Honey, are you OK? How'd you do that? Does it hurt?' Paul worried.

I was more worried about the fact that Michael's fingers had pulled out, leaving me feeling empty and unfulfilled. I desperately hoped that this was not going to be the end of his illicit ministrations. I needed more. Damn it!

Annabel moved the phone away from her ear. 'Julie, sweetheart? Lord! Are you all right?'

'Oh, yes, thank you, Annabel. I'm fine. I think I'll just nip upstairs to the bathroom and get cleaned up if that's OK.'

'Of course you can. Take all the time you need. Darling,' Annabel began, addressing her husband, 'seeing as you're not doing anything, could you go up and show Julie where the clean towels are? I've reorganised them since she was here last.'

'No problem, dear,' Michael replied affably. My heart leaped. My anticipation of what might follow doubled. Annabel merely smiled, wholly unaware of the irony that she was the one creating the situation that would allow her husband to be unfaithful. She simply went back to her phone conversation.

I got up from the table and walked towards the stairs, but not before Paul gave me a reassuring squeeze of the hand and an affectionate wink. I nearly felt guilty as I walked up the stairs and out of sight, holding my now see-through skirt away from my legs. But then Michael patted my behind and all I felt was that luscious, exciting need to obey my body's desires.

'Hold on a minute, Ivy,' I heard Annabel say into the telephone as we neared the bathroom. 'Darling?'

We both stopped. 'Yes?' her husband queried.

'If you can't find us, Paul and I will be in the garden checking over the seating plan for tomorrow's party.'

Michael's lust-filled eyes met my own. We both grinned. 'Yes, dear,' he replied.

The bathroom was rather small – yet big enough for our specifications. The dappled-glass window overlooked the back garden and the other problem was that the lock was broken. Then again, thinking about people busting in on the two of us screwing was enough to make me even wetter. Filled with heady lust, I yearned for him to ram his cock into me right then and there.

But my torment was not over yet.

'Let's get you cleaned up then,' Mr Grant said, sounding rather matter of fact.

For an instant I was crestfallen. Surely he could not simply mean to help me tidy myself up?

'You dirty girl,' he then uttered softly.

Once again, I was red hot, tingling with anticipation. Michael's handsome face was flushed darkly with passion and, for the first time, to my thrill, I noticed flecks of silver running through his jet-black hair. I had never had an older man before. Michael must have been at least fifty – that was almost thirty years older than I was. Yet he was still so virile, so potent. My head swam with the images of what he could do to me, especially with all the experience he must have accumulated over that time.

I let him take control, knowing instinctively that was what he wanted. I would let his powerful cock fuck my young, nubile body until we were both weak with delight. I wanted him to fill me up with his seed, to come all over me, to do me every which way possible.

He started to unzip my spoiled white skirt. I stepped out of it gratefully. My flesh-coloured knickers left little to the imagination as it was, but I still wanted rid of them.

'Fuck me,' I blurted, almost forgetting that we needed to keep quiet. I shocked myself with my bad language. Paul thought women who swore were uncouth and I would never come out with such a thing in front of him.

'Oh, not yet, Julie. I have other things in mind.'

Excitement bubbled within me. 'Anything,' I breathed.

'First, I want you to take off your blouse.'

I did as he asked. My breasts were heaving, threatening to spill over the balcony of my silk bra. I yearned to touch them.

'Unhook your bra,' he ordered next.

I smiled and, keeping eye contact, I reached behind my back and released the catch. My pretty bra tumbled to the cold bathroom tiles and landed with a soft thud.

Michael stepped closer to me – but not close enough. Even so, I could feel the breath that pushed out from his nostrils tickle my bare nipples in a delicate caress. Yet still he did not touch me. He just stood there, staring, enraptured by the sight of my tiny breasts, the nipples as hard as bullets, as red as wine. A muscle worked in his lean jaw and the only other indication I had of how turned on he must have been was the straining of his cock against the fabric of his expensive suit trousers.

'Now take off your knickers.'

The order both shocked and aroused me. If I obeyed, I was removing the last real barrier between us. Once I was completely naked there would be no stopping the inevitable. Could I really go through with this? My thoughts went to Paul, who at this very moment could not possibly be having as much fun as I was. He was probably making sympathetic noises as Annabel complained about all the work that needed doing for the wedding. Michael was waiting. A smile crept on to my face and I shoved Paul's image and any guilt out of my mind.

Feeling giddy, I locked eyes with Michael and slid my hands towards my knickers. My fingers pushed at the fabric, moving it over my hips, where I then let them fall to the floor. I stood there with my knickers round my ankles, feeling wonderfully brazen and exhilarated. Surely now he could not resist me? But Michael simply put one hand to his chin and rubbed, as though he were in deep thought. His head shook gently.

'What's the matter, Michael? Do I not please you?' I raised an eyebrow. 'Tell me what to do to please you,' I said, enjoying myself immensely.

'It's not enough,' he said. His steely eyes were brimming with his intentions. 'I need to see more of you.'

I frowned, and then I realised just what he meant. I reached over to the bath and picked up Annabel's lady's razor. How fitting, I thought mischievously. Next, I twisted the hot water tap on and let the liquid trickle over my fingers. It was pleasantly warm. I brought some of the water to my pussy and let it dribble over me. My natural blonde pubes were very tidy anyway, but I was aroused at the thought of being totally bare. No man had ever had the guts to ask me to do that before.

The lukewarm water was still shockingly cool against my ultra-hot skin. I did not take the opportunity to massage my clit, though – I knew the waiting would make it all the more exquisite. Carefully, with the help of some shaving foam, I rid myself of the only other barrier between us. It was highly erotic, having Michael watch me shave my plump mound. Soon, I was completely smooth, much to Michael's supreme delight. He moistened his lips as he watched me pour more water over my fanny and then dab myself dry with a deliciously rough towel.

Suddenly, all this tantalising waiting grew too much for me. I rubbed my breasts with one hand and massaged my clit with the other. The moans escaped unbidden from my parted lips. It felt wonderful to play with myself in front of a man who so obviously adored my body and who so badly wanted to fuck me.

'Naughty, naughty girl,' said Michael. His head shook from side to side. 'I see that I shall have to force you to keep your hands to yourself.'

Putting his own hands to his throat, Michael undid his tie. The grey silk came free with a rasp. My breasts heaved. I felt completely vulnerable standing there like that, shaved bare and totally nude while he remained clothed in his powerful suit.

'Close your eyes,' he instructed.

Trembling with excitement, I did as he asked. I felt the silk tie wrap over my eyes. He tied it tightly. In my darkened world, I heard him unbuckle his belt.

'On your knees,' said Mr Grant.

I sank down to the ground. My clit leaped with delight from the sensations this action gave it. But it ached to receive even more attention.

'Hands behind your back,' came the next order.

I was obviously too slow in responding because my hands were abruptly yanked behind my back. The leather belt was wound around my wrists and tied clumsily. I knew I could not get free, even if I had wanted to. My cunt throbbed. It needed a cock.

Suddenly I felt something velvety smooth graze my mouth. It was Michael's cock. He moved it playfully over my lips, the pre-come from the tip left wet trails in its wake. Hungrily I opened wide and flickered my tongue over the huge, bulbous head and tasted the tang of the pre-come. I found the eye and tickled there, enjoying Michael's groans. He thrust forward, shoving himself into my mouth. I nearly gagged as he stuffed my mouth entirely with his cock, nudging at my throat.

So here I was, bound and blindfolded and gagging on my future father-in-law's huge, salty cock that slowly pushed in and out of my mouth. But my juices were trickling freely, dripping on to the cold bathroom tiles, which were abusing my knees. I was completely exposed and vulnerable. But I had never been so turned on before in my life. Even though I was the submissive one, the one being used, I felt so powerful. Only a woman could give a man such pleasure. As Michael fucked my mouth, his shuddering, pleasure-filled breaths made me feel so horny. In that instant, I wished that I could be watching this hugely erotic scene myself.

At that moment, I heard cheery voices in the garden and the scrape and bump of furniture being dragged about. It was Paul and Annabel, sorting out the final preparations for our wedding.

Michael pulled out of my mouth. He had not come.

'What's wrong?' I moaned.

'Get up,' he growled hoarsely.

I stumbled, feeling undignified. Large hands gripped my arms, steadying me. He turned me around and flattened me out over the sink. The cold marble made my stomach flinch as it dug into me. Still blind, with my arse out like an offering, I felt Michael reach over my head. There was a creaking as the window was pushed open wide. A cool breeze washed over me. The pre-come that he had smoothed over my lips dried, making my skin feel taut. My nipples tightened.

'Fuck me, Michael,' I hissed. The word sounded strange coming out of my mouth. Strange but good. Liberating. This is what I wanted Michael to do to me, what I wanted Paul and I to do. Fuck. 'Please. Pin me down and fuck me sore.'

'Darling!' Annabel's voice sang from outside. 'I've sent Father Boyle up to see Julie. He has a few things he wants to discuss before the wedding.'

I tensed. Father Boyle? Father fucking Boyle? Damn it. We'd have to stop. Get dressed. Where the hell was my bra?

'Michael, we should stop. Before the priest comes. Please.'

The head of his cock nudged my pussy. The head seemed huge as he pressured my hole to let him in. I felt myself stretch to bursting as he entered me roughly. I could not restrain my cry. Both of Michael's hands were on my narrow hips, dragging me back and down on to him. But when I cried out with the delightful pain of his entry, one hand shot out and clasped my mouth shut.

'Mr Grant?' That was Father Boyle's gentle southern Irish accent. Explosive shock registered within me. I tried to struggle out from under Michael's strong grasp, but he held me down firmly and rutted his dick deeper, harder and faster into me. And the worse thing was, it felt good. And I did not want him to stop.

'Good morning, Father,' said Michael, quite amiably. 'I'll be with you in a moment. As you can see, we're just a little tied up here.'

I struggled again. Again I was held down. Finally I gave up. I could not resist. I could not pretend that, although I was horrified and my cheeks burned with embarrassment, I was not turned on. I was definitely turned on and I relaxed, bucking energetically back on to Michael's cock.

'I ah – I can see that Mr Grant. I shall wait outside for you then? Perhaps in the garden? Yes, I will be in the garden with your wife. Whenever you're – ah – ready.'

Michael's fingers gripped the flesh of my arse. Then his arms reached around me, pulling me close, squeezing my breasts. 'Suit yourself, Father. Although I'm sure Julie wouldn't mind if –' Michael thrust hard and grunted '– you stayed. You did come to –' another thrust and a loud moan '– see her after all.'

I was getting hotter by the second, wondering whether seeing this would turn Father Boyle on. Surely it must. I caught myself wondering what his cock looked like. Was it big or small? Thin or wide? Were priests circumcised? Michael was right; I was a naughty girl.

'Well, if you're sure.'

If I hadn't have been blindfolded, my eyes would have widened to the size of a Eucharistic wafer.

'She's sure. Aren't you, Julie?'

'Stay,' I blurted. Then I bit my lip, waiting for his reaction, not believing I had asked a priest to stay and watch as I was screwed.

There was a pause. Michael continued to slip in and out of me. His pace had slowed and now he rolled his hips around, causing me to utter a deep-throated moan. 'Oh, Jesus Christ!' I cried.

Although I was blind, I was sure I sensed Father Boyle cross himself. That thought made me sit back on to Michael even more.

'Shit,' he muttered.

I felt Michael shudder as I brought him dangerously close to orgasm. *Thwack!* Michael's bear-like palm smacked my arse so hard I was sure it would leave fingerprints. 'You naughty, naughty girl.'

Michael's fingers dug into my skin. He lifted me up with the force of his thrust, causing the cold surface of the sink to dig further into my stomach. But I was hardly aware of it – the fire between my legs was much more distracting. My clit pulsed, yearning to be touched. Michael's fingers obliged. He massaged slowly and gently at first, still pushing into me from behind and stroking me towards certain bliss.

'So, Father,' Michael began, sounding nearly breathless, 'do you have a bet on the National this weekend?'

'Well, I ought not be a betting man, given my – ah – position,' replied the priest.

Michael was speeding up, slamming in and out of me. My breathing was erratic. His fingers still massaged my clit expertly. I knew my cheeks were aflame; they tingled now. I licked my lips in anticipation of the oncoming orgasm.

'We – ugh – we all sin now and again, Father. Isn't that – ugh – isn't that right?' said Michael.

There was a pause. At that moment I was blind and I felt nearly deaf as the delicious, dizzying, mouth-watering feeling of my approaching orgasm blotted out almost everything else. Michael grunted behind me. His breath was hot on my neck. I could feel his balls slap against me.

'I have to say, I do enjoy a –' I heard the priest swallow '– a quick flutter now and again.'

That did it for me. I cried as I reached orgasm. I was throbbing inside as the sweet sensation flooded through my whole body.

'I will most likely be backing – ah – Red Marauder this year,' Father Boyle continued.

Just then, Michael shuddered and I felt him pump his come deep into me. He sighed noisily and then pulled out. I slumped on the sink, chest heaving, my pert breasts squashed against the cold marble.

'A wise choice, Father. He might be one of the older horses in the race, but he does have a marvellous technique.'

I giggled at the irony.

I did marry Paul the next day. Michael watched on proudly, holding his wife's hand as he eyed up one of my bridesmaids. After the ceremony, I felt brave enough to give Paul a long, deep kiss. I surprised him by tickling his tongue with a lick of my own. Father Boyle did manage to marry us, although he looked quite abashed and often stumbled on his words – much to my amusement.

On our wedding night, when we arrived at our hotel in the Bahamas, Paul was pleasantly shocked to see my smooth pussy. I told him it was my wedding gift to him and he screwed me with a lovely, renewed vigour. After that, we had a very exciting sex life and Paul never asked nor guessed where I learned my tricks. In spite of all the obvious benefits I reaped from the session in the bathroom that day, at least I can say that I get along with my father-in-law!

Clawing at the Temple Doors
Sophia Mortensen

I catch your eye in the bar above the WH Smith in Victoria Station. It's Friday evening and you're passing time until the 18.20 arrives to take you back up north, but you can barely face it; it's always so packed, even in First Class. All those boring geezers around you, and all those City boys in suits sharper than yours, so much younger than you, calling their lovers on their mobiles. They're all so full of themselves. The company of men has begun to bore you but, in your heart, you wish you were one of those boys. You could have made it as a big shot in the 80s, but it didn't happen, did it? Didn't want to ruin your political credibility. And now you're 49 years old and – like Lucy Jordon – you've never been driven through Paris in a sportscar, with the wild wind in your hair. And it rankles, doesn't it, and you're desperate to do something before you hit 50 in your greyer than grey Gieves and Hawkes.

Ever get the feeling you've been cheated? You silly bugger. It seems you couldn't do anything right. They were out to get you, whatever you did. You see, all the time you were stuffing your off-the-pegs in the Corby trouser press you could have been hanging out in bars and grooving with girls like me. But you couldn't do that, with all those government briefings and reports and policy documents, it was just rush, rush, rush. And all that time something was being neglected, wasn't it?

And it was hurting you to the point you couldn't concentrate. And that secretary of yours would have been OK to let it out on, except she was so masculine – and maybe a little too much like you. What a pity! You wanted someone you knew would lie back and take it; give herself over to your right honourable old chap. That bit on the side never worked out, did it? Still, probably with good reason. Had to keep your nose clean. Couldn't be a love rat. But a man with as many responsibilities as you needs to let it all out every now and then. What's a guy to do?

Ever see Alan Partridge? Don't you think it's a bit close to home? Or is there no time in your life for laughter? You don't look like you laugh much, come to think of it. I tell you what . . . I've decided we're going to have some fun. I'm going to blow your mind; save you from your moribund destiny. Here's what happens.

I've clocked who you are and I want you. You're drinking your pint slowly, gulping on it like you're swallowing your embarrassment at never being able to let go. I imagine you dancing at a rave in 1987 – you're all stiff like the guy in that Madonna film, unable to get into the groove. But I know what that's all about – you've got no give and take; you haven't been trained to be aware of your whole body. You're divided up into parts like a clockwork doll and you walk with the shoulders of your suit rather than letting your hips move you forward. You plan and scheme and angle in where you can, snapping and brutal like a shark. That's all well and good in the boardroom, smoothing the way for deals with your cronies, but it doesn't cut it with the lovely chicks on the dance floor. They want to see the slinky moves. You can't manage those, but you crave the lovely chicks all the same.

You try to ignore foolish pop stars but once, just once, you stood in front of the mirror at home in your dressing room and grabbed your crotch, just for the hell of it. You tried to imagine what it would be like to be a tattooed sex icon with an audience. It was after one of those terrible days in the House. You tried to concentrate on being that icon – feeling that sexual power – but images of the PM's question time kept creeping into your mind and you gave up, defeated. Oppressed by your sense of responsibility your imagination was instantly vanquished. Still, it wasn't all bad: supper was ready and the missus had cooked something with scallops and fennel.

Now you've remembered what it is you're missing, and you catch me looking at you and something gives; something that leads you to thinking that tonight could be different. You've got more time on your hands now and, although you should be heading back to your constituency, you just for once fancy a bloody change. And who can blame you?

Even from a distance I can see you've registered that I'm sexy. And you immediately think you have no chance, because you're almost 20 years older than I am and you think I'm looking for one of the flash City boys. You're wrong. It's you I want. It's the way you need it so badly that turns me on. I can give you what you've never had and that would make me very happy. It's all that stuff you never had as a youth. All the stuff that's been stored up over the years, ready to burst. You don't know any sexy women ... physically they're all female versions of yourself: sexless beasts with awful layered short haircuts, straight outta Croydon.

I walk up to you and time stops.

'It's Mr________, isn't it?' You're immediately defensive. You gruffly acknowledge I've spotted who you are. Go on, look me in the eyes. That's better.

'Train delays again, eh?' I announce. 'Still, it's not your fault.'

You ask if I'm waiting for someone.

'No. I'm on my way to Brighton but I just can't face the packed trains. I'd thought I'd wait around for a bit. Read a magazine or something.' I wave a copy of the *Lancet* at you. That perks you up. You thought I was a Cosmo girl, didn't you, with my glossy lips and tanned skin and sparkly hairgrips? You thought I would have nothing intelligent to talk to you about. Wrong again.

'Me too,' you say, with some irony. 'This time on a Friday is impossible. For the sake of my sanity I'm going to take a later train today.'

You go on to talk about cars and motorways, comparing what's worse at this time of the week, and I start looking bored. Get over that stuff. It's not your problem.

'Do you mind if I talk with you a minute?' I ask in a voice as beguiling as I can muster. 'It makes me dizzy to try and read when there's so much noise around, and anyway it's boring being on your own.' Go on, take the bait. I've leaned on the bar and you've noticed what a lovely shape I am; the suit jacket has fallen away and is revealing my curvy frame and soft, figure-hugging top. You're looking. That's great. You're thinking that maybe it would be nice to spend some time chatting with a nice-looking young woman. Oh, it's the power I like so much; the power I have over men like you. And, despite your better judgement, you know this little game is going to go my way, no matter how much you think you're in control, because my confidence is enough to draw you in and hypnotise you.

Five minutes later and you and me are seated at the anonymous-looking tables. You have bought me a drink and we have been talking about the new City Hall. The TV monitors are playing a loop tape of Ali G. You don't talk about it. It's all beneath you, the youth culture of modern life. I want you to let go and be able to smile, or even laugh. What a winner that would be. You ask me questions about my education, and of course I lie. I say I went to UCL and studied the history of medicine. I weave tales of cadavers and formaldehyde until you feel dizzy but in safe hands. Medical hands.

And while you're in this state of trust – almost willing to think of me as an equal in terms of education and class – I pull from my bag a copy of George Bataille's *Story of the Eye*. You've never heard of it. I pull a face that makes you feel stupid and dull. Yesterday's man. I talk about surrealism. You say you never had time to really go into it, but you know all the main artists. You rattle some names off but in fact they're the usual names people come up with when they betray that they know so little about it: Dali, Magritte. Yeah, yeah. I mention Man Ray. He was a photographer; you know that much. You have a little reprieve. Luis Buñuel has you stumbling for a moment and you glaze over until I talk about Catherine Deneuve in *Belle de Jour*. Something registers. You saw it at a student film night back in the late 70s and were confused by it. French ladies in Citroens meeting Japanese businessmen in hotels when they didn't even need the money. Insects buzzing in jars. What was it all about?

I shift closer to you just for a second before I stand up to go to the ladies. You look me longer in the eyes this time. You're besotted, aren't you? You want access to all sorts of things you can't put into words. You are seized by the desire for liberation like you've never been seized by anything in your life – but you can't ask for it, although somewhere inside yourself you have a premonition of having to beg.

Dear Mr ex-Cabinet Minister. All the social climbing;

all the rigmarole and protocol and long-distance travel are nonsense if you can't grab that special thing that is the opposite of death for one fleeting moment. And now, this evening, you suddenly decide you want to live it up. You want Itchycoo Park in the daytime; picnics with girls in gingham and the scent of wet grass. You want to reclaim your cock, hard in your pants at age 18, and all the girls you never did 'cos you were under the cosh of your own making. Go back in time. It's the local art school dance in 1972, boyo, and there are so many people around cooler than you, but just this once you're going to get lucky. And in that fleeting second, as we look into each other's psyches, I know that you are getting ideas above your station.

1972. *Up Pompeii* and *The Benny Hill Show* and *Casanova* on the box. What d'you think of that? You like it, don't you, even though it's all such low culture? You'd never admit it to your friends, but you liked seeing all those tarty starlets running about showing their knockers. And suddenly, in your head, you're 19 years old – full of wonder and spunk. The hypnosis has begun. And that's the age I get you when I draw you to a page in *The Story of the Eye*. It's the scene in the church. Simone is wanking in the confessional; Sir Edmund is faintly bored but loving her death wish. You take the book and read it. You can't believe what this woman has handed you. You think of Sir Stephen ... now where did you read that? Wasn't that some erotic literature as well? For some reason you think about an artist called Sebastian whom you read about in the papers the week before. Had himself crucified for real in the Philippines. Imagine that, sir. Imagine such a thing happening. A man, sir. Crucified. Hung out to dry by all and sundry, sir. You shudder. She smiles broadly. Something trembles in your pants but it could be fear. She walks away. You count the seconds until she returns.

You've never read anything like this before. Now it's all spilling over. You've briefly flicked through other pages: people locked in wardrobes; young girls sitting in saucers of milk. Can you imagine your partner reading such an inflammatory thing? Christ, no, but this one, she's a right little goer. She comes back still smiling and looking so smart in that pinstriped suit. She softly takes the book from your grasp.

'Why are you showing me this stuff?' you ask. You're suddenly shocked and confused. You've only just met. You were talking about medicine and politics and now you're reading pornography in a crowded bar.

'This is the real surrealism, not Dali's melting clocks,' she replies. She leans closer into you and strokes your hair. The effect is unnerving. You want to give in to it – someone so attractive showing you tenderness. She continues: 'There's so much you seem to have missed out on. You were born at the ideal time. Primed for revolution and excitement. I wish I could have seen all that stuff,' she says. 'The sixties and seventies. All that music! All those great movies! Did you ever drop acid?'

You don't answer, and that last question really winds you up. You weren't always like this, grey suit and grey hair. You were an idealist. Your foundations were built on something more solid than a few silly experiments with drugs. How could she know what it was like then? Everyone took acid, didn't they? It was part of the whole movement, the raising of consciousness – not like it is today. You feel upset. All those sit-ins and protests and all that Marxist debate. It's got us all nowhere. What a waste of time. These days you prefer the opera, and that's a little bourgeois thorn in your side. You've turned into your father.

You immediately think she's using her youth to have a dig at you but you look at her and realise it's just naive enthusiasm on her part. She's quite wide-eyed and wants to hear all about it. You feel powerful again. See, you don't have to be paranoid, but you still want to teach her who's boss. She's confusing you but something inside you likes the tease and challenge. You want to read aloud from the book and fuck her to delirium on the seats in front of the young smooth blades. Give those arrogant little shits an eyeful. You can still do it. No Viagra required; you've got enough libido to satisfy her for a year, haven't you? Oh, God, it's been so long since you've been able to let go. All that hoo-ha earlier in the year. Blimey, you just want to have a bit of fun.

It's crunch time. The plates are shifting in your consciousness. You're seized with the realisation that you *can* allow yourself to think about all the stuff you've pushed under the carpet for so long; the things that keep coming back even though you don't invite them, and when you least expect them.

Everything's going to give. You're going to be a man broken down before you can be built up again. She'll do it before the midnight hour and you're powerless to stop her. Your mouth is dry even though you keep trying to quench your thirst with your pint. You're trying to think of anything except what it's going to feel like when you explode inside this woman. And you will. This very clever, captivating woman with a medical degree and a fibre optic cable into your most secret emotions. You cannot keep twisting around on your seat like that; you are aware that she knows what's going on under your suit trousers. It's hard like a rod of iron. It's never been this way – so hard – before, not even when you used to chase northern tarts wearing too much make-up around, being grateful for when you could spunk into their candypink faces. You like that, don't you? You like them tarty and dirty and with their legs wide open, showing their juicy pink slits, all ready for you. But she's not tarty. She looks well groomed; not that much make-up but lovely thick luxuriant straight hair and shining lips and eyes that have the very devil in them.

You breathe out slowly in a hiss and close your eyes. It's what happens when desire becomes overwhelming. You tell her you can't take it any more and she knows what you mean. Just for a fleeting moment she discreetly slips her hand between your legs and brushes over the beast. She looks you in the eye to register her approval. Now it's time. Cometh the hour, and all that.

You leave the bar and glide down the short escalator in the station. Your arousal is so intense you're willing, just this once, to miss the bloody train; to go with this woman and see what happens. But, Christ, what are you thinking? You are not even drunk. Would she have slipped something into your drink? One of those sex drugs? Or maybe ecstasy. You've often thought about trying it. You've thought about your wife's niece, wondering if she does it. She's at that age. You imagine being sixteen again. Things are a bit different now, eh? The kids aren't concerned about politics any more. They want to vote for pop idols, not Prime Ministers. In the concourse, young people are heading out on the town. The girls are all so sleek these days; all grooving around in hipster flares and stardust eyeshadow; bright eyes and frosted candy lipgloss and perfect skin that the light dances over when they laugh. If only young people knew what they had, knew how very beautiful they were. You feel sad for a moment but Smart Woman won't let you put up any obstacles to what you've started. She's pretty sleek herself. You've got to admit it ... it's your lucky day, mate. No turning back. You've had a belly full of being on your best behaviour, of trying to do everything right and getting no thanks at all. Fuck 'em.

She has hailed a cab. You're going to her place at some smart apartment block in Chelsea. You register that familiar sound of the diesel engine as the cab pulls away – but not to a board meeting this time; not a press conference where you have to talk figures to a bunch of rat-faced reporters. This cab is going to take you and her to the magic kingdom.

She looks confident and beautifully groomed as you enter the apartment block foyer. She's carrying a polished black-leather Samsonite case like someone in a Bond film called *Fuck and Let's Die*. No one bats an eyelid: it's the ex-Cabinet Minister and his smart new aide. She's advising him on budget forecasts for his first consultancy post since the resignation. Her manicured nails click against the plastic of the key fob. Those square, sharp little claws press into your flesh and you like it. She's taking control already. Up to the apartment and you find yourself needing a drink to calm your nerves. Supposing you can't get it up? No, that will never happen; not now you've seen some of the stuff in that book. It's got you so excited you want to read more. It's very different. What happens to that priest? You'll have to buy a copy to find out. The big Waterstone's in Piccadilly will have it.

This is OK. Right by Bibendum and the Conran shop. You've been around here before with Members of the House. Must have been an R in the month because you had oysters. She unlocks the door and you enter. There's no going back now. So you're going to be unfaithful again. Oh well. You can do your stuff, release some of that tension or, if it doesn't work out, you can just leave

... It's still early; still time to hire a car or find a hotel or something.

But this is not the apartment you were anticipating; it's gloomy in here and the décor is odd – more like somewhere you'd expect some avant garde film student to live. Maybe it isn't hers. Maybe it belongs to some guy whose going to jump you or something. It all suddenly feels wrong. What do you think you're doing? The walls in the hallway are deep red and decorated with prints by Francis Bacon. You enter the main living room. It's full of foreign artefacts: ethnic stuff, low-level seating and lava lamps. You hate it. You have a sudden longing for the pale wood and understated classic design of your own drawing room and study. This place needs an airing. It looks like a hippie hovel, a den of iniquity. Now it's dark.

She betrays no emotion even though she's clocked your reaction. You cannot quite get a handle on this woman. Has she played you for a sucker? Is she going to rob you? You feel odd, disjointed, a little dizzy. You get the notion that she isn't quite what she seems – that there is no medical qualification, no racks of sophisticated clothing, no crate of Chablis in the kitchen. What there is, however, is still an insistent tension in your trousers and some very curious music in the CD player. Who did she say it was? Someone you have never heard of, that's for sure. Coil or something. So what if it's not like your place? You're not moving in; you're going to be here less than two hours.

She's watching you eye the room with that calculated arrogance that comes so naturally to you. She tells you to make yourself comfortable. Take off your shoes and jacket; loosen your tie and relax; she's mixed two vodka tonics and has calmly taken up a position opposite you.

You swallow it too fast. It goes down a treat. You remember a sentence from that scandalous book: 'The paralysed wretch drank with a well-nigh filthy ecstasy at one long gluttonous draft.' Hmm, that about sums it up, doesn't it? You burst out laughing suddenly. She smiles and fixes you another drink, then stands there magnificent and commanding, drumming the glass with her nails as you squirm slightly on the sofa. You wish she wouldn't look at you like that. She's not being what you would call the perfect host, although you cannot quite put your finger on what's wrong. You would have expected her to lead you to the bedroom by now but she looks as if she is waiting for something, watching you too closely for comfort.

You feel something begin to happen in the base of your spine. You try to speak but all you can do is giggle. It's unnerving as well as exciting. A fluid ripple shoots from your groin to your lips. Something feels odd. You don't dare stand up. You reach out for the glass but swipe the air instead. You notice her Italian leather heels are sinking into the carpet just enough to exact a frisson of fear and excitement in you. You make a lunge at them and start planting kisses on her ankles. Just what *is* going on? She hasn't touched you yet and you are aching for her attentions. Is she some kind of magician? You don't make a habit of letting people – especially women – get the upper hand. And you certainly never let anyone see you out of control. But you are transfixed by this creature, yet you can't work out why. And just when you think she is going to prolong the agony even further, she very gently runs her hand through your hair and tugs it slightly.

You complement her stroking by pressing yourself against her like an unneutered cat. You are hypnotised and consumed by your own desire. The glasses have steamed up but you don't want to take them off because everything is looking so pin-sharp and colourful at the moment. She runs her hands down each side of your body; your shirt is made of the finest cotton and the quality doesn't go unnoticed.

'Pink. My favourite,' she says.

'What are you doing to me?' you ask. 'I feel strange. I feel . . . I feel like it's going to be a long night.'

'It's Lughnassa. It's time for the harvest. It will, indeed, be a long night.'

You look very confused now. Especially as you feel like you want to roll around naked on the long-haired rug by the window and be stroked. It's drawing you to it. You want sensual rapture. She won't mind. In fact, she's encouraging it, even though she's saying nothing. For the first time in decades you feel you can be yourself. Christ almighty, there's thunder brewing. You begin to strip off as best you can, shirtsleeves all tangled up in your watch and everything, as you rip at it in frustration, giggling.

Off come those terribly expensive lined trousers, (the ones that wifey likes you to wear because you look so slim and smart), and you launch yourself in a dive that is at once both sporting and abandoned on to the synthetic weave. It's all going to change from here, isn't it? An ex-Cabinet Minister rolling around on the carpet in an altered state. Goodness me!

She seems perfectly sober but you feel a little like an insect under a microscope. You try to be indignant but you can't raise the anger. It's just not there. You want to be outraged; what she has done is a crime, but how would you prove it? You make an attempt to be arrogant but all you feel is immediately fraudulent. You imagine what everyone would say if they could see you. Another burst of the giggles. You splutter your drink all over the carpet. She still watches you, waiting for the moment she feels is the perfect instant to release the bats from the belfry. Not yet; you've got to get over the silly bit first. You have to let your psyche adjust before she thinks you are ready to fully appreciate what's going on.

'How time is slipping underneath our feet: unborn tomorrow and dead yesterday, why fret about them if today be sweet!'

You look up, half-naked and startled. You blink behind your spectacles and look as if you have gone into shock. You haven't heard that for a long time, have you?

'What's the next bit?' you ask. 'Something about a caravan.'

'One moment in annihilation's waste, one moment, of the well of life to taste. The stars are setting and the caravan starts for the dawn of nothing, oh, make haste!'

'Yes. Yes. I'd forgotten that. *The Rubaiyat of the Omar Khayam*. Wonderful. It's about . . .'

'Seizing the day?' I offer.

'Yes. But it's so magical and uplifting.' Now, there's two words you have rarely used in your lifetime.

'Magical is good,' I say. 'And more than a little of doing what you want now and again.'

It is at this point I notice that you still have your socks on. Black and conservative. At least they are not decorated with Disney cartoons. If there were any hint of that sort of idiocy I would have to take a knife to them, and you, for being such a gross disappointment. Or maybe saw your foot off like the beautiful Japanese sado-girl with her garrotting wire in *Audition*. But it's OK – they're just slightly dowdy; nothing that's going to provoke a psychotic reaction. I haven't had one of those for a while.

I've changed my clothes and you haven't even

noticed that I've been out of the room. You've been so busy, playing with the plants and staring at the carpet and running your hands over your body like an houri in a temple. You haven't noticed that I have shifted into loungewear for slinky grooving. I allow myself the luxury of settling down on the rug with you. I take one of your hands and run it over my top. It's Dolce and Gabbana. It's beautiful. My therapist, the criminal psychologist, bought it for me for my birthday. He shouldn't really; he says it's 'unprofessional' to buy his clients presents but he likes me to look nice when I curl up on his lap and tell him all my troubles. And I'm definitely going to tell him about you. Feels good, that top, doesn't it? And ... oh yes, it doesn't take you long before you realise that I'm wearing no bra over my 34E cup assets.

They're a right treat, aren't they? You cup them as if they were the ripest, most precious fruits. You've never seen anything like them. Oh, God, I can see what it's doing to you. And I can see that you have a reasonable excuse to be arrogant, with something of that size nestling down there. What a treat for me that you are getting hard. I play a little with you, but cruelly. I'm testing you, even if it's not to my ultimate advantage. You have to learn.

You throw yourself in a most uncharacteristically amdram fashion to the floor and all the desperation starts to come out. Oh dear, have I administered a psychic emetic? An expectorant combination of narcotics and poetry and magic? Looks that way. I begin to stroke you and tell you it's OK. I can't help but snake my hand to your boxer shorts. And it takes only the lightest of caresses before you are pushing your cock against my hand. You want it, don't you? You want everything there is going of this stuff. All in one go. You're a writhing bundle of civil servant frustration clawing at the temple doors. It's been a long time coming.

You give in to desire and kiss me deeply. The suit, the timetables, the reports from traffic division, the drudgery – it's all gone, just for tonight. Think of it as a holiday. But even though I'm going to let you have anything you want this evening, I still have to exert a little superiority over you for now. A girl like me is always going to be prepared, and I like to give people surprises, so I reach into my box of tricks that I've brought with me in the Samsonite case. There's some lube there; all I have to do is select the correct size of appendage for the harness I'm already wearing. I calm you and ease you back down on to the lovely silky rug. You squirm and writhe so beautifully. You've had a snog and you're feeling slightly more relaxed. It's all OK. You're getting in touch with your feminine side, aren't you? And, before you know it, I've whipped down those Paisley-patterned boxers and I'm gently but insistently priming you for your debauchery. And this is what you wanted, isn't it, to have the responsibility taken away from you? That is the king of all sensations.

I'm very skilled at this. I can lube my little black rubber friend into you before you know what's what. And the power I have over you is making me flood with girl grease. And it's soaking right down between the tops of my thighs. It's warm in here and a heady bouquet of ripe scents is rising from the nexus of the action. Your temperature has gone up by several degrees. All the deodorant and aftershave is evaporating and we're down to sweat and musk and pheromones. That's better, isn't it? Oh, I must say, I quite like the cut of your jib – you squirming about underneath me. Who's the daddy now, eh? I stroke myself while I'm giving it to you. You are overwhelmed with the need to see me touching myself but that's a treat I'm saving for you for later. For now, it's just you, being fucked, having to work, going through the barrier of where 'no' used to be.

I've placed in front of you a print of Felicien Rops's *The Temptation of St Anthony*. As you look up to take a breath from your ignominy, you spot it leering back at you. Suddenly it all makes sense. A voluptuous girl on the cross is defiant in the face of a miserable patriarchy emaciated by moaning and denial. It makes sense to you right now because you are opened up in head and sphincter, a martyr to your cause. Stephen Stylites, but given in to temptation rather than pointless suffering. It reminds you of what you want, of what you've missed, of what it is never too late to grasp: art and lust and life and love and wild summery abandon. And, as your body builds itself up to an explosion that will send your world spinning off its axis forever, a flash of blinding light cascades at once in your amygdala; at once in your prostate. In all this darkness there is revelation. The all-seeing eye that is at once both omnipotent and dread-filled is looking back at you. You want the eye inside you, like the girl in the book. Your long-dormant imagination has sparked itself into being. You get it. You jet out your gorgeous release into the rug and you are shaking and crying out and begging me to kiss you deeply and take away the greyness for ever. It's pumping and throbbing and dirty sweet, and I praise Satan in my triumph.

You are incandescent with joy. I am your salvation and nemesis. The corruption is complete. The dark will welcome you.

It's not the evening you expected, but it's a start, isn't it?

Moons of Shakti Tsaurah Litzky

The other night, after a super, de luxe session of sixty-nine, Danny asked if I'd ever been with a woman. 'Your tongue is so fast, Sissy. It's a hovercraft, a humming bird.' Danny was a poet and I stopped him before he could say my tongue was a little hand of God.

'That's because my tongue is so hungry for you, baby,' I said. 'You are my blessed fountain of sweet cream. I was born to churn your butter.' I bent my head down to take him in my mouth again.

I didn't tell him about Margo, or how she had a flaming arrow tattoo that pointed from her pierced navel down to her waxed pussy. I didn't tell him how she used to rub liquorice oil on her pointy little nips because liquorice is my favourite candy. For years we hunted together, stalking all species of domestic and imported, classic and exotic cock. We also loved to pleasure each other; we felt it kept us balanced, kept us from getting too crazy over the vagaries of men. We never moved in on each other's romances and, if we met a man we both liked, we'd flip a coin or once in a while decide to share.

One St Patrick's day in Provincetown we sucked and fucked Jim Finn until he fainted. We often kid around about how our wild times have prepared us for our lives in the here and now. She became an efficiency expert while I am a yoga teacher. That was many lifetimes ago; now Danny and I will have been married ten years in two weeks and Lulu, Margo's love child by Stevie Ray Vaughan, is applying to college.

I wonder why I never told Danny about me and Margo. I have told him about our midnight campaigns in crowded bars and dance halls, and the shared men, but I never told him about Margo's big black strap-on that she named the Hornet or how often I slept with my hand on her belly, my head nesting between her small, white breasts. He has always liked her. Maybe I didn't want him to imagine us together, even though I often enjoy imaginary flings with skateboard boys, test pilots, UPS men or petty thugs like Jean Paul Belmondo in *Breathless*.

Maybe I didn't want Danny getting hard and thinking about the moist valley between Margo's wide thighs. Am I turning into a conventional, jealous wife? Will I start to look through his credit card receipts? Will I begin to inspect his shirt collars for lipstick? Jealousy is a twisted labyrinth that leads only to loss of self-respect. How disgusting, particularly since Danny loves me so and I am crazy for him: his intelligence, his decency, his magician's hands and his fine tool, his roto-rooter, his cock-a-doodle-doo. I even love his poetry and how he recites Gregory Corso in bed. He tongues every centimetre of my coochie and my back hole too. He especially loves to plant his fat, hard cock deep inside my ass crack, to dive between the moons of Shakti, as the yogis say. I delight in it as well and encourage him. 'Come on, John Glenn,' I say, 'how about some moon diving?'

One of the extra special benefits of being married to Danny is that he is just so imaginative, always coming up with new and exciting games for us to play. The very first game Danny made up for us was 'baby'. We would climb into bed together wearing only white underpants, pretending we were babies in diapers. We would lie facing each other, then he would gather me up in his arms and rock me back and forth. I would giggle and coo and say goo-goo and da-da and pretend to cry. He would rock me some more until my pretend tears stopped. After a while, we reversed positions. He always looked so sweet, his eyes closed, his head cuddled against my chest. Sometimes, after a while of this rocking we would get very aroused, and off came the white underpants. Other times we just got tired and fell asleep holding each other. As the trust between us grew, Danny invented wilder, more exotic games. For a long time our favourite game was Attila the Hun and the beautiful shepherd girl. Then last year, when Danny started working on his book of poems, he invented a new game – Microphone.

Danny believes the best way to test a poem is to read it out loud. After dinner, he goes into his study to write. Whenever he finishes a new poem, as soon as he prints it out, he yells loudly – Microphone! This is my signal to meet him in our bedroom. I stop whatever I'm doing and rush in. Still, usually when I get there, he is already completely undressed, lying on his back on the bed. He never bothers to pull back the covers. He is already holding in one hand a copy of his just-completed poem. With the other hand he languidly strokes his fine microphone. I strip out of whatever I'm wearing. I take my time so he can watch me, folding each garment carefully, bending over so he can see the hairy crack of my ass when, finally, I put my underthings on the chair. I go to my closet and take out the long black silk shirtwaist dress that is hanging there. It is just the perfect thing to wear when reading poetry.

I put it on over my naked body. I pirouette in front of Danny so he can see my flesh ripple and move beneath the fine silk. I never button the shirtwaist all the way up. I want him to see the swell of my cleavage. Often, I pull just one breast out to salute him. Then I stand at the foot of the bed and I take the poem from his hand. I begin to read in a slow, even voice, taking care to pause for breath at the end of each line, just as he taught me. But, no matter how clearly I read the poem, when I am finished, Danny always says, 'You did not read loud enough. I couldn't hear a word you said. You'll have to use the microphone, but it is dusty. You will need to clean it first.'

Eager to obey, I move forward between his legs, bend my head down and take that dirty microphone into my mouth. I dust it up and down, north to south. I open wider, taking in as much as I can. I use saliva, what the yogis call jade fluid. It has magical properties. With my tongue I gently wash every pit and groove of this well-used tool. Then I run my tongue round and round the staff, round and round the fat pointed cap on top, shining it. I always swallow the few sweet drops of Danny's love milk that I find there. Then I take him in my mouth again and suck it; suck it up and down until it shines as bright as the lingam of Shiva. Danny's tool is growing so big. It is now a giant microphone. I give the top a last loving kiss and release it. I move my upper lip very slowly up and down the long seam that runs from the bottom to the top of the mike.

Danny cries out. He is moaning, reciting some kind of poem in a language I don't understand. Studying tantra taught me about the wisdom nerve – a long nerve connecting the upper lip to the clit. As I caress Danny with my upper lip, my clit grows wiser and wiser, wetter and wetter. Soon, my whole lotus is soaked. I'm so excited. I want to swallow the microphone down my throat, but this seems to be always the moment when Danny says loudly, 'Now!' This is my cue to release him.

I strip off the dress, step out of it. I bend and dry that

steel-hard microphone between my breasts. Then, circling its wide base firmly in one hand, I use the other to pick up the poem that has fallen to the floor beside the bed. Once again I read the poem, but this time directly into the tiny mouth of the microphone. When I am done, Danny claps his hands. 'Loud and clear,' he cries out. 'I couldn't have read it better myself. Sissy, you did great.' This makes me very happy, but then I look down and notice the microphone has gotten dusty again. Danny notices me looking, glances down and sees. 'Oh, oh, I guess you better use some of that extra-strength cleaner between your legs,' he says. Then I climb astride and take him deep inside me. He reaches his hand up to my mouth because I like to suck his fingers as I ride. We both love to play Microphone but Danny's book is nearly finished. I am already wondering what new game he will invent for us when it is done.

If anything, our passion for each other has increased. He tells me he still loves my legs, although my thighs are now cross-hatched with purple veins. Even if he is balding and has acquired a pot belly, he is as beguiling to me as the great Lord Shiva. I tell him even Buddha had a belly and it's so erotic.

Only last month, Margo was telling me that, after all this time, Danny is still a stud muffin. I knew it was her way of complimenting me on my good luck; her way of telling me she was happy for me. I know she would never disturb my happiness and yet I had never told Danny about our girly-girl sex play. Sometimes when Danny and I are fucking I truly understand how sex is a divine pathway to cosmic consciousness; now here I am worrying myself about Danny imagining Margo, here I am wandering lost in the dark, serpentine tracks of my reptile brain.

I should be ashamed. I thought all those acid trips

had elevated my consciousness. I must transcend this petty jealousy. I should sleep with Danny *and* Margo; that would certainly put my elevated consciousness to the test. Maybe Margo would like to join me in giving Danny a special party for our anniversary. I remember my cousin Bruce telling me how, for his birthday one year, his wife Adelaide gave him her friend Poppy. Adelaide told Bruce his birthday present was in the bedroom and, when she led him in, there was Poppy naked in their bed with a big red bow tied around her waist. Adelaide excused herself and went to play bingo. I am more selfish then she; I want some fun too.

I still dream of Margo – her slim, delicate upper body; those small, soft breasts that I can cup so easily in my hands; and then her surprisingly wide hips and big solid ass and her sturdy, thick peasant legs. It is as if it took two women to make her: top by Modigliani, bottom by Rouault. When Margo walks down the street, men turn and stare, then they follow her. I'm barely five feet tall, thin, wiry, intense and dark haired. Someone once said she was the Cadillac and I the Porsche. I wonder if she still thinks about my body too?

I decide to call Margo at her job and see if she would be willing to help me make a very special anniversary party for my Danny. 'Sissy,' she said when she heard my voice on the phone, 'you rascal, I've been meaning to call. It's been too long, everything is topsy-turvy. My boss Otto decided he wanted a sex change so he's in Sweden and I'm running the whole shebang. I'm so busy I can't breathe. Let's meet for drinks. I need a bucketful. How are your classes at Leaping Lotus and how is Danny, your big, fat poet man?' Her words always all pour out in a rush in a breathy little girl voice that is so incongruous coming out of her large body.

'It's Lilting Lotus, Lilting Lotus,' I tell her, and then I

tell her about the Tantra for Tension Taming class I'm teaching, and that Danny's book, *Breathing Without Air*, is nearly done and, I added, that he wasn't fat but substantial. 'Whatever you say, Sissy,' Margo answered, laughing.

When I ask about Lulu, she says, 'Lulu keeps surprising me. Last year she wanted to be a trapeze artist, now she wants to be a geneticist.'

'Lulu is like you,' I tell her. 'Smart enough to do anything.' Then I describe what I have in mind. There is a long silence on the other end of the phone, then Margo says, 'You know, Sissy, our lives are so different now. I'm a mother, you're a wife, we have careers, gynaecologists, bank accounts, but I still think –' she paused '– of your bush.' I imagined her blushing in that way of hers, her whole face becoming bright, vivid pink. 'And there's still a flame burning for you deep inside me,' she continued, 'but why fan it? It could flare up, singe our lives. Besides, it might be no good between us after so long. Maybe we should just remember what we had, a bird in the hand and all that.'

'But Margo,' I said, 'we're not birds; we love each other and we can handle it.' I didn't tell her that I wanted to test myself, to see if I could conquer my base jealousies. Instead I said, 'We've never hurt each other. Remember how we would flip a coin if we were both wet for the same guy? I'll never forget how we seduced the Sager twins and then switched partners.'

'They were identical,' Margo said, 'except Laurie had that King Kong dick.'

'But Mike's balls were bigger and covered with hair,' I added.

'Yeah, I remember,' said Margo. 'I got some stuck in my teeth. It's true.' She went on, 'We had such great times, we always enjoyed sharing. OK, let's do it. I can't resist. I'll enter into one more conspiracy with you for auld lang syne, besides, I always wanted to see what Danny's cock looks like.'

Oh, no, I thought, and suddenly my mouth was dry and I couldn't speak. A little green snake was twisting around my throat, strangling me, but I took a few deep, Bhastrika breaths to elevate my mind. The little snake was gone and at least I was able to make myself laugh. 'Ha, ha,' I laughed feebly, 'this will be your chance, ha, ha, ha.'

We were on the phone all the time over the next two weeks, planning our surprise. Margo let me take the lead. She told me she was looking forward to it. She'd been so busy on her job that she hadn't had sex for three months. She wanted to tongue me again and it was going to be a lot of fun. My anxieties were dissipating. In the middle of senior yoga class, while I was demonstrating Praying Mantis lotus to seven senior ladies, I found myself imagining me and Danny and Margo and I farted loudly and fell over on my head.

I would tell Danny to be home from his copywriting job no later than seven because I was cooking a special anniversary dinner. Margo and I decided it would be just too, too crude if he walked into the apartment and found us embracing in the bedroom. This was a play that deserved a prologue. I would greet him at the door in my purple leather corset, the one that started under my breasts and went down to my hips. Panties would not be part of the picture, just a purple garter belt, black fishnets and my knee-high black patent leather stiletto boots. I decided to go for the mondo tacky effect, so I got strawberry incense and pink candles. I bought red satin sheets and a red strobe light for the ceiling fixture.

On the big day Margo came over an hour before Danny was due. I was already in my outfit when I answered the door. 'You look a four grand a night hooker,' she said.

'Thanks for the compliment,' I told her. Then I took her into the bedroom. I lit the candles and incense and switched on the strobe light. 'Fabulous,' she commented. 'It looks just like a whorehouse.' She took off her trench coat. All she had on was a pair of black lizard pumps and thigh-high black sheer stockings. Her long strawberry blonde hair was cascading down her back and she had golden glitter on her face and all over her body. She put her coat and dress away in the closet and then she took a slow stroll over to the bed, shaking those big-mamma hips at me. I couldn't help but notice that her legs were still perfect, firm and white as snow, not even one tiny spider vein in sight. I took a deep breath and pushed that thought from my mind.

'You are one hot ticket,' I told Margo. 'You look like Wonder Woman.' I made myself go to her. I put my hands over her delicate breasts and gently kneaded them.

'Ahh,' sighed Margo. 'This is going to be a great thing.'

'I'm going into the living room,' I told her, 'before I get carried away.'

I sat on the living room couch admiring the fine curve of my thighs in my fishnets.

When I heard Danny's familiar footsteps in the hall and the sound of his key in the lock, I ran to the door and flung it open. He was standing there holding a big bunch of red roses. 'Happy . . .' he started to say and then he said, 'Wow, wow,' and then, holding the bouquet out towards me, 'Roses are red, the sky is blue, look at you,' as he eyed me up and down.

'Get in here, you poet head,' I said. I grabbed him by the arm, pulled him inside, pushed shut the door. I took the roses from him and, holding them between us, leaned over to give him a kiss. He has a big, fleshy Mick Jagger mouth. I call him lover lips or sometimes Mr Mouth. I led him to his chair. 'Just sit,' I said, 'I'll be right back.' I dashed into the kitchen and put the roses in a jar of water and carried it back into the living room and put the jar on the television set.

I turned to face him, bowed low so he could see my tits shimmy and then, with a dramatic flourish, pulled out the joint that was tucked into the top of my corset. I lit it for him with the candle that was burning on the coffee table and watched him toke some down. He put the J down in the ashtray, then he opened his large arms out to me. I tumbled happily into his lap.

'You're the queen of all my dreams, my sweet pea, my ecstasy,' he said. (It is so romantic being married to a poet.) Then he swallowed my mouth up in those lover lips. I found his fly, unzipped, pulled out his pride. My Danny's cock isn't all that long, but it is wide – a fine staff, substantial and decent, dependable like its owner. No premature ejaculation for my Danny; he could go all night. I lifted my pelvis up and took him in all the way. I sheathed him, I stroked him, massaged him. I washed him and wooed him with my jade fluids. 'Oh, Sissy, dear wife, star of my life,' he gasped, breathing hard and I felt him throb within me. I did not want him to come so I lifted off, put my arms about his waist, hugging his stout belly. I put my lips over his and slowly fucked his mouth with my tongue. I really took my time and when I felt him pushing into me, his prick metal hard, I stopped. I knelt, took his socks and boots off those big, caveman feet and stripped him down.

'I have a special surprise for you,' I said and led him by his cock head into our bedroom. Margo's opulent form glowed larger than life in the candlelight. She looked like a goddess from some ancient civilization:

Hera come down from Mount Olympus. I was startled, overwhelmed by her beauty. In spite of myself I felt my heart sink, then I got that queasy feeling in my belly that means I'm frightened. Margo was so lush, so female, so much more woman than I ... How would Danny react? What would he do?

For once he was without a quick and clever rhyme. His mouth gaped open, he was staring at Margo, then, 'I don't believe this,' said Danny. 'I must be sleeping and this must be a dream.'

My stomach got even more queasy, I could barely breathe but I managed to say, my voice suddenly very reedy and thin: 'It's no dream, lover lips, we planned an anniversary show just for you.'

'Is that what this is?' said Danny, grinning. 'I thought I died and came back as Henry Miller.'

'Happy anniversary,' said Margo.

'Well, thanks,' said Danny, eyeing her appreciatively. 'You must be the cake. I like that decorative arrow.' I felt so sick I wanted to melt into the floor. I must have been crazy, insane, to do this to myself, but then Danny turned to me. He put his big arms out and grabbed me. 'Margo's the cake and you are my feast of delight,' he said. 'I'm luckier than Henry Miller with all his fancy women and his three wives. I have the best wife in the world, and she's so sexy. Sissy, every year you get more gorgeous.' He kissed my shoulders, my neck, worked his way down to my breast above the corset. Suddenly the strawberry scent in the room mingled with the odor of musk and roses. From some distant temple I heard the deep, passionate chords of the sitar and oud. I nestled, joyful, into his neck, traced the line of his collarbone with my tongue. I kissed the little hollow at the base of his throat and then pulled out of his embrace.

'Let the show begin,' I said. Margo sat up, her whole face smiling, shining. She threw her head back and shook her flood of hair sensuously side to side, then she lifted one of her sweet, pert breasts and offered it to me. I did a little undulating dance as I moved over to the bed. I found Margo's roseate nipple as I had so many times before. She had not forgotten the liquorice oil, and I put her teat in my mouth and sucked and sucked, while she spread her legs wide before Danny's eager eyes. She fingered herself as I nursed. I liked to flick the tip of her nipple with my tongue and she must have liked it too because she started to moan and open and close her legs spasmodically as she fucked herself with her fingers.

Finally I pushed her hand aside with my own, found her fat clit and pulled on it first gently and then harder, harder. Her back curled with pleasure as she lifted up to meet my touch. Even though I was still sucking at her tit, I was able to turn my head just enough to see Danny. He was cradling his cock in the palm of his hand and the expression on his face was so beatific. He looked like he had just deciphered the Rosetta stone, channelled the lost poems of Atlantis or won the Pulitzer Prize.

Margo was writhing beneath me now, quivering, rolling her body from side to side. I didn't want her to roll away, so I took my mouth off her breast and put my head between those big legs. Her juices were thick: sweeter than honey, sweeter than ambrosia and mead. I moved my tongue north and there was her clit, eager, standing up, yearning for me. I made my mouth small and tight and sucked that clit like it was the nipple of Mother Kali as Margo bucked hard beneath me. She let out a big sigh and came, filling my mouth with the syrup of life. The nectar of joy flowed from Margo's pussy into me, making me golden and open. I put my hands on her strong hips and lifted my head up for breath.

'What a pleasure party,' Margo moaned. 'I love you both.'

Suddenly, Danny cried out, 'You two are so beautiful, so beautiful, don't stop yet.' I turned to look at him. He was moving his hand so quickly up and down his cock, all I could see was a blur.

'Don't stop, don't stop, please, oh baby, oh Sissy, oh Sissy, oh baby, I'm almost ready,' he moaned. I had to smile. He was so adorable in his urgency. Then I got up on my hands and knees and waved my tight little ass at him; I lifted my rump higher and higher. Margo, sensing what I had in mind, leaned over and with her hands spread my ass cheeks wider than the skies of paradise. I wanted to invite him, to say, 'Dear Danny, come, dive between the moons of Shakti,' but he had moved across the floor towards the bed so quickly that, before I could even speak, he was there.

Hunting Me Julie Shiel

He told me to dress in the vinyl outfit and returned to watching the television. 'Yes, sir,' I replied and went into the bedroom. I pulled the clothes he had bought me from the bag and laid them out on the bed, the black vinyl shining against the red velvet of the bedcover.

First I wiggled into a tight black vinyl corset top that accented my already large breasts even further. Next was the garter belt, again in black vinyl, and black fishnet stockings attached. The black vinyl thigh-high boots came next. They had platform high heels and clung to my legs tightly. The vinyl creaked sensuously with each move I made as I pulled them up over my knees. I stood a little unsteadily and pulled a pair of net panties over the boots and my ass. Easy access for later, I thought with a smile. Finally, I pushed my fingers into the black vinyl opera-length gloves, sliding them up my arms. I loved the feel of the material clinging to my body. It felt sensuous, a constant pressure holding me in a sort of light bondage that was absolute.

I stood before the mirror, a pale blonde in black vinyl, five feet seven inches in my stocking feet, with the boots adding another five inches. I stared in shock at myself. I worked at a bank, wearing skirts during the day and jeans in my free time. My transformation was complete. While I had dressed up in lingerie and fetishwear before, nothing had been so dramatic and so sexy as the vinyl I now wore. It made me feel decadent and sluttish. Satisfied with my image, I walked to the doorway of the bedroom. 'I'm ready,' I told him and he turned. He simply gazed at me for a few moments, smiling appreciatively, before telling me it was time to go. 'Go? Go where?' I asked him apprehensively.

'You'll see,' he answered. It was December, and cold outside. I also feared being seen dressed in this manner, so I threw on a long black overcoat. It had recently snowed and there were still frozen patches here and there that presented a challenge while wearing the boots. He helped me down the stairs and into the car. A short drive later and we were at my best friend's house.

'I don't want her to see me like this,' I protested, but he insisted that we go in for a 'short visit'. It was Friday night and she had a house full of company gathered in the living room drinking. She had been drinking as well and was a bit tipsy. Dawn and I stood talking in the back hallway while he went in to say hello, and I heard him being greeted raucously. It sounded like there was quite a party going on. On his return he told her that I had something to show her. She insisted I take off the coat but I was reluctant. He pulled it from my shoulders instead and I stood blushing before her, dressed in the black vinyl.

'You look hot!' she exclaimed, and had me turn around. Giggling, she told him that she wanted me first. I laughed, but she pulled me close and kissed me. It wasn't the first time we had kissed, but I knew he was watching and I was a little nervous. She pushed her tongue into my mouth and I relaxed, deepening the kiss, moaning as I felt myself growing wet. She wrapped her fingers in my hair to pull me closer and I pushed my body against hers. As we broke the kiss, she giggled again, and the two of us smiled at him teasingly.

'Time for us to go,' he told her. 'We'll see you later.' Dawn giggled and nodded her agreement.

'Have fun,' she told us. 'Maybe I'll win.' She grinned. I was puzzled as to what she meant by that remark but he draped the coat over me once more and pushed me out through the door.

'You'll pay for that,' he told me as we left, swatting my ass. I laughed mischievously.

'What are you up to?' I asked nervously. He told me I would find out later and guided me along the sidewalk.

Once we were in the car again, he begn heading out of town. After we had passed the city limits he turned down a side road lined with trees and veered off on to a narrow dirt track. He was driving me into the state forest where he worked part time as a game warden during the summer season. We often went for picnics and hiking in good weather, but I had never been there during the winter. He was silent as we drove further into the wood, the headlights illuminating the deeply rutted track directly in front of us and the snow-laden trees arching over us on either side.

I asked him once again what we were doing but he didn't respond and I fell silent, admiring the winter scene. Finally we came to a stop in a place I had never been before. It was a dead end with a picnic table in a small clearing. The moon was almost full and bathed everything in a silvery light. The snow was undisturbed here, and its whiteness cast the trees in stark blackness save for their icy boughs.

We got out of the car and he pulled my coat off me. I stood shivering.

'Run for me,' he commanded.

'What?' I asked stupidly. Surely he didn't expect me to run through the snow and ice in these boots?

'Run. I'm giving you a five-minute head start.' He grinned and looked pointedly at his watch.

I returned his smile uncertainly, but thought, OK, if

he wants me to run, I'll give it a go. I turned and began picking my way across the stone-covered clearing towards the thicket of trees, trying to walk in the few patches of ground where the snow had melted. The going was pretty slow between the high-heeled boots and the slippery ground, and I wondered if he was still watching me as I entered the woods. I could move a little quicker in the forest, away from the stones, and began zig-zagging a trail through the trees, grasping their trunks to steady myself as I slipped among the snow. The woods were dripping with white, with fewer bare patches below the branches of the frozen trees. Everything was lit by the moon, shining off the snowy ground. I felt exposed, knowing that the black vinyl outfit I wore would stand out against the snow, and began working my way towards a tangle of bushes. I shivered, both from the cold and from the sharp thrill of excitement that ran through my body.

I hadn't got far when I heard a noise behind me. I heard a crash of frozen branches breaking and sought to hide behind one of the larger trees. As I turned, I saw him loping through the woods easily, reminding me of a wolf hunting its prey. That's just what it is, I thought. I knew he had seen me, so I turned to run into the thicker bushes, the branches slapping and breaking against my vinyl-clad body. I ran through the monchrome landscape, the beating of my heart loud in my ears, my feet slipping and sliding as my boots sought to dig into the snow. He caught me before I reached the safety of the thicket, grabbing me around the waist. I fought to free myself and twisted in his grasp. We were silent; the only sounds were those of the creaking vinyl, the crunch of ice-crusted snow and our breath in the darkness. Suddenly he shoved me against a tree. I released my grasp on his fingers where I had been trying to prise him loose, and he took the opportunity to pin my arms behind me. He held me against the tree with his body, one knee between my legs, his weight pressed against my ass. Reaching into his pocket he produced a pair of handcuffs and quickly snapped them across my wrists.

Knowing he had me under his control, I ceased my struggles and stood panting heavily, partly from the exertion, partly from excitement. Our struggle had aroused me to the point of being almost senseless with desire. Again reaching into a pocket, he pulled out some rope and looped it through the chain linking the handcuffs. Tying it fast, he gave it a tug and eased off me.

'Sixteen minutes,' he said, glancing at his watch with a smirk. I glared at him.

'Walk,' he ordered, giving me a gentle push back through the woods. He held on to the leash he had made, holding it just tight enough that I was aware of it. I began picking my way through the forest once more, even more gingerly this time since my hands were now cuffed behind me.

I asked him what he was going to do with me, but he didn't answer. He simply continued marching me through the woods, tugging on the rope ever so slightly to steer me in the direction he wished me to go, using his free hand to steady me as I slipped in the snow. We reached the forest's edge and he walked me back towards the car but, instead of allowing me back into the warm, he dragged me to the picnic table, then swept one hand across it to clear it of snow.

I lay across the table face down with my hands cuffed behind me. He kicked my legs apart, then ran his fingers up the vinyl to my panties, feeling the dampness there. He reached up and yanked my panties over my ass and down my legs, having me step out of them. I was incredibly aroused by this time and hot liquid rushes were pooling at my centre. I knew I was soaking wet with my ass exposed and hoped he would take me right there on the table.

Instead, I felt the first sharp sting of his hand striking my ass. I yelped and jumped, but he held me down with one hand in the small of my back. I wiggled my fingers uselessly in the constraint of the handcuffs. His hand came down on my ass again, but lower this time. I could feel my skin heating up as he fell into a rhythm. He struck me with his open hand, low on my ass where my thighs began, stimulating my pussy as well. With each strike I felt myself growing wetter and I began moaning louder, pushing back to meet his punishing hand.

Finally he stopped, leaving me panting and moaning into the picnic table. He ran his fingers across my pussy, feeling how wet I was, then pushed a finger inside me. I began begging him in vain, 'Please . . .'

'Please what?' he asked.

'Please, sir,' I answered promptly. 'Please fuck me.' I was willing to beg, to plead, to say anything he wanted to hear if I could only feel him inside me. I wanted him to take me from behind, right there, as I lay pinned against the table, my hands cuffed behind my back. I just wanted to feel his cock spreading me apart. I fell into frantic moaning.

He found my clit and began rubbing it gently, prompting a fresh wave of begging and moaning, louder and more sincere this time. I felt my orgasm building inside me as he rubbed me, my muscles contracting, my body shaking as I fought to go over the edge. He stopped and pulled me off the table, ignoring my whining.

He walked me to the car, opened the back door and told me to get in. I thought perhaps he wanted to take me there instead of on the table, so I climbed in eagerly, my ass in the air and my head down on the seat. The warmth of the interior was welcome after being in the frosty air.

'Lie down,' he ordered and, pouting a bit, I did so. Pulling the rope that was still attached to the cuffs, he wrapped it around each vinyl-boot-clad ankle and tied them together. Pulling on it, he was satisfied with his hog-tie and shut the back door.

I was filled with frustration by this time, and when he got into the front seat I began asking to be let loose. He ignored me as he began to drive back out of the park. 'What if a cop pulls us over?' I asked. He commented that the officer would likely get a very good look at me and a hard-on for his trouble. I fell silent, imagining the possibilities.

'What are you going to do with me?' I finally asked.

'I'm selling you,' he responded.

'Selling me? To whom?' I decided to go along with it.

'To the highest bidder.' I fell silent. 'You'll go down well in a Mexican whorehouse with your blonde hair and fair skin.' He didn't crack a smile at any of this and I began to grow a bit worried. He had spoken of his fantasy of auctioning me off before, and I knew he was one to live out his fantasies. Still, he wouldn't, I tried to reassure myself.

'Please don't sell me,' I appealed to him.

'What reason do I have to keep you?' he asked me. I could play this game.

I could tell from the smoothness of the car that we must have hit the main road. Other than that I had no idea where he was taking me. The uncertainty was exciting in its own way. 'I can please you,' I told him. 'With my mouth, with my ass, with my pussy, with all of me.'

'I could simply take all of you if I wished,' he replied. This was true. I fell silent for a moment.

'I'll slide my tongue down your cock,' I began. 'Flick you with my tongue ring, lick down to your balls, taking each one into my mouth. Then I'll slide back up and around you, pushing my tongue into the tip.' He gasped and I knew I was getting to him. 'Then I'll swallow you hard, pushing you against the back of my throat and the roof of my mouth.' I heard a soft moan from the front seat.

I paused for a moment. 'That's a start,' he told me. The car came to a stop and he got out, then came around and opened the back door. He undid the ropes that held me hog-tied and I breathed a sigh of relief, stretching out my legs. I started to wiggle from my position lying face down in the back seat, but stopped when he delivered a light smack to my exposed buttocks.

He leaned over me and tied a cloth over my eyes before guiding me out of the car. I stumbled in the heels and he steadied me, still holding my handcuffed wrists behind me. He threw the coat across my shoulders. 'Walk,' he ordered. 'Quickly.'

I could hear cars driving by as he guided me down a sidewalk, then into a house. I heard voices and music, then the laugh of my best friend coming from another room. I was disoriented, but very aroused.

'Are we at Dawn's? Why did you bring me here?' I asked.

'You'll find out,' he replied. He sounded amused. He led me past the voices and I could feel myself blushing at the picture I knew I presented.

'How long?' someone called out, to which he replied, 'Sixteen minutes.' I heard jeering and catcalls, fading as we passed into another room.

Still leading me by my bound hands, we came to a stop, and then he suddenly pushed me on to a bed. I squeaked in protest at the unexpected movement, then squirmed on the bed to get to my knees. It was silent for long minutes.

I felt his fingers slowly wrap themselves into my hair as he pulled my head up from the bed. He reached his hand between my legs and began rubbing my pussy, commenting on my wetness. I pushed against him, begging him for more.

'You're my good little slut, aren't you?' he asked. His voice was that low gravelly tone that sends chills through me.

'Yes, sir,' I moaned. 'I'm your good slut. Use me.' I heard him undo his belt, then the muffled sound of his pants sliding down his thighs to land on the floor.

'And who am I?' he whispered. I hesitated, then answered him somewhat reluctantly.

'You own me,' I responded.

'You'll beg to be mine,' he whispered into my ear, flicking his tongue across it and eliciting a moan from me. I felt his cock at the entrance to my pussy and pushed back urgently. He pulled away from me, rubbing his hard cock against my clit. He slapped my ass sharply. 'Not yet,' he told me.

My whole body was shaking with my need to come. 'Oh please, sir, please, I'll do anything, just please fuck me,' I began pleading senselessly.

Suddenly he grabbed my hips and shoved his cock into me. I screamed at the penetration, pushing back against him. He felt huge inside me. He began fucking me in long deep smooth strokes, occasionally slapping my ass.

'Please,' I moaned into the pillow.

'What do you want?' he asked me as he shoved into me harder.

'I need to come,' I begged him. I was still wound up from being taken to the edge over the picnic table.

'Not yet,' he said, and pulled out of me. I sobbed in frustration as I stayed in the position he had left me in, head down and ass up. Reaching for the key, he unlocked the handcuffs and I stretched my arms and pushed myself up on to my hands. That didn't last long. He pounced on me, twisting me on to my back and pinning my hands above my head. Still blindfolded, I lay gasping for breath. He leaned in and kissed me hungrily before sliding himself down my body. I pushed my hips up to him as his lips traced my breasts through the vinyl. His teeth caught my nipple and tugged on it lightly, teasingly, bringing it to stiff attention. Moving lower, he pushed the top up over me, exposing my breasts as his hands cupped each one and his lips traced down my stomach.

I moaned as he neared my wet pussy. He lightly flicked his tongue across my clit and I jumped, shoving myself towards him. 'I said not yet,' he told me as he pulled away. His voice sounded strange, as if full of some emotion. I was near insane with arousal and knew it wouldn't take much for me to reach orgasm. 'Beg for it,' he ordered.

'Please let me come,' I began. 'Please, sir, I'll do anything, please me me come ...' I trailed off into sobs.

'You can do better than that,' he mocked me. He pushed a finger into me, wiggling it inside me.

'Oh, please, sir, I'm your slut, I'm your slave to use, please use me hard,' I continued. 'Please fuck your whore, please let me come!' I wrapped my fingers into the sheet, pulling on the bed as I strained to reach orgasm.

'Better,' he told me as he lowered his tongue to my clit, pushing another finger into my aching pussy. I came screaming, writhing on the bed and begging incoherently as the waves of my orgasm washed over me.

Replacing his fingers with his cock, he once again pushed into me, continuing to rub my clit. As he spread me apart I continued coming, clamping down around his cock as he moved inside me. As my orgasm subsided to moans, I continued begging him, telling him I belonged to him and asking for him to come deep inside me. He slammed into me faster and harder as his own orgasm grew closer. He held me pinned down to the bed, his body over mine, and groaned as he pushed into me, holding himself there as he came in pulsing waves.

'Oh, yes please, sir,' I moaned. 'Come hard inside me.' He arched his body over mine as he shoved his cock into me a few more times.

He withdrew from me and I whined in protest, not wanting to release him. He moved up on the bed and I felt him rub his wet cock across my lips. I opened my mouth hungrily and began licking my juices off him. I love how I taste, thick and sweet, and I could taste his come mixed with my own. I ran my tongue down his length, swirling around his cock. Sliding down, I began licking his balls, taking each one into my mouth, and he groaned and jumped a little at the sensation.

Licking my way back up, I pushed my tongue into the tip of his cock. He gasped. Finally I opened my mouth around him, then closed it suddenly, flicking my tongue around the end. The sounds of his arousal were stirring me again and I moaned, letting him feel the vibrations of my mouth on his hard cock.

'Fuck yourself,' he ordered. I was quick to comply, spreading my legs and rubbing my clit hard and fast. 'Good girl,' he whispered.

He began fucking my face as I masturbated, falling into a rhythm, pushing against the roof of my mouth and the back of my throat. I felt another orgasm rising within me and my moans became more urgent. I spread my legs further, lifting my hips from the bed and pushing a finger inside myself.

'Faster.' His voice was low and gasping. 'Come for me, slut.' His words sent me over the edge and I was coming again, hard, my screams muffled by his cock. I released him from my mouth and he moved quickly, slamming into my pussy. He was hard and rough with me, leaning on my outspread thighs as he fucked me. I sought to pull him into me deeper and dug my vinyl-clad nails down his back, into his ass. I could feel him swelling inside me, growing bigger and harder as my orgasm subsided.

'Do it again. Now!' he ordered. I sobbed, drained and not believing I had the strength for another, but I obeyed him. I pulled off one vinyl glove and pushed my fingers between us, again rubbing my sensitive clit, and still he pounded into me.

Abruptly he pulled out from me and I whined. Taking a pillow, he shoved it under my ass. 'Don't you dare stop,' he ordered. Getting his finger wet with my juices, he began working it into my anus. At first I pulled away, but he insisted and I began to relax. I felt the head of his cock at my opening and he began pushing into me slowly, working himself in an inch at a time.

My arousal had slowed at the uncomfortable sensation of him sliding into my ass, but I continued rubbing my clit. At last he was fully inside me and began moving, slowly at first, then faster. He held my hips, using them as leverage to push himself up me. I began rubbing myself faster as my desire grew once again. I began shoving against him to meet his thrusts.

'You like me fucking your ass, don't you, slut?' he asked me.

'Oh, yes,' I moaned. 'Fuck your slut!' Suddenly I exploded with another orgasm. It was different than the others in that it hit me suddenly rather then building up. Taken by surprise, I cried out. He moaned and slammed into me harder as I came, reaching his own orgasm.

I lay shaking and exhausted. He leaned over and kissed me softly, then removed the blindfold. Instead of the face I expected, I found myself looking at Steve, one of his closest friends. I jumped and scrabbled backwards against my Master. I stared at the two of them in shock.

'Steve won the bet,' he told me. 'Sixteen minutes.' He grinned. My mind replayed the events of the evening, trying to match up which of them had done what to me, and found it didn't really matter.

He pulled me against his chest and brushed the hair from my forehead. 'But I think I might keep you, after all,' he told me with a smile.

Cavern in the Green

Wylie Kinson

My insides turned cold when I saw the pink message slip marked 'urgent' waiting for me on my desk: Report to Mr Parker's office at once, it said. I thought I was about to lose my job. I set my morning coffee down and regretted not having been with the firm long enough to accumulate streaky brown stains on the inside of my ceramic mug. My shoulders dropped as a tight knot of nervous tension grew in the pit of my stomach. I wondered if Jonah had been sent the same message. I resignedly surveyed my small, bright office as I walked out, mentally calculating how many boxes I'd need to clear out two months' worth of accrued clutter.

'How the hell did Old Man Parker find out?' I muttered under my breath as I punched the elevator button. I pictured his stern, heavily jowled face and unforgiving eyes looking exactly as they appeared in the portrait that hung prominently in the lobby of this grand old office building. I had never met him personally. He was in semi-retirement and didn't appear in the office very often, but the senior employees loved to scare the new recruits with stories of his uncompromising, iron-fisted approach to business.

As the ancient elevator groaned upwards, I reflected on yesterday's adventure and the lusty antics that would lead to my likely dismissal.

I couldn't help but smile at the mental picture of

Jonah in his tight, muscle-gripping, form-fitting neoprene and rubber wetsuit. I had hardly given a second glance to the guy in the short time we'd been acquainted, but as we sat on a tourist-filled scuba boat for a day of diving and underwater exploration, my eyes refused to veer from his broad-shouldered manly physique.

He grunted through clenched teeth as he tugged the confining suit up over his tight, perfectly rounded butt. My eyes were drawn magnetically upward to where a fiery lion's head, captured in mid-roar, was tattooed on the back of his right shoulder. It appeared very out of character for a reserved fellow like Jonah, a member of the boring accountant crew at Parker International. I wondered how many girls in our office new about this wild cat. Not many, I'm sure. Cavorting with co-workers was a serious offence at our stuffy firm and Old Man Parker wouldn't tolerate the shenanigans of inter-office romances.

Parker International had over seventy employees so I didn't cross paths with Jonah that often. Apart for the obligatory 'good mornings' as we passed in the hall or shared an elevator, our conversations never ventured beyond discussing the weather. New to the company, and a new resident to Bermuda, I'd not yet subscribed to the office gossip grapevine, so I knew little about him.

'Well, it seems we have more in common than the daily forecast,' he said when he spied me on the dock yesterday morning.

'Oh, um, hello Jonah,' I stammered, embarrassed to be seen by a fellow co-worker on a Tuesday morning.

'Taking some vacation time?' he asked.

'Um, yeah, sure,' I lied. Vacation after only eight weeks with the firm? If that's what he wants to believe ... 'How about you?'

'Well, if you promise not to tell –' he lowered his voice to a whisper '– it was such a nice day that I called in sick.'

'Me too!' I laughed, relieved. 'Our little secret.'

We shared a wink and boarded the boat. I didn't bother to tell him that it was actually my thirtieth birthday and skiving work was my way of fighting the I'm-thirty-and-still-single blues. It was either a day in the sun or a bottle of vodka, my sofa and the soaps.

'Good morning, folks!' the boat operator shouted enthusiastically over the drone of the engine. 'Welcome aboard the *Sea Nymph*. I'm Dave and I'll be your guide today. Looks like most of you are visitors to Bermuda,' he said, quickly surveying his roster. 'Let me tell you a little about our day's activities. We'll start with a sixty-five foot wreck dive, and then we'll head over to Smugglers Island for a picnic lunch and a tour of the old stone fort.'

As Dave continued the briefing, my eyes loitered on Jonah's sculpted profile. Why had I not noticed this man's firm square jaw and succulent full lips before? The hot sun could not alone be responsible for the trickle of sweat that rolled southerly between my breasts.

'Do you dive often?' I asked Jonah when he caught my gaze lingering on his sun-bleached hair. 'I've never seen you out here before.'

'I usually go out myself but my boat is in dry dock for maintenance. This all-day tour was the only thing available at the last minute. How about you?' he queried, surveying me with his own bold admiring stare.

I was pleased I'd chosen to wear my new electric-blue bikini, which set off the colour of my deep blue eyes and bronzed skin.

'I've only lived in Bermuda for a couple of months, but I try to get out every weekend,' I explained as I slipped my long legs into my form-fitting wetsuit. 'I used to dream of days like this when I was cooped up in my windowless New Jersey office. I promised myself that if I got the job at Parker, I would take full advantage of living on a Caribbean island.'

I was well aware of how the snug suit accentuated my small waist and curvaceous hips and chest. Jonah locked his steely blue eyes on to my shiny black zipper as I teasingly slid it over my tanned, lean torso. I could feel the heat of his stare as I paused flirtatiously at the vee of my breasts. The suit was so tight that it created extra cleavage to my already endowed form and, despite the cool ocean water we would soon plunge into, I decided to leave Jonah with the view.

'Excuse me,' said Dave, the boat guide, singling us out. Jonah and I, entirely engrossed in mutual admiration, didn't notice him approach. 'According to my roster, you two are the only locals on the tour today. It's obvious you know each other, so if you'd like to buddy up on the dive, feel free. That way our big group won't slow you down.'

Jonah and I exchanged coy smiles and nodded eagerly at Dave's suggestion. As dive buddies, Jonah and I took to the task of assisting one another into our cumbersome dive equipment. It could have easily been done solo, but we both wanted the cheap thrill of physical contact.

After a glorious dive on an ancient Spanish vessel, our tour group headed to Smugglers Island, famous for its labyrinth of underground caves. During our picnic lunch, Dave told us a little about the island. Rumour had it that Old Man Parker's grandfather discovered pirate's gold hidden in one of these caves in the 1880s, making his family richer than the British Royals. It made sense. If Parker inherited his grandpappy's face and disposition, they sure didn't make their money with charm and good looks!

'Would you like a private tour?' Jonah whispered in my ear. 'I've been here before and know my way around.'

'Sure!' I hope I didn't sound like an eager schoolgirl, but I'd been dying to spend some time alone with Mr Hotty since I watched him peel the wetsuit off his glistening sun-kissed skin.

Jonah entwined his fingers in mine as we grabbed our bags and slipped away unnoticed from the group. We walked a short distance through dense tropical greenery until we came to a curtain of vines. Jonah parted the vines to reveal an enormous opening in the side of a twenty-foot rock wall. We dropped our beach bags and walked hand in hand down a rocky embankment to the bottom of a huge cavern.

Through the filtered light I saw a parade of glistening tall stalagmites that endowed the perimeter of the cavern floor, their blunt knobbly heads mocking us in phallic display. Stalactites dripped from the ceiling like dirty icicles caught in a spring thaw. A deep rock pool in the cavern's centre held water so still and crystal clear it hardly betrayed its liquid content.

'Amazing, isn't it?' Jonah said with childish delight, looking towards me for approval. 'I used to play pirates in here when I was a kid.'

Largely ignoring the geological wonder surrounding me in favour of the awesome sight of Jonah's rippled abdomen, I lewdly hoped he'd search for my treasure.

'Come on, let's take a dip,' he whispered suggestively.

'Won't it be cold?' I asked, gaping at this sun-starved lake.

'I'll keep you warm,' he promised as he slipped noiselessly over the rim.

Recognising an opportunity for close body contact, I followed.

'This is freezing!' I gasped, as the water rose over my taut stomach. I felt the goose bumps rising on my flesh, but Jonah was focused on other tell-tale signs of my chilly discomfort.

'Ooh, you are shivering,' Jonah remarked as he hungrily admired my erect nipples peeking through the bikini. 'I'd better warm you up.'

I struggled with my moral conscience for all of ten seconds when Jonah circled his sinewy arms around my back and cupped his hands under my bottom. I've never acted so loose and horny before! I've never had sex on the first date and, except in my frequent erotic fantasies, never allowed an almost stranger to handle me this intimately. But what the hell! I'm thirty today, I thought, and I can't think of a better way to celebrate than with a little (or a lot) of dirty, almost stranger sex. I mentally hummed 'Happy Birthday to Me' as his head lowered to take my erect nipple in his mouth, sucking it through the fabric of my bikini. My head dropped back as I gasped in sheer ecstasy. The contrasting sensation of the cool water and the heat of Jonah's mouth had my insides tingling with desire. His lips and tongue explored the sensitive skin of my neck and shoulders while he untied my bikini top to reveal two creamy white orbs, crowned with dark pink circles. He locked one strong leg around mine for leverage as we bobbed slowly up and down in the undulating saline pool. I could feel his bulge grow to stalagmite proportions as it bumped against my thighs. He continued to nibble and suck at each nipple with his hot mouth. I silently begged him to continue that technique a little lower on my anatomy.

As if reading my thoughts, his long tapered fingers

found their way into my bikini bottoms and he stroked the delicate plump flesh of my sex. The temperature difference between the outside and the inside of my pussy was enough to cause the water around us to boil. His exploring fingers circled and teased my clit before settling into an erotic stimulating rhythm. My teeth feasted playfully on his firm shoulder and once again I admired the fierce lion's head tattoo. I clung to Jonah for fear of slipping beneath the surface and drowning in pure bliss. His skilled tongue returned to lavish my breasts until my legs began to quiver and my climactic juices generously contributed to the crystal clear waters of the pool. My gasps echoed within the cavern like an orgasmic haunting. He slid two long fingers inside me and played me like a puppet while I enjoyed the intensity of my orgasm.

So much for the boring accountant stereotype – Mr Number Cruncher certainly knows what keys to press on me.

Once I'd recovered, I eagerly coaxed Jonah to sit on the edge of the pool. While he hoisted himself out of the water, I tugged firmly on to the waistband of his shorts, leaving him bare-assed naked.

He perched on the rim of the pool and allowed my mouth to nuzzle his enormous cock. The damp earthy smell of the cavern mixed with the musky smell of his sex was proof alone that Mother Nature was a sexually charged female. I licked the salty water from the underside of his smooth erect penis while he tangled his fingers into my wild curly blonde mane. My tongue flicked playfully over his balls before I took them in my mouth and sucked until his groans echoed off the solid rock walls. My arms were wrapped around the tops of his thighs and my breasts bobbed on the water's surface, occasionally brushing against his hairy muscular calves, sending electric currents straight to my groin. I circled the tip of Jonah's hardness with my mouth, tickling the tiny slit with my tongue. Slowly I took more of his length until it filled me. I retracted, inch by salty wet inch, until only the tip of the head remained. I replayed this technique again and again, each time gripping firmer and pumping faster with my mouth until Jonah spasmed in ecstasy. He graciously pulled out to water my neck and chest with his warm seed.

As Jonah assisted me out of the pool, I had an inspiration that would make spelunkers everywhere mad with envy. I wrapped my cool fingers around Jonah's semi-erection and led him to a three-foot stalagmite that was erupting from the cavern floor. I seductively slipped out of my skimpy wet bottoms and, caressing the head of the growth, teased, 'Did you know that these take hundreds of years to grow one inch?' I watched as he grew at a much faster rate. He looked at me wild-eyed, not knowing what to expect. I'm sure his perverse male mind had me mounting the calcium carbonate formation and riding it like a bull stallion. Not this time. I wanted hot pulsing flesh inside me. I turned my back to him and, gripping the knobbly stalagmite, leaned over and spread my legs. Even in the dim cavern light, my glistening pussy winked a delicious invitation.

In one giant stride Jonah was next to me again. He moved behind me to fondle my breasts and nip the back of my neck like a mating lion. That explained the tattoo. The crinkly hair of his chest rubbed the sensitive skin of my back. With one hand, he reached down to tickle my hungry clit. I felt him hard again – so soon! One forceful thrust had him so deep inside me I gasped with a mix of shock and delight. I urged him to impale me once more. Jonah used slow deep thrusts to work us both into a climactic frenzy. Happy Birthday to me!

We eventually stumbled naked and exhilarated from the cave.

'I can't believe we've never exchanged more than "It looks like rain" to each other before this,' Jonah commented between our high-school-sweetheart kisses.

'We certainly caused a heatwave today,' I quipped.

Our passionate playfulness was suddenly interrupted by a distant noise. We both jerked back abruptly, recognising our predicament.

'Is that the boat?' I asked, panicking.

Jonah nodded, wide-eyed.

'Oh, shit!'

We grabbed our beach bags and sprinted through the enveloping greenery, frantically wrapping ourselves in beach towels. We reached the dock just as the boat was pulling out.

'Hey, wait for us,' I yelled. Not that being stranded on a semi-secluded island with Jonah would be a bad thing. In fact, I'll be fantasising about it for weeks.

'Hey you two,' Dave scolded with relief. 'Thought we'd have to return with a search party! I rang the return-to-ship bell a bunch of times but you obviously didn't hear me.' A look of dawning came over Dave as he noticed our towelled attire and he suppressed a knowing smile.

'Mr Parker will see you now. Go right in.' The cardigan-clad spinsterish secretary looked at me disapprovingly as I recovered from my reverie. Her stern, pinched appearance had me wondering if she'd been reading my mind.

The feeling of dread returned like a punch in the gut

as I rose from the smooth leather sofa in the reception area and approached the massive double oak doors.

Who could have told? Jonah couldn't have ratted us out because he had as much to lose as I did. Who could have seen us? There were no messages on my answering machine indicating someone checking up on me yesterday.

I kept my eyes lowered on the highly polished hardwood floor as I swung open the doors to the lion's den. Is he going to swallow me whole or give me a humiliating lecture about my lack of professionalism?

'Good morning, miss. Come in, come in,' intoned Parker in his stentorian British-accented grumble.

I looked up and was stunned to see Jonah standing next to the old man. That traitor. That bastard! How could he? I threw him daggers with my eyes as I faced my impending dismissal.

'Jonah has come up with a wonderful employee incentive idea.' Old Man Parker interrupted my murderous glare. 'No one seems motivated by employee-of-the-month privileges, perfect-attendance bonuses, etcetera, so he's suggesting that all employees get a paid day off on their birthday.'

My eyes volleyed between the two of them. I was shocked speechless.

'He tells me that you inspired this idea and suggested I give you full credit.' He stuck his massive wrinkled paw towards me in gratitude.

'I, um, don't know what to say,' I stuttered, returning his one-pump shake. 'Thank you, sir.'

'Well, I'm just glad that my grandson has a good team of workers. He'll need people like you around him when he takes over the company next month.'

Grandson? Grandson! Well, that's what I get for fucking before a proper introduction.

'I'm sure your *grandson* will do an outstanding job, sir.' I smiled generously for both of them. 'And I'm happy to be his source of inspiration anytime,' I added, with a sexy wink for Jonah's eyes only.

I turned towards the exit and, just as the great double doors clicked shut, I heard Jonah whisper behind me, 'Happy Birthday.'

LOOK OUT FOR THE ALL-NEW BLACK LACE BOOKS – AVAILABLE NOW!

All books priced £6.99 in the UK. Please note publication dates apply to the UK only. For other territories, please contact your retailer.

BEDDING THE BURGLAR
Gabrielle Marcola
ISBN 0 352 33911 X

Maggie Quinton is a savvy, sexy architect involved in a building project on a remote island off the Florida panhandle. One day, a gorgeous hunk breaks into the house she's staying in and ties her up. The buff burglar is in search of an item he claims the apartment's owner stole from him. And he keeps coming back. Flustered and aroused, Maggie calls her jet-setting sister in for moral support, but flirty, dark-haired Diane is much more interested in the island's ruggedly handsome police chief, 'Griff' Grifford. And then there's his deputy, Cosgrove, with his bulging biceps and creative uses for handcuffs. **A sexually charged tale of bad boys and fast women set in the teeming backwaters of 'gator country!**

MIXED DOUBLES
Zoe le Verdier
ISBN 0 352 33312 X

When Natalie Crawford is offered the job as manager of a tennis club in a wealthy English suburb, she jumps at the chance. There's an extra perk, too: Paul, the club's coach, is handsome and charming, and she wastes no time in making him her lover. Then she hires Chris, a coach from a rival club, whose confidence and sexual prowess swiftly put Paul in the shade. When Chris embroils Natalie into kinky sex games, will she be able to keep control of her business aims, or will her lust for the arrogant sportsman get out of control? **The gloves – and knickers – are off in this story of unsporting behaviour on court!**

Coming in December 2004

CREAM OF THE CROP
Savannah Smythe
ISBN 0 352 33920 9

Aspiring artist Carla Vicenzi has caught the eye of Alex Crewe, a serial seducer who owns an exclusive retreat where artists hone their craft. Alex wants a high-profile exhibition, but corporate shark Crewe embodies all the values Carla despises. As she tries to resist his advances, he woos her the old-fashioned way, unaware that she can be dirtier than him. Eventually they are drawn together by forces neither of them can resist, and their resulting affair is explosive, pushing each of them to their sexual limit. Meanwhile Carla's dishy but dumb boyfriend is lured into depravity by Ruth, Alex's slinky PA. Amid the scheming and double-crossing, Carla still manages to find time to seduce a few of New York's fittest firemen! **A story of lust and honour, revenge and greed, set against Manhattan's glittering skyline.**

EDEN'S FLESH
Robyn Russell
ISBN 0 352 33923 3

Eden Sinclair is director of the exclusive Galerie Raton in Atlanta's prestigious mid-town district. As summer temperatures soar she finds it increasingly difficult to adhere to her self-imposed celibacy, and spends a lot of time fantasising about the attractive young artists who pass through the gallery. Among them is Michael MacKenzie, the flame-haired sculptor whose sexy masculinity sets her pulse racing. Almost delirious with unrequited passion, Eden sets out to seduce him – despite her professional promise never to become involved with her clients. Things become even more charged when she finds out gallery owner Alexander is having an affair with her best friend. In downtown Atlanta it's going to be a summer of saucy surprises and steamy encounters.

Also available

THE BLACK LACE SEXY QUIZ BOOK
Maddie Saxon
ISBN 0 352 33884 9

- What sexual personality type are you?
- Have you ever faked it because that was easier than explaining what you wanted?
- What kind of fantasy figures turn you on – and does your partner know?
- What sexual signals are you giving out right now?

Today's image-conscious dating scene is a tough call. Our sexual expectations are cranked up to the max, and the sexes seem to have become highly critical of each other in terms of appearance and performance in the bedroom. But, even though guys have ditched their nasty Y-fronts and girls are more babe-licious than ever, a huge number of us are still being let down sexually. Sex therapist Maddie Saxon thinks this is because we are finding it harder to relax and let our true sexual selves shine through.

The Black Lace Sexy Quiz Book will help you negotiate the minefield of modern relationships. Through a series of fun, revealing quizzes, you will be able to rate your sexual needs honestly and get what you really want from your partner. The quizzes will get you thinking about and discussing your desires in ways you haven't previously considered. Unlock the mysteries of your sexual psyche in this fun, revealing quiz book designed with today's sex-savvy girl in mind.

Black Lace Booklist

Information is correct at time of printing. To avoid disappointment check availability before ordering. Go to www.blacklace-books.co.uk. All books are priced £6.99 unless another price is given.

BLACK LACE BOOKS WITH A CONTEMPORARY SETTING

- ❑ SHAMELESS Stella Black ISBN 0 352 33485 1 £5.99
- ❑ INTENSE BLUE Lyn Wood ISBN 0 352 33496 7 £5.99
- ❑ A SPORTING CHANCE Susie Raymond ISBN 0 352 33501 7 £5.99
- ❑ TAKING LIBERTIES Susie Raymond ISBN 0 352 33357 X £5.99
- ❑ ON THE EDGE Laura Hamilton ISBN 0 352 33534 3 £5.99
- ❑ LURED BY LUST Tania Picarda ISBN 0 352 33533 5 £5.99
- ❑ THE NINETY DAYS OF GENEVIEVE Lucinda Carrington ISBN 0 352 33070 8 £5.99
- ❑ DREAMING SPIRES Juliet Hastings ISBN 0 352 33584 X
- ❑ THE TRANSFORMATION Natasha Rostova ISBN 0 352 33311 1
- ❑ SIN.NET Helena Ravenscroft ISBN 0 352 33598 X
- ❑ TWO WEEKS IN TANGIER Annabel Lee ISBN 0 352 33599 8
- ❑ PLAYING HARD Tina Troy ISBN 0 352 33617 X
- ❑ SYMPHONY X Jasmine Stone ISBN 0 352 33629 3
- ❑ SUMMER FEVER Anna Ricci ISBN 0 352 33625 0
- ❑ CONTINUUM Portia Da Costa ISBN 0 352 33120 8
- ❑ FULL STEAM AHEAD Tabitha Flyte ISBN 0 352 33637 4
- ❑ A SECRET PLACE Ella Broussard ISBN 0 352 33307 3
- ❑ GAME FOR ANYTHING Lyn Wood ISBN 0 352 33639 0
- ❑ CHEAP TRICK Astrid Fox ISBN 0 352 33640 4
- ❑ THE GIFT OF SHAME Sara Hope-Walker ISBN 0 352 32935 1
- ❑ COMING UP ROSES Crystalle Valentino ISBN 0 352 33658 7
- ❑ GOING TOO FAR Laura Hamilton ISBN 0 352 33657 9
- ❑ THE STALLION Georgina Brown ISBN 0 352 33005 8
- ❑ DOWN UNDER Juliet Hastings ISBN 0 352 33663 3
- ❑ ODALISQUE Fleur Reynolds ISBN 0 352 32887 8
- ❑ SWEET THING Alison Tyler ISBN 0 352 33682 X
- ❑ TIGER LILY Kimberly Dean ISBN 0 352 33685 4

❑ COOKING UP A STORM Emma Holly ISBN 0 352 33686 2
❑ RELEASE ME Suki Cunningham ISBN 0 352 33671 4
❑ KING'S PAWN Ruth Fox ISBN 0 352 33684 6
❑ FULL EXPOSURE Robyn Russell ISBN 0 352 33688 9
❑ SLAVE TO SUCCESS Kimberley Raines ISBN 0 352 33687 0
❑ STRIPPED TO THE BONE Jasmine Stone ISBN 0 352 33463 0
❑ SHADOWPLAY Portia Da Costa ISBN 0 352 33313 8
❑ I KNOW YOU, JOANNA Ruth Fox ISBN 0 352 33727 3
❑ THE HOUSE IN NEW ORLEANS Fleur Reynolds ISBN 0 352 32951 3
❑ HEAT OF THE MOMENT Tesni Morgan ISBN 0 352 33742 7
❑ THE WICKED STEPDAUGHTER Wendy Harris ISBN 0 352 33777 X
❑ DRAWN TOGETHER Robyn Russell ISBN 0 352 33269 7
❑ LEARNING THE HARD WAY Jasmine Archer ISBN 0 352 33782 6
❑ VELVET GLOVE Emma Holly ISBN 0 352 33448 7
❑ UNKNOWN TERRITORY Annie O'Neill ISBN 0 352 33794 X
❑ VIRTUOSO Katrina Vincenzi-Thyre ISBN 0 352 32907 6
❑ FIGHTING OVER YOU Laura Hamilton ISBN 0 352 33795 8
❑ ARIA APPASSIONATA Juliet Hastings ISBN 0 352 33056 2
❑ THE RELUCTANT PRINCESS Patty Glenn ISBN 0 352 33809 1
❑ HARD BLUE MIDNIGHT Alaine Hood ISBN0 352 33851 2
❑ ALWAYS THE BRIDEGROOM Tesni Morgan ISBN0 352 33855 5
❑ COMING ROUND THE MOUNTAIN Tabitha Flyte ISBN0 352 33873 3
❑ FEMININE WILES Karina Moore ISBN0 352 33235 2
❑ MIXED SIGNALS Anna Clare ISBN0 352 33889 X
❑ BLACK LIPSTICK KISSES Monica Belle ISBN0 352 33885 7
❑ HOP GOSSIP Savannah Smythe ISBN0 352 33880 6
❑ GOING DEEP Kimberly Dean ISBN0 352 33876 8
❑ PACKING HEAT Karina Moore ISBN0 352 33356 1
❑ MIXED DOUBLES Zoe le Verdier ISBN0 352 33312 X
❑ WILD BY NATURE Monica Belle ISBN0 352 33915 2
❑ UP TO NO GOOD Karen S. Smith ISBN0 352 33589 0
❑ CLUB CRÈME Primula Bond ISBN0 352 33907 1
❑ BONDED Fleur Reynolds ISBN0 352 33192 5
❑ SWITCHING HANDS Alaine Hood ISBN0 352 33896 2
❑ BEDDING THE BURGLAR Gabrielle Marcole ISBN0 352 33911 X

BLACK LACE BOOKS WITH AN HISTORICAL SETTING

- ❑ PRIMAL SKIN Leona Benkt Rhys ISBN 0 352 33500 9 £5.99
- ❑ DARKER THAN LOVE Kristina Lloyd ISBN 0 352 33279 4
- ❑ THE CAPTIVATION Natasha Rostova ISBN 0 352 33234 4
- ❑ MINX Megan Blythe ISBN 0 352 33638 2
- ❑ DIVINE TORMENT Janine Ashbless ISBN 0 352 33719 2
- ❑ SATAN'S ANGEL Melissa MacNeal ISBN 0 352 33726 5
- ❑ THE INTIMATE EYE Georgia Angelis ISBN 0 352 33004 X
- ❑ SILKEN CHAINS Jodi Nicol ISBN 0 352 33143 7
- ❑ THE LION LOVER Mercedes Kelly ISBN 0 352 33162 3
- ❑ THE AMULET Lisette Allen ISBN 0 352 33019 8
- ❑ WHITE ROSE ENSNARED Juliet Hastings ISBN 0 352 33052 X
- ❑ UNHALLOWED RITES Martine Marquand ISBN 0 352 33222 0
- ❑ LA BASQUAISE Angel Strand ISBN 0 352 32988 2
- ❑ THE HAND OF AMUN Juliet Hastings ISBN 0 352 33144 5
- ❑ THE SENSES BEJEWELLED Cleo Cordell ISBN 0 352 32904 1

BLACK LACE ANTHOLOGIES

- ❑ WICKED WORDS Various ISBN 0 352 33363 4
- ❑ MORE WICKED WORDS Various ISBN 0 352 33487 8
- ❑ WICKED WORDS 3 Various ISBN 0 352 33522 X
- ❑ WICKED WORDS 4 Various ISBN 0 352 33603 X
- ❑ WICKED WORDS 5 Various ISBN 0 352 33642 0
- ❑ WICKED WORDS 6 Various ISBN 0 352 33690 0
- ❑ WICKED WORDS 9 Various ISBN 0 352 33860 1
- ❑ WICKED WORDS 10 Various ISBN 0 352 33893 8
- ❑ THE BEST OF BLACK LACE 2 Various ISBN 0 352 33718 4

BLACK LACE NON-FICTION

- ❑ THE BLACK LACE BOOK OF WOMEN'S SEXUAL FANTASIES Ed. Kerri Sharp ISBN 0 352 33793 1 £6.99
- ❑ THE BLACK LACE SEXY QUIZ BOOK Maddie Saxon ISBN 0 352 33884 9 £6.99

To find out the latest information about Black Lace titles, check out the website: www.blacklace-books.co.uk or send for a booklist with complete synopses by writing to:

Black Lace Booklist, Virgin Books Ltd
Thames Wharf Studios
Rainville Road
London W6 9HA

Please include an SAE of decent size. Please note only British stamps are valid.

Our privacy policy
We will not disclose information you supply us to any other parties. We will not disclose any information which identifies you personally to any person without your express consent.

From time to time we may send out information about Black Lace books and special offers. Please tick here if you do not wish to receive Black Lace information. ❑

Please send me the books I have ticked above.

Name ....

Address ....

....

....

....

Post Code ....

Send to: Virgin Books Cash Sales, Thames Wharf Studios, Rainville Road, London W6 9HA.

US customers: for prices and details of how to order books for delivery by mail, call 1-800-343-4499.

Please enclose a cheque or postal order, made payable to Virgin Books Ltd, to the value of the books you have ordered plus postage and packing costs as follows:

UK and BFPO – £1.00 for the first book, 50p for each subsequent book.

Overseas (including Republic of Ireland) – £2.00 for the first book, £1.00 for each subsequent book.

If you would prefer to pay by VISA, ACCESS/MASTERCARD, DINERS CLUB, AMEX or SWITCH, please write your card number and expiry date here:

....

Signature ....

Please allow up to 28 days for delivery.